The Borribles

Michael de Larrabeiti was born in Lambeth, brought up in Battersea and educated at Clapham Central Secondary School. He has worked at many things but mainly on camera in documentary films and as a travel guide in France, Spain and Morocco. In 1961 he was the photographer on the Marco Polo Expedition, travelling four months overland to Afghanistan on a motor cycle. He began writing in 1970 and now lives in an Oxfordshire village, earning a living by turning his hand to anything that pays wages. He is, in his own words, 'married with two Borribles'.

Michael de Larrabeiti

The Borribles

Piccolo Books

First published 1976 by The Bodley Head
This Piccolo edition published 1983 by Pan Books Ltd,
Cavaye Place, London SW10 9PG
© Michael de Larrabeiti 1976
ISBN 0 330 26857 0

Printed in Great Britain by
Collins, Glasgow

For Whiteboncé, Spikey and Fang

"If you're my friend,
follow me round the bend."
Borrible proverb

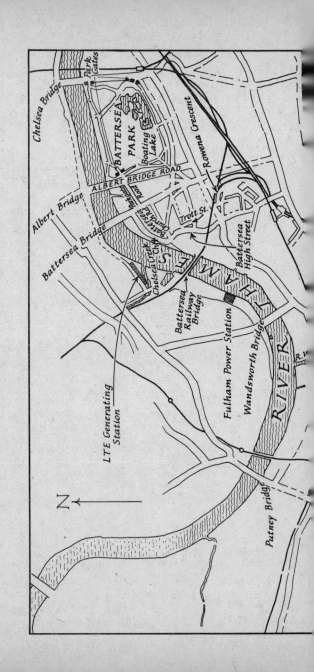

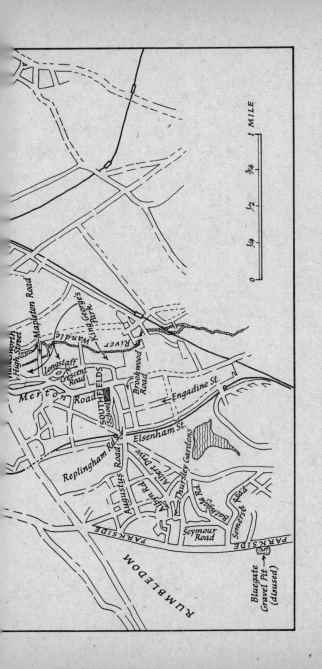

Chapter 1

The swirling rain-clouds rushed on revealing the bright moon and the two Borribles dodged behind the bushes and kept as quiet as they could. There was danger in the air and they could feel it. It would pay to be cautious.

"Strewth," said Knocker, the chief skirmisher and lookout of the Battersea tribe, "what a bloody cheek, coming down here without so much as a by-your-leave."

Lightfinger, Knocker's companion, agreed. "Diabolical liberty I call it . . . nasty bits of work, covered in fur like nylon hearth rugs . . . snouts like traffic cones. Just like rats, aren't they?"

"There's a big one, just getting into the motor, he's shouting at the others, he's the boss all right. Tough-looking, do you see?"

"Yeah," answered Lightfinger, "they do what they're told, don't they? Look at them move."

Presently the two Borribles saw the large car drive away in the moonlight, passing along the shining tarmac which led between the trees to the limits of Battersea Park. The car stopped for an instant at the gates and then turned left into Albert Bridge Road and disappeared on its way southwards into the quiet streets of the outer London suburbs.

The two Borribles stood up and looked around. They weren't too happy in parks, being much more at ease in crowded streets and broken-down houses. It was only occasionally that the Borrible lookouts checked on the green spaces, just to see they were still there and that everything was as it should be.

When Knocker was sure they were alone he said: "We'd better see what they were up to over there. There's something going on and I don't like it."

All at once the patch of ground at his feet began to tremble and clumps of grass began to pop up and away from their roots. There was a noise too, a scraping and a scrabbling, and a muffled voice swore and mumbled to itself. The carpet of grass rose and fell violently until a squat protuberance established itself between turf and top soil. The bump hesitated, as if it didn't know whether to continue upwards or retreat downwards. It grunted, swore again and, as if undecided, took off on a horizontal course, forcing the turf up as it wriggled along.

At the first sign of trouble Knocker and Lightfinger had taken refuge behind a bush but as the bump moved away they came from cover and followed it.

"It's got to be . . ." said Knocker, "it can't be anything else, and down here in Battersea, it's bad, double bad."

The mound now stopped and shook and struggled and became bigger, and as it grew more clods of grass fell from it.

"Watch yourself," whispered Knocker, "it's coming out. Get ready to jump it."

Lightfinger and Knocker crouched, waiting with patience, their minds racing with schemes. The turf rose higher and higher till it was as tall as the Borribles themselves, then it burst and the grass fell away like a discarded overcoat and revealed a dark and sinister shape of about their own size.

It looked like a giant rat, a huge mole or a deformed rabbit, but it was none of these for it stood on its hind legs and had a long snout and beady red eyes, like the things that had gone away in the car.

Knocker gave a shrill whistle and at the signal both he and Lightfinger leapt forward. Knocker got an arm-lock round the thing's head and pulled it to the ground while Lightfinger fell onto the hairy legs and bent one over the other in a special lock that could dislocate a knee with no trouble. The thing shouted so loudly that it would have woken the neighbourhood if there'd been one in Battersea Park. Knocker squeezed it round the neck and whispered: "Shuddup, you great fool, else I'll smother yer." The creature shuddupped.

Knocker sat the prisoner up and got behind it so he could tie its arms back with a length of rope he took from his waist. He and Lightfinger were very careful with the animal because there was no telling how strong it was. Lightfinger moved so that he was sitting on the thing's legs, looking into the eyes, which were like marbles rolling around at the wide end of the snout.

"All right," said Knocker when he was ready, "give it a duffing."

Lightfinger grabbed it by the scruff of the fur and pulled its snout forward. "Name," he asked gruffly.

The snout moved a little and they heard a voice say in a distinguished tone: "Timbucktoo."

"Tim who?" asked Lightfinger again, shaking the snout good and hard.

"Timbucktoo."

"And where are you from, you moth-eaten carpet?" asked Knocker, though he knew the answer.

Timbucktoo shook himself free of the two Borribles and, though his hands were bound, he got to his feet and glared haughtily down his snout, his red eyes blazing.

"Why, I'm fwom Wumbledom of course, you dirty little tykes. You'd better welease me before you get into sewious twouble."

"I knew it," said Knocker turning to Lightfinger with excitement. "A Rumble from Rumbledom. Ain't it strange as how they can't pronounce their 'r's?"

"So that's a Rumble," said Lightfinger with interest.

"I've often wondered what they looked like . . . bloody ugly."

"It's the first time I've been this close to one," said Knocker, "but you can't mistake them, nasty."

"You wevolting little stweet-awabs," exploded the Rumble losing his temper, "how dare you tweat me in this fashion?"

" 'Cos you're on our manor, that's how, you twat," said Knocker angrily. "I suppose you didn't even know."

"I only know what you are," said Timbucktoo, "and what I am and that I'll go where I like and do what I like without having to ask the permission of gwubby little ignawamuses like you. You'd better untie me, Bowwible, and I might forget about this incident."

"He's a real pain," said Lightfinger. "Let's throw him in the river."

The moon was clear of clouds again and glinted on the nearby Thames. In spite of himself the Rumble shivered. "That will do you no good. I can swim, you know, like an otter."

"So you should," said Knocker, "you look like one," and he cuffed the Rumble once more and told him to hold his tongue.

Knocker thought deeply, then he said, "I s'pose the river's the best idea for getting him off our manor, but maybe we ought to take him back and find out more about him, what his mob are up to. I don't like the look of it; suspicious this is, Rumbles down here in Battersea, it's wrong. We ought to give Spiff a chance to give this thing the once over."

"I think you're right, brother," said Lightfinger, and they hauled the Rumble to its feet and pushed it towards the Park Gates. When they reached the sleeping streets they kept to the dark shadows between the lamp-posts and marched rapidly in the direction of Battersea High Street.

Borribles are generally skinny and have pointed ears which give them a slightly satanic appearance. They are pretty tough-looking and always scruffy, with their arses hanging out of their trousers, but apart from that they look just like normal children, although some of them have been Borribles for years and years. They have sharp faces but their eyes are burning-bright and dart about all over the place, noticing everything and missing nothing. They are proud of their quickness of wit. In fact it is impossible to be dull and a Borrible because a Borrible is bright by definition. Not that they know lots of useless facts, it's just that they are quick and tend to dislike anyone who is a bit slow.

The only people likely to get close to Borribles are ordinary children because Borribles mix in with them to escape detection by "the authorities" who are always trying to catch them. Any child may have sat next to a Borrible or even talked to one and never noticed the ears because Borribles wear hats, woollen ones, pulled down over their heads, and they sometimes grow their hair long, hanging to their shoulders.

Normal kids are turned into Borribles very slowly, almost without being aware of it; but one day they wake up and there it is. It doesn't matter where they come from as long as they have what is called a "bad start". A child disappears from a school and the word goes round that he was "unmanageable"; the chances are he's off managing by himself. Sometimes it's given out that a kid down the street has been "put into care" because whenever he got home from school the house was empty; no doubt he's been Borribled and is caring for himself someplace. One day a shout might be heard in a supermarket and a kid with the goods on him is hoisted out by a store-detective. If that kid gets away he'll become a Borrible and make sure he isn't caught again. Being caught is the end for a Borrible.

So Borribles are outcasts but unlike most outcasts

they enjoy themselves and wouldn't be anything else. They delight in feeling independent and free and it is this feeling that is most important to them. Consequently they have no real leaders, though someone may pop into prominence from time to time, perhaps because he has had a good idea and wants to carry it through. They manage without authority and they get on well enough together, though like everybody, they quarrel.

They don't get on with adults at all, or anybody else for that matter, and they say why should they? Nobody has ever tried to get on with them, quite the contrary. They are ignored and that suits them down to the ground because that way they can do what they want to do in their own quiet and crafty way.

Knocker and Lightfinger had been on night patrol in Battersea Park when they'd stumbled across the Rumbles and the discovery had annoyed and scared them. Borribles like to make sure that no other Borrible tribe is encroaching on their territory, that's bad enough. They are always frightened that they might be driven away from their markets and houses and have their little bit of independence destroyed, so scouting round the frontiers is a regular duty.

Unearthing a Rumble was something very upsetting. They are the real enemies of the Borribles and the Borribles hate them for their riches, their power, their haughtiness and their possessions. If the Rumbles were coming all the way down from Rumbledom to colonise the Park, what price Battersea High Street?

Knocker and Lightfinger harried Timbucktoo along in front of them. They went past Morgan's Crucible Factory, along Battersea Church Road and by St Mary's down by the river, and then into the High Street. They saw no one and no one saw them, it being well into the early hours of the morning. They made for an empty house standing opposite the end of Trott Street. It was tall and wide and the bottom windows were boarded up and a sheet of corrugated iron covered the main doorway. The facade of the building was painted over in grey, and in black letters was written, "Bunham's Patent Locks Ltd. Western 4828."

It was a typical Borrible hideaway, derelict and decaying, and Knocker and Lightfinger lived there. Borribles live where they can in the streets of the big cities, but they like these abandoned houses best of all. When a house is already occupied they will often use the cellar and they camp in schools at night too because they are left empty and unused, like the schools in Battersea High Street.

The two Borribles halted on the pavement and looked up and down the street. Nobody. They opened a gate in the railings and Knocker pushed Timbucktoo down some stone steps leading to a basement. The captive rolled over and over like some hairy cushion until he landed on his snout at the foot of the stairs. The area was covered in rubbish that had been dropped from the street above by passers-by and luckily it broke the fall of the furry Rumble. He sat up and rubbed his head, then spying the litter he began patting bits of paper with feverish movements of his paws.

Knocker stopped halfway down the steps and turned to speak to Lightfinger. "Look at him, he must be suffering from shock."

"Perhaps you hit him too hard," suggested Lightfinger.

"Nonsense," answered Knocker and he went down and lifted the Rumble to its feet.

The chief lookout opened a door that led from the area into the basement part of the house and dragged the Rumble in by the neck, with Lightfinger pushing from behind. The door was closed and Knocker switched on the electric light. Borribles always have electric light even in deserted houses; there are good technicians amongst them and they simply tap into the nearest power supply.

The Borribles had entered a large cellar which had a few orange boxes for use as chairs and tables. Two doors opened from the room, one into an underground larder, which served the Borribles as a store-room, the other to some stairs which led to the rest of the house. At the bay window were hanging scraps of old blankets with not too many holes in them. They prevented the light shining into the street and alerting the police that someone was residing in a house that was supposed to be empty.

Knocker pushed Timbucktoo down onto an orange box and he and Lightfinger looked at the expressionless snout.

"What we gonna do with him, now we've got him here?" wondered Lightfinger.

"Yes," said the Rumble, looking up, his eyes glinting crimson, "you won't get away with this you know, it's iwwesponsible. You Bowwibles must be insane. I'll see you get your ears clipped."

Lightfinger and Knocker winced. Borribles are very sensitive about their ears, for if a Borrible is caught by the police the first thing that happens is that his ears are clipped and he starts to grow like any ordinary child. Left alone, Borribles don't grow physically and their small size is a great advantage.

"Clip me ears, will yer?" said Knocker tight-lipped and he went into the store cupboard. A second later he was out again, carrying a roll of sticky tape. He went over to the Rumble, grasped its head and wound the tape round and round the animal's snout so that it could no longer speak.

He stood back to admire his work. Lightfinger relaxed and cupped his face in his hands, and rested his elbows on his knees.

"There," said Knocker, "that's the way to deal with a talking mattress."

"I'm glad all animals can't speak," said Lightfinger, "we'd have meningitis within the week, or run out of sticky tape."

"I'll go and get Spiff," said Knocker. He ran up to the ground floor of the house and tapped on the door of the large room that overlooked the back garden. It was dark and dingy that garden and Knocker knew it was a wilderness of weeds growing through the old fragile rust of oil drums and the twisted frames of broken bicycles. While he waited Knocker pulled a damp strip of patterned paper from the wall; plaster came with it. The door opened a crack and another Borrible appeared. He was perhaps an inch taller than Knocker and his ears were very pointed. He was dressed in a bright orange dressing-gown made from new warm towelling. His carpet slippers were comfortable.

"Who are you? Ah, Knocker, what do you want then?"

"Sorry to wake you there, Spiff," said Knocker, "but me and Lightfinger found something in the Park, and think you ought to have a look at it. It's down in the basement."

"Oh Lor'," groaned Spiff, "can't it wait till morning? You haven't got the law on your trail, have you?"

"No," said Knocker tensely, "it's nothing like that. What we've got is worse. It's a Rumble! There was a whole lot of them in a posh car and we caught this one coming out of the ground. Cheek, isn't it, coming down here without a by-yer-leave and digging?"

Spiff had become more and more intent on what Knocker had been saying until finally he seemed quite beside himself.

"One of those toffee-nosed Rumble-Rats, eh? You get back downstairs, me lad, and I'll come right away. I'll just put me hat on."

He closed the door and Knocker scooted back down the dark uncovered stairs. He understood Spiff's caution: no Borrible ever left his room without putting on a woollen hat to cover the tops of his ears. It wasn't that they were ashamed of them, quite the contrary but they liked to be prepared for an emergency. Any unforeseen circumstance could force them into the streets and it wouldn't do to be spotted as a Borrible.

"He's coming," said Knocker as soon as he re-entered the room. "He's a good house-steward, you know, short-tempered sometimes, but very crafty."

"You can't get anything past him and that's a fact," said Lightfinger. "Some say he's artful enough to catch himself. Do you know he won all his names in fights with the Rumbles? Nobody knows how many, nobody . . . strange that. He hates 'em."

"There's lots of stories about his names and not very Borrible some of them," said Knocker, "but I don't believe the half of it." He sat down and looked at Timbucktoo and thought about names and the gaining of them, a major preoccupation with him.

A Borrible name has to be earned because that is the only way a Borrible can get one. He has to have an adventure of some sort, and if he is successful he gets a name. There are all kinds of things a Borrible can do; it doesn't have to be stealing or burgling necessarily, though it generally is. It could be a witty or funny trick on someone, and it is preferable if that someone is an adult.

The only thing that Knocker had against the rules was that it was difficult to get on any adventures once you had a name. First chance was always given to those who were nameless and this irritated Knocker for he had a secret ambition: to collect more names than any other Borrible.

A noise on the stairs disturbed Knocker's reflections. He stood up and at the same moment Spiff flung open

18

the door and strode theatrically into the room. His head was adorned with a magnificent hat of scarlet wool and he clutched the orange dressing-gown tightly to his chest. Spiff had the clear face of a twelve-year-old child but his eyes were dark with wisdom. He stopped short as soon as he saw the Rumble and he pushed his breath out over his teeth and made a whisper of a whistle.

"At last," he said like he was praying, "at last. It's been a long while since I had my hands on one of these stinking rodents." He turned and beamed at Knocker and Lightfinger. "You lads have done marvellous, you've captured one alive and well, though he won't be for long, the little basket. Found him in the Park, eh? With hundreds of others, digging holes, that's how it starts, brothers. Down here on our manor, taking it all for granted, think they are the lords of creation, don't they? Go anywhere, do what they like, we don't count." He prodded and screwed the Rumble with a rigid index finger as he spoke. He turned to Knocker; "You know what this is?"

"A Rumble."

"Some people call them Rumbles." Spiff was bitter. "I know what I call them; bloody scavengers, no better than you or me for all their la-di-dah manners. Years of them I've seen, sneerin' at us, down their hoity-toity snouts. Thieves they are, just like us, only they call it finding. A copper would call it stealing by finding. They're a bit quick at it too, mate, I can tell you; why an old lady has only got to put down her bag of peppermints to scratch herself and there they are, gone in a flash. Bloody hypocrites! Drop a gob-stopper and you won't hear it hit the ground, one of these little bleeders has scooped it up in mid-air. Keeping the place clean they call it, huh, so clean there's nothing left for anyone else."

Knocker and Lightfinger looked at each other. They had never seen Spiff so angry.

"Oh, come on, Spiff," said Lightfinger carelessly, "it can't be that bad, the Rumbles have never done me any harm."

Spiff jumped a foot from the floor. "Don't you know anything about the old days," he cried, "the struggles and fights we had to win free? Why those times were terrible."

"Oh, I know about it all right but that was your time, not mine," and Lightfinger leaned against the wall, crossed his ankles and shoved his hands into his pockets.

"Don't care was made to care," said Spiff sententiously, "and history repeats itself, in fact it don't repeat itself, it just goes on being the same."

"Well, what are we going to do with this rabbit, anyway?" asked Knocker.

"Lock it up in the cupboard," said Spiff rubbing his chin. "I'll call an Annual General Emergency Session tomorrow. You two can run down the street with the message right now, before you go to bed. I know the others won't like it but this is an emergency and we will have to act and think together for once!"

Spiff took one last look at the Rumble, then he shoved his Borrible hat further onto his head, spun on his heels and left the room. Knocker got the prisoner to his feet and locked him in the store-cupboard, then he and Lightfinger left by the basement door and spent the next few hours informing all the Borribles in the High Street what was afoot. The Annual General Emergency Session was set for the next morning at ten o'clock. Finally the two exhausted lookouts got to their own room at the top of Spiff's house and they climbed into a bundle of old blankets and sacks that formed their bed.

"Ho, ho, oh, ho," yawned Knocker, "what a day."

"Goo' night," said Lightfinger, and was immediately asleep.

*

A Borrible's main business is to stay alive. This is an occupation that takes up most of his time; getting food from what is left about, finding stuff before it is lost and knocking food off barrows and out of the store-rooms of supermarkets and such like. That is why Borribles live round shopping centres and along street-markets like Brixton and Petticoat Lane. Then again much of their provisions come from the gear that falls off lorries, which happens a lot in London with the bumpy roads.

So important is that aspect of their life that they have many proverbs about it and they are all gathered together in *The Borrible Book of Proverbs*. Some of these sayings are very ancient, like "That which falls off a lorry belongs to he who follows the lorry," and "That which is found has never been lost." One of their favourites is, "It is impossible to lose that which does not belong to you," and Borribles use that one a lot to people who complain about their thieving.

By eight o'clock on the morning following the capture of Timbucktoo Rumble, Battersea High Street market was in full swing. There were barrows and stalls along each side of the road and so little space was left for traffic that not a car dared venture down there. The barrows had been shoved very close together and it was easy for a Borrible to crawl underneath them from one end of the street to the other, picking up fruit on the way. Some Borribles mingled with the shoppers on the pavements, others looked into carrier bags and asked questions, creating diversions while their mates "did the shopping". It was a good way to get breakfast.

The coster-mongers shouted at each other and at prospective customers, urging them to buy. There were barrows selling fruit, ironmongery, fish and large crabs; the shops had their doors wide open and friends were drinking tea in Notarianni's café and chatting their heads off. The pie-and-eel shop, Brown's, was doing a fine business and people from the different blocks of buildings, Archer House, Eaton House and White House, were loafing about the street and talking about passing bets in Ernie Swash's. The noise was so great that it rose right up the side of the house where Knocker and Lightfinger were sleeping and woke them in their bed on the floor.

Knocker sat up and shoved his companion. "Come on, breakfast." They had both been out so late the night before that when they came back it had been bright morning. Some of the costers had been putting out their barrows and loading them up, so the two Borribles had had no trouble in getting provisions. Breakfast was there beside them: one grapefruit, two oranges and two large doughnuts with jam.

Lightfinger rubbed his eyes and the sacks and blankets dropped from him. He reached for an orange, bit it open and sucked hard, making a lot of noise. The orange was wonderful, it had been chilled to ice crystals by the lorry journeys to and from Convent Garden.

"Ooaah," he groaned with pleasure, "that's lovely."

"We'd better hurry up," said Knocker, "we don't want to miss the meeting."

Halfway down the High Street was an old and disused brickbuilt hall. It had last been occupied by photographers called "Scots of London," but they had gone long since and now the shop fell within the province of the Borribles. It was here that Spiff had asked the other stewards of the High Street to meet him, and as it was a special meeting any other Borrible who wanted could come and listen and eventually make comments, if he wished.

Inside the hall Spiff stood on the stage talking away as fast as he could go. He was listened to, very seriously, by about a score of his colleagues. Other Borribles, ragged, dirty and inquisitive, slipped in through the side entrances and stood about, wondering what was going on. They did not have long to wait.

Spiff stepped to the front of the stage and held up both his arms like a politician. He shouted several times and gradually the noise in the hall became less and less until eventually there was a kind of excited silence. The stewards behind Spiff took their seats and leaned forward attentively. Spiff looked all round and then began to speak, relishing the occasion, for if he had a weakness at all, it was a delight in speechifying.

"Brother and sister Borribles, I am pleased to see so many of you here, for today is a day of decision. Our way of life is threatened and we must either act together or perish."

The hall went quieter and the tension rose.

"Not to beat about the bush, I'll give you the facts, then I'll tell you what me, and the rest of your elected representatives, have decided, and then, in due order, we shall put it to the general vote. Right, the facts. Last night, our chief lookout and his assistant . . ."

All heads turned to Knocker and Lightfinger.

". . . while on a routine inspection of the Battersea area discovered that we had been invaded by the Rumbles."

The crowd drew in a deep breath and then let it out again in a long explosion and Spiff looked round for effect and more silence.

"It seems that a large force came down here, all the way from Rumbledom, and occupied the Park for several hours. They were digging! Now, in my opinion, this can only be a preparation for a take-over of Battersea, an erosion of our freedom, a new and subtle kind of slavery and a clipping of ears. Things have been bearable as long as the Rumbles have stayed in Rumbledom, where they belong, but this is something else."

Murmurs of assent came from the assembly but Spiff held up his hand and went on.

"There is only one answer, my friends, pre-emptive defence. We must attack before we are attacked. We, my brother stewards and I, have evolved a plan to destroy the Rumbles at the heart of their organisation. However . . ."

Spiff broke off for a second and admonished the ceiling with a grubby finger.

". . . to carry out this plan we shall need to search carefully among the ranks of the nameless. From those who have not yet had their first adventure we must select the bravest, the slyest, the craftiest and the most resourceful. It is not only the enemy we have to fear, but the enormous distance between us and him, dangerous terrain. The Rumble is confident in his stronghold, blinded by his own conceit, safe, so he thinks, in the security of his own riches and comfort, but that is where we shall strike, with a handful of chosen Borribles. We shall need dedicated volunteers but remember, those who go may never return. Blood will be spilt."

At this there was a terrific hush in the hall and the Borribles looked at each other with trepidation. An adventure was one thing, death another.

"We feel," went on Spiff, "that Battersea should not bear this brunt alone. All London Borribles are involved. To this end messages will be sent out over the city and certain tribes will be asked to send their likeliest un-named champions to us for training and instruction. Likewise, from among the ranks of the Battersea nameless, we shall choose one who shows the greatest promise. We intend to approach the following groups: the Totters of Tooting, the Wendles of Wandsworth, the Stumpers of Stepney, the Whitechapel Wallopers, the Peckham Punch-uppers, the Neasden Nudgers and the Hoxton Humpers. Details of the raid will be worked out when all the candidates have arrived."

Spiff stopped for breath and the hall became alive and buzzed with conversation. Who, people wondered, would be chosen as the Battersea representative on the expedition? An honour, yes, but what a danger too.

Knocker swore to himself; "Wish I didn't have my name already, that's a real adventure that is, wish I could go."

Spiff called for quiet again, and got it, after a while. Now he prepared for his moment of high drama. He made a sign to the side of the stage and the prisoner was brought on for all to see. There was a stunned silence. The Rumble was still taped round the snout but its beady eyes glowed a fearful red and it stood upright and unmoved.

"This," shouted Spiff, "is the enemy, no braver than us, no more dangerous, but he is difficult of access, well-protected in his burrows, he is rich and he is powerful, thinks himself superior to all Borribles by divine right. This is the enemy who wants to take Battersea into his grasp. Even now they may be digging under the streets to emerge in your very back-yard, even now they may be undermining your way of life, silently, like dirty moles."

Spiff took a deep breath and shook his arms in front of his body as if he was emptying a sack of cement and the crowd stirred with emotion. Spiff raised his voice a further notch. "This is the enemy, brothers, and we all know that he must be stopped at all costs, yes, but more than that, he must be eliminated, and who are the Borribles to do it? Why we are!"

An enormous cheer gushed from the audience. "Throw it in the river," came a voice from the back of the hall, "with a bicycle round its neck."

This suggestion was so popular that it was taken up on all sides.

"Yeah," came the shout, "in the river, steal a bike someone."

Spiff smiled indulgently. "I understand your feelings, brothers," he looked at the Rumble, "but I have a better plan. Let me explain. The one thing that these objects fear above all others," he touched the Rumble lightly

25

with a disdainful finger, "is discovery! They would hate to be unmasked and shown for what they really are. In their mythology the greatest possible disaster is what they call the Great Rumble Hunt. Their whole world is built on a false confidence, friends; the Great Rumble Hunt will destroy that confidence, and we, the Borribles of Battersea, will start that Rumble Hunt. But," Spiff had to shout across the cheering, "this is to be a war of nerves, we want them to know that something really nasty is on the way . . . us! And that is where this little rodent comes in. We propose to stick a notice onto the fur of this—carpet bag, and send it back along the chain of Borribles, right back to Rumbledom, where it will be discovered in an exhausted and dishevelled state as proof that we mean business. The message will say, 'The Great Rumble Hunt is on. Beware the Borribles!' All those in favour say 'Aye'."

Another enormous cheer rose from the assembly. Borribles clasped each other, jumped up and down and shouted, "We'll show 'em, we'll teach those rabbits to come down here." Only Knocker was unhappy, wishing he could get rid of his name.

The stewards on the stage left with Spiff and the prisoner and the hall gradually emptied as the various groups of Borribles made their way back to their own houses, cellars and sheds, to discuss the morning meeting and to wonder who would be chosen as the Battersea champion to go with the others. Those who were not known for their bravery kept very quiet and decided not to call attention to themselves, for there are Borribles who go right through life without ever earning themselves a name. But there are others of a different stamp, and they ran back to the market directly from the meeting, stole some paper and, without delay, sat down and wrote a note to Spiff begging for the position.

Knocker walked back to his house, alone. Lightfinger had gone off on a food raid but Knocker wasn't hungry.

He felt thwarted. He knew that there was absolutely no chance of him being considered for the expedition to Rumbledom. He went into the basement of the deserted house and made his way upstairs. As he passed Spiff's door it was thrown open and the steward appeared, beaming.

"Right, lad," he said, "in here, just the bloke we want, look lively, the others want a word with you."

Knocker stepped inside the room and found it crowded with the stewards who had been on the stage with Spiff. The prisoner had disappeared. Knocker took off his woollen cap and held it in his hands; he had good pointed ears showing a high range of intelligence and alertness. The stewards nodded approval. They were sitting round the room comfortably relaxed on upholstered orange-boxes and little grape-barrels. Spiff settled into a fine armchair that must have fallen off a very expensive furniture lorry or removal van.

"Sit down, lad," he said. "We wanted to thank you for your good work last night, champion that was, champion." He consulted a sheaf of papers. "Now to business; we want to ask your advice. As you may know, there are eight Rumbles in the Rumble High Command. I feel that if we can eliminate them, the rest of the Rumble social structure will fall to pieces and they won't have time to interfere with us any more. So that's why we are sending eight Borribles only, one for each High Rumble. There will be one from Tooting, Hoxton, Wandsworth—you heard all that already. But, Knocker, who are we going to send from Battersea?"

"The point is," said one of the other stewards, "you are out and about a lot, you see a lot of Borribles in action, who do you think would be a good choice?"

Knocker thought for a while. "It's tricky," he said at length, "there's quite a few who are good. There's a bunch of bright lads down by Morgan's Crucible Works, some others under the railway arches at Battersea Park Station, but I think the brightest of the lot, out of the whole Borough, is one who lives up on Lavender Hill, bright as a button and smart as paint."

"Whereabouts does he hang out?" asked another steward.

"Underneath the nick," said Knocker, who had been saving up the surprise.

"Underneath the nick!" cried a dozen voices. "He must be mad."

Knocker laughed. "Oh, no. Bright. There's a stack of rooms that are left empty each and every night. It's centrally heated, blankets galore, constant electricity and hot water. You name it, he's got it. In fact he's got some of the Woollies thinking he's a local lad and in the daytime he often does the odd errand for 'em. You see he doesn't even have to do a lot of thieving; he's got almost everything he needs on the spot."

"I should have known about this before," said Spiff, looking a big disgruntled.

"I'm sorry," explained Knocker, "but I was hoping to make the boy a lookout for us. I was waiting for the right adventure to come up so that he could get a name, and I think this must be it."

Spiff looked round at the other stewards.

"Carried," he said, and they nodded. "Right, that's settled. Now, Knocker, I want you to send a runner up to Lavender Hill and get that wazzisname down here. As soon as the champions come in from the other Boroughs we shall have to begin a training session. As well as that, I want you to get some volunteers to do some spare-time thieving. We're going to need lots of things for the expeditionary force, grub, weather-proof clothing, good catapults, watches, compasses, anything that might be useful. You are our best lookout so I want you to organise the provisioning of the expedition. I know you've got your own thieving to do, and so have the others, but do what you can. This expedition cannot afford to fail."

Knocker nodded. His heart was bursting with pride,

he was being involved, which was more than he had dared to hope. "Is there a chance of anything else, Spiff?"

"What do you mean? You can't go on it, you know, that's a rule."

"I know that. It's, well, you said they would have to be trained. I'm a good Borrible lookout, well, I could train them . . . couldn't I?"

Spiff gave Knocker a long look, a look that went right through the Borrible and saw everything. "Hmm," he said, smiling a secret smile, "you are keen, aren't you? How many names have you got?"

"Just the one," answered Knocker feeling uncomfortable.

Spiff chuckled and looked at the other stewards. "He reminds me of me," he said. "Well, brothers, shall he train the team?"

The motion was passed and Knocker was delighted. He wasn't the chief lookout for nothing and he knew how to get his own way. He got up to go, feeling proud and also grateful to Spiff. The steward detained him.

"Here, take this envelope, it's instructions about the Rumble, he's downstairs in the cupboard. Send him packing, try not to let anyone see him, they might chuck him in the river anyway."

Knocker ran downstairs and opened the cupboard. Sure enough the Rumble was there, his paws still tied behind him and a notice glued onto his fur, which had gone all spiky and dirty.

Two assistant lookouts came into the room and leaned against the wall to watch as Knocker read his instructions. When he had finished he removed the tape from the animal's snout and sat it on a grape-barrel.

"You are being sent home, Rumble, alive. Take that message to your leaders and tell them what you have seen and heard."

Knocker turned to the lookouts. "You two can escort

him on the first stage of the journey. This envelope has instructions from the meeting. Take him to the Junction and hand him over. Then he can be taken to the Honeywell Borribles and they can take him up to the Wendles beyond Wandsworth Common, from there the Wendles will take him to Merton Road. This letter goes with him and explains what should be done at each stage. Finally, he should be released as near Rumbledom High Street as possible and allowed to find his way home. Any questions?"

The two lookouts shook their heads.

"Right," said Knocker, "as soon as you've got rid of him come back to me and report. It is very important that he gets back in one piece, though it doesn't matter what he looks like; the rougher the better. We've got to frighten the fur off them."

Timbucktoo jumped to his feet at this. "You don't fwighten me, Bowwible, nor your fwiends. You don't know what you're taking on. We'll be keeping a watch out for you, you'll be skewered on our Wumble-sticks before you get a sight of Wumbledom Hill. You may be safe down here in your gwimy stweets and stinking back-alleys, but Wumbledom is a wilderness with twackless paths that only we can follow. This means war."

Knocker cuffed the Rumble round the ear, almost affectionately. "Go on," he said, "you old door-mat, before I knock that snout of yours through the back of your bonce."

At a sign from Knocker his two assistants hauled the Rumble from the room on the first stage of his long and perilous journey; a journey on which he would be passed from hand to hand like a registered packet in the London post.

Chapter 2

During the fortnight that followed the lookouts' room in the old empty house marked "Bunham's Patent Locks Ltd" became the centre for the collection of all gear that might turn out to be useful on the expedition. Under the watchful eye of Knocker it was stacked and sorted. Accepted or refused, everything was entered into a large ledger; anything left over was going to be raffled so there was great interest in the High Street, and many of the Borribles were excelling themselves in collecting material. Of course a lot of others took no interest at all and if they found something useful amongst their loot, well they just kept it.

There were life-jackets from the sports' section of Ardens and Nobbs, thick warm coats from Walker's, sleeping-bags, unbreakable nylon rope for climbing up trees and the sides of houses, stout boots, oilskins, woollen underwear, sharp knives, sou'westers, ski-goggles, corduroy trousers with knee pads and small shoulder satchels converted into rucksacks.

Looking at his inventory Knocker felt pleased; every eventuality had been foreseen. The store-cupboard was full and the lookouts' room was piled high with valuable items. The only space left clear was a small area round his desk and a kind of corridor to each of the doors.

One day his contented musing was interrupted by Lightfinger who came into the improvised warehouse and sidled between the goods towering above his head.

"You look tired," he said.

"I am that," answered Knocker. "I think I've got everything now, though I suppose I'm bound to have forgotten something."

"Well, you haven't finished yet, mate," said Lightfinger. "Spiff wants to see you right away, upstairs."

Knocker ran up to the ground floor landing and knocked on Spiff's door.

"Come in," cried the rough voice and Knocker did so.

"Ah, there you are, Knocker, sit down, good news, they're here."

"Who?" asked Knocker who was very tired and whose mind was still counting hot-water bottles and ice-axes.

"Oh, come on," said Spiff. "The Champions, the Brightest of the Borribles, the Magnificent Eight, the two thirds of a Dozen, call 'em what you like, they're here."

"Where?" asked Knocker, sitting up in his chair.

"They're in the store-room under the gym at forty-five Rowena Crescent, other side of Prince's Head. I want you to put them through basic and advanced lookout training, even if they are lookouts already. Make sure they are first-class thieves, good at shoplifting, Woollie-dodging; and see they know the Borrible proverbs by heart, all the usual kind of things. Then take them on a few courses in Battersea Park, I know they don't like the countryside, but they've got to get used to it; Rumbledom's rough. I'll give you a fortnight, that's all. There'll be another bloke to help you, he's from the Northcote Road lot, was brought up in a paratrooper's family before he was Borribled, he could be useful. By the way," Spiff threw over some books and Knocker caught them in his lap, "you'd better read those from cover to cover, they're the Rumble manuals, their whole history from the word go, gives the layout of their place, the structure of their command, the way they fight with their Rumble-sticks. Nasty prodders, they are, with a four-inch nail at the end. Everything's there. Get on with it, Knocker. I'll come and see you in two weeks' time. If there's anything you need, send a runner."

Knocker gathered up the books and got up to leave, but he was stopped.

"Oh, yes, in the first volume I've made a list of the Eight High Rumbles of Rumbledom, their names. We thought it would be a good idea if we gave each of your Borribles one of those names to win, so if they ever get that far, your blokes will know exactly which Rumble he's got to do for. Good idea, isn't it?"

"How shall I give them out? Did you decide that?"

Spiff laughed to himself mysteriously. "You'd better put the names into a hat and let them draw for them, then there can be no arguments about the targets they are given." The steward hesitated and then laughed again. "That is except two of them, those you'll have to put into a separate hat. You'll see them marked on the list. Go on, buzz off, Knocker."

Knocker whistled as he went down the stairs. He would dearly have loved to go on the expedition and to have earned a new name and a new story, but fancy going through life with a Rumble title, that would be strange. Then he reflected that it was not the name after all but the story it carried with it that mattered. He could think of some fine Borribles with the most extraordinary monikers but when you saw them or heard their names you didn't think of the word alone or its sound, you thought of the life and the deeds that lay beyond it, the story.

Stories are very important to Borribles. Most of the time they can't have a real adventure because they are too busy, but they read tales that deal with exciting things, like westerns or spy-stories or science fiction. For a Borrible the next best thing to an adventure of his own is hearing other Borribles recount their adventures and how they won their names. That's why they like doing outlandish things, so they can tell their stories afterwards and exaggerate what happened. They like winning their adventures of course but, just like most other people, they very often lose, but that is all right as long as it makes a good story.

Knocker left the house and made his way up the High Street. There was no doubt in his mind as he threaded his way along the pavements; the eight champions who were going on this adventure would have wonderful stories to tell. The Rumble names they were going to win would remind them of their targets during the expedition and, in years to come, if they were successful, everyone who heard the names would know how they had been won. "Yes," concluded Knocker as he turned into Rowena Crescent, "a clever idea."

Outside number forty-five Knocker stopped to make sure his hat was on firmly. The gym was a long low building looking like an empty pub and faced with green tiles. Above the door and the three long windows was a notice board. Knocker looked up at it, though he knew what it said: "Rowena Gym. Tough Guys for Stage and Screen and T.V. Stunt Men. Kung Fu. Laetitia Martin, prop."

Knocker could hear grunts and groans coming from inside. That would be adults trying to break into the big-time. In the pavement he saw the tell-tale grilles showing him the basement where the Borribles would be. Tightening his grip round the Rumble books Knocker went through the main entrance and down a corridor that was tiled in the same dirty colour as the front of the building. A porter threw open the door to his office and stood right in front of the pint-sized Borrible. He looked huge with his legs spread and his hands on his hips. He had a cauliflower ear and his breath smelt sickly sweet with brown ale.

"And where d'you think you're going, mush?"

"It's all right," lied Knocker, "my big brother's here and I got to give him these books. I'm late already."

The man thought slowly, then, "Hmm, okay, but don't hang about. Kids ain't allowed in here, specially little squirts like you. I'll clip you round the ear, I will."

Knocker shuddered at the idea, pulled his hat down hard and bobbed away.

At the end of the corridor Knocker found two staircases, one going up, the other down. Knocker allowed one of his books to fall to the ground and as he picked it up he looked under his arm and saw that the doorman was still watching. Knocker went up to the first floor, waited a while, then crept back down the stairs. The corridor was now empty so he descended the dank cement steps until it became so dark that he had to feel his way. He groped along a wall until he came up to a rough wooden door which did not give when he pushed it. He gave the Borrible knock, gently at first and then, when nothing happened, he knocked a little louder, one long, two shorts, then a long, "Dah . . di-di . . dah."

There was a slight noise behind the door, a bolt clanged, a lock clashed and an eye peered out through a slit.

"Borrible?" asked the person behind the door.

"Borrible," answered Knocker.

The door was opened enough for Knocker to pass through and then it was closed and bolted behind him. He found himself in a long dusty room with exercise bars covering each wall from floor to ceiling. From the central beams hung thick ropes for climbing. Mats were piled on the parquet flooring and Knocker could see all kinds of equipment for improving the efficiency of the human machine. The room was lit by long narrow windows situated under the grilles that Knocker had seen in the pavement outside. The light that slanted across the room was grey and faltering, losing itself before it reached the corners. It was so dull that Knocker could hardly make out the eight shapes sitting quietly on a bench at the far end of the gym.

The chief lookout turned to the Borrible next to him. "Northcote Road?" he asked, and his companion nodded.

"Name is Dodger," he said and smiled.

"That sounds like a good name," said Knocker, "you must have had a good adventure getting it. You must tell me one day."

"Everyone knows how you got your name, Knocker, that's one of the best Borrible stories ever told."

It is usual for Borribles meeting for the first time to exchange compliments on their respective names and the winning of them. Until they have a name Borribles are known simply as "You, Oi", or "Mush", sometimes as "Fingy", or even "Wazzisname". To call a named Borrible by one of the foregoing is an unforgivable insult and will lead to fighting. Borribles are great scrappers, mainly because they are used to it.

An even greater insult for a named Borrible is to hint that he acquired his name only because he'd found it, or someone had thrown it away. And to an un-named one it is very galling to have it suggested that he is nameless because no one has yet had the devious ingenuity to invent an epithet bad enough for him.

Knocker inspected the Northcote Road Borrible and liked what he saw. It seemed to him that they would get on. He smiled.

Instead of the usual woollen cap Dodger wore an army beret of a dark red colour and stuck into it was the badge of the Parachute Regiment, shining bright.

"Army background," observed Knocker.

"Oh, yes," said Dodger proudly, "Parachute Regiment and SAS until I became a Borrible. Might not have run away at all if they hadn't wanted to pack me off to some school. Up'ntil then I'd spent all my time watching the soldiers doing their training. That was the life."

Knocker laughed. "Well, we'd better get going, we haven't got all that long." They turned from the door and strolled down the long hall, their feet kicking into piles of rubbish and releasing stale smells from old cartons.

"How did you get in here?" asked Knocker.

Dodger pointed to the ceiling. "I had the bolts off a couple of those grilles in the pavement. Easy. That way we won't have to go past 'Punchie' the porter every day."

"I'll ren ember next time."

The Eight sat motionless on the bench. Some leaned back against the wall with their eyes closed; some held their heads in their hands and others sat looking straight in front of them, staring at Knocker.

At a sign from Knocker Dodger switched on some electric lights and the Borribles blinked their eyes. "Stand up. Hats off."

When they had done what Knocker had asked he walked down the line and inspected their ears to see if they showed signs of the intelligence he was expecting. It was a manoeuvre that gave him time to think. He would have admitted to no one, apart from Spiff perhaps, that he was flabbergasted. One of the champions he noticed was black. Of course he knew that many Borribles were black, more and more all the time. There were a lot in Battersea, Tooting, and a greater number even in Brixton; he just hadn't thought of one on this expedition. He had no one to blame but himself for this oversight, he was chief lookout and his mind should have been open to all possibilities, not drifting around in preconceptions. Mentally he kicked himself for being a fool, but he hadn't finished kicking himself yet. When he stopped at the end of the row he found that the last two Borribles were females. Here his surpise nearly got the better of him, but he pursed his lips and pretended to be thinking. One of the girls smiled and to cover his embarrassment Knocker looked closely at her ears. They indicated a high degree of intelligence and great individuality—and that could mean trouble. Now Knocker knew why Spiff had laughed and why he had said he'd have to put the names into two different hats.

Knocker went back to where Dodger stood, handed over the Rumble books, and took the list of names from his pocket. He looked at it, making the eight champions wait. Finally he said: "You will be here for two weeks. We are going to see how good you really are. When Dodger and I have satisfied ourselves about your basic knowledge we will move on to more specialist skills, but before that I want to be convinced that you are good: good with a catapult, good with your hands, good with your feet. I want you to be the best runners, the best fighters, and I want to see how you deal with adults in tricky situations. You'd better be the best if you want to go on this trip, because if I don't think you are, you ain't going."

Knocker looked along the faces, scrutinising them one after the other. "Anyone hears an order from me or Dodger, jump. That's against the grain for a Borrible, I know it, but there hasn't been an adventure like this in years and if you want to be in on it you've got to do what I say. Any questions?"

There were no questions.

"Good, now to the names. It was decided at the stewards' meeting to give you your names now—provisionally."

There was a stir in the line and eyes flashed.

"This is to make it more convenient for me during training and for you all when you're out on the adventure. These names will not be confirmed until your return—if you ever make it. These names have been lent to you on trust. One false step at any time and your name will be withdrawn, and you will never be given another adventure."

There was silence, the eight faces looked at him and waited. They were tense and excited, but these Borribles were too canny to give much away in their expressions. Knocker liked that. He went on.

"These are fine names, names that a have good ring to them and will remind you, and others in the future, of this adventure; but more important, the name that each of you will be given is also the name of the Rumble that is your individual target. While you remember your own name you cannot forget the name of your enemy."

Knocker paused. He knew that each Borrible standing before him could hardly wait for the moment when he would carry a name; the one word which could sum up and symbolise a whole life. "All right," went on the chief lookout, "the names will be distributed by drawing lots, six names in one hat, and two names in another. Dodger."

Dodger and Knocker removed their hats and Knocker tore each name separately from the sheet that Spiff had given him. He put six names into his own woollen cap and two into the red beret of the Paratroops. Dodger held the beret while Knocker shook his own hat vigorously to mix the names fairly and squarely. "I'll start at one end and move along," he said, "it's all the luck of the draw."

He studied the face of the first person in the line. By chance it was the one he had recommended to Spiff, the Battersea Borrible from the Lavender Hill nick. Knocker had always liked the look of him, although they didn't know each other very well. He was slightly built, even for a Borrible, his skin was clear and his hair was dark and tightly curled, like wire-wool. His eyes were sharp and blue and they moved quickly, but were never furtive. He smiled a lot and Knocker could see that it would take a lot to get him down. He glanced at Knocker, winked, then, plunged his hand into the hat

39

and pulled out a scrap of paper. He opened it, read it to himself and then smiled at the chief lookout. He rolled his tongue about, getting the feel of his name for the very first time.

"Bingo," he said, "the name's Bingo."

"That's a good name," said Knocker and stepped sideways. He stood in front of the black Borrible. "Where you from?" asked Knocker.

"Tooting, man, Tooting, and you?"

Knocker raised his head sharply. "I'm from here."

The Tooting Borrible, or Totter, had hair standing out in a thick solid uncut mass all round his head like a black halo. His teeth protruded and he seemed to be smiling all the time, but really his expression was one of cheerful slyness. Knocker liked that. He shook the hat again and the Totter took a piece of paper.

"My name is going to be O-ro-coc-co," he said, splitting the word into separate syllables and pronouncing them with care.

The next person was smaller than Bingo even. He had a triangular face with a pointed chin and his mousy hair lay flat across the top of his head He had a way of wagging his head in a most knowing way; there wasn't a trick he didn't know, said his eyes. Knocker stopped in front of him with the hat and the Borrible said, "I'm from Stepney, the best place in the world."

Knocker nodded only and offered the hat. The Stepney Borrible looked at the name on the paper he had drawn and whistled, then he said, "Good, I've got the best, Vulgarian, the Chief Rumble. Don't reckon his chances when I catch up with him."

"I see you've read the books, so you know why you're here?"

"Course, to get a name, and because they said that this was going to be the best adventure ever." And the Borrible glanced up and down the line and the others nodded in agreement.

"You've got to convince me that you're good enough first. Then you go," said Knocker.

"Perhaps you ought to start by showing that you're good enough to train us," said a brittle voice to Knocker's right, but Knocker ignored it and moved on a step.

"I'm from Peckham," said the next one without being asked and he thrust his hand into the hat and pulled out his name. Knocker watched him closely as he read the paper. He seemed strong and resourceful. He had dark heavy eyebrows and a red face with a firm jaw and enormous shoulders and arms. The kind of bloke who would not mince his words, not very witty perhaps, but dogged and persistent.

"Well," said Knocker, "which one have you got?"

The Peckham Borrible did not even show pleasure as he said, "I've got the name I wanted, Stonks, the Keeper of the Great Door of Rumbledom. He's the strongest one, ain't he? He'll need to be when I hit him."

When Knocker came face to face with the next person he wrinkled his nose. There was an unmistakable smell about this one and Knocker guessed immediately where he came from.

"You're from Wandsworth, aren't you? A Wendle?"

"So what, some of the finest Borribles in the world have come from Wandsworth."

Knocker recognised at once the brittle voice that had spoken out of turn a little earlier. "And some of the worst," he retorted, smiling a smile that had no warmth in it.

In common with most other Borribles he wasn't overfond of the aloof Wandsworth Brotherhood. They lived along the banks of the River Wandle in disused sewers and smelly holes they had scooped out below the streets of Wandsworth. But no one knew exactly how they lived, for they were the most suspicious and warlike of all Borribles and did not encourage visitors

41

and rarely spoke to anyone outside their own tribe. Their skin always had a green tinge to it which came from living so much underground and being so often in and out of the filthy Wandle water. Once the Wandle had been a pleasant stream, but years of industrialisation had turned it into a treacherous ooze of green and muddy slime. The mud was a mixture of poison waste, decomposed rubbish and undigested lumps of plastic which rolled slowly along the surface skin of the river as it slid like a thick jelly down to the Thames. The Wandle mud would entrap any stranger who was foolhardy enough to wade across without guidance. No one but the Wendles knew the secret paths along the river and they would only take the traveller across for a price. Every Wendle carried the smell of the Wandsworth marshes with him—and that smell was the smell of treachery and decay. Knocker had seen few Wendles, none of them had been this close and he didn't like what he saw: the green tinge to the flesh, the dark eyes of an indeterminate colour, and the cold, proud bearing of the born scrapper. There seemed to be no spontaneous warmth in the Wendle and warmth was normally the first thing that was noticed in a Borrible.

"Take your name, anyway," said Knocker flatly, and he held out his hat.

The Wendle narrowed his eyes and screwed up his mouth to prove that he didn't care a damn about Knocker or anyone else and he pulled out his name. He nodded, then he laughed loud, pleased and hostile.

"Out with it," said Knocker impatiently. "What is it?"

"What a name I have," he cried, "I shall cover it in glory."

"Or mud."

The Wendle ignored Knocker and looked up and down the line of adventurers. "Napoleon Boot," he said loudly. "Call me Napoleon Boot."

"And I suppose you know why you're going to Rum-bledom?" asked Knocker.

"Why am I going?" The other was angry. "What's wrong with you? Because I hate them, that's why. I always have hated them, and if you always had 'em leering down at yer from Rumbledom, like I have, you'd hate 'em as much as I do. I don't need these other seven to come up the Burrow with me. I'll tear it apart on me tod."

Knocker shrugged. He was glad to move on to the last of the male Borribles. He looked at the face and liked it. It was square and flat, and the eyes were optimistic under the spiky brown hair. This Borrible looked like he could take a lot of knocks and still come up smiling.

"Well," he said, "as I'm last, I hardly have to take my name out, do I? I mean I've seen the books, too, like the others, even in Hoxton, so I know my name then, it's Torreycanyon."

Knocker gave the empty hat to Dodger and took the beret with the two names only in it. He stood in front of the two Borrible girls, and felt embarrassed. He was used to girls of course but not to be trained as lookouts. He didn't like the idea of girls on this adventure and wondered how it had happened. He looked from one to the other of them; he was forced to admit that they were tough-looking, and certainly their ears were amongst the most beautifully shaped he had ever seen, denoting strong character, unbendable wills and great slyness and cunning. He couldn't fault them there. But, he thought, they'll never be able to support the rigours of the trek, the dangers, the rough living out-of-doors, every night a different bivouac. And what effect would they have on the team as a whole? That really worried him. He knew Borribles, they would quarrel and fight just as well as they could steal.

Knocker glanced back down the line and found the

others watching him closely. Orococco was smiling, his white teeth shining against his black skin; even the Wendle, Napoleon Boot, was smirking.

"Where are you girls from?" asked Knocker.

"Whitechapel," said the first.

"Neasden," said the second. Knocker held out the hat to the girl from Whitechapel. "Take one of these," he said. The girl took out a piece of paper and read her name simply, with no comment. "Chalotte," she said, her voice cool and relaxed. Her green eyes flickered over Knocker's face and she smiled. Knocker thought she was beautiful; her hair fell to her waist and was blond, her skin shone and her legs were well-shaped and long.

He gave the last piece of paper to the girl from Neasden. "Sydney," she said when she'd looked at it. Knocker looked at her. Her hair was dark and shiny and her eyes were grey and her face was kind.

"Why did Whitechapel and Neasden send you two?" he asked, disguising his shyness behind a sarcastic tone. "Haven't they got any male Borribles out there?"

Chalotte said, "The message that came to Whitechapel specified a female Borrible."

"And the Neasden message."

Chalotte nodded. "If you look at the Rumble books you'll see that two of the High Command are female. That's why we were asked, I should think."

"Hmm," said Knocker. He went to move away from them, and then turned suddenly, raising his voice. "There will be no favouritism, you will be treated just like the others, no difference at all. You will march like the others, you will train like the others and sleep on the ground like the others, and you will wear the same combat clothes. When you leave you must expect the same conditions—exactly. You will march as long, eat as little and fight as much as every other member of the expeditionary force. No favours, so ask for none. You will take the same risks as the others, and maybe perish with them. Do you understand?"

If Knocker had hoped to frighten Chalotte and Sydney with this outburst he had failed. They looked at each other and then looked at the chief lookout.

"That is why we came," said Chalotte and quoted a Borrible proverb. "No name earns itself."

"Yes," said Sydney, "we know the score. Any time you think we aren't up to scratch you send us back."

Knocker turned again and walked to where he could address all of them. "Right," he began, "now you have your names, training will last a fortnight, all day and every day. I'll give the details tomorrow. First thing you must do is learn your enemy. We have the Rumble books here but we have something that is better, Spiff's notes and studies of the enemy and their way of life. We will start reading right away. In his notes you will find a detailed description of each of the Rumbles of the High Command. Now you know your names you know which one is yours and you must know exactly what he or she looks like. You will have to distinguish between him and a thousand others right in the middle of a punch-up. Another thing, we shall be training with the Rumble-stick or sticker, the enemy's weapon, a four-inch nail stuck into the end of a lance of wood. They use it like a spear, or as a quarter-staff and dagger combined. The Rumble is good with it, cuts his teeth on it—you've got to be better. From now on we work hard. Your survival will depend on this training."

The next two weeks were weeks of exhausting activity. The eight members of the expeditionary force never stopped working. Every morning at five Knocker had them on their feet for half an hour's physical jerks, just to get the blood circulating properly through their brains. After breakfast they had a morning training session inside the gym, the subject chosen by Dodger or

Knocker. They did things like Rumble-stick combat, adult evasion and impromptu excuse making. They perfected their tactics for stealing in pairs and in fours and they practised racing starts and fast running, for all Borribles are rapid movers. Before lunch they slipped out for a quick run, just a mile or so to improve their wind. To keep them in trim Knocker made them responsible for stealing their own midday meal and they ate it all together in some uncomfortable spot along by the river on some windswept bomb-site, or in some draughty house with no windows. This was to get them used to the conditions they would meet when they set out on the adventure itself. Knocker watched the girls closely but they never complained and they did everything just as well as anyone else.

After the midday meal they went back to the gym for a short rest of half an hour or so and then Knocker would test them on Borrible knowledge and on Rumble studies. This was the kind of information that each expedition member was expected to have at his fingertips. He tested them a lot on this so that every one of them had a mind as sharp and as hard and as useful as a brand new tin-opener. They learned practical information too about how to avoid capture, how to escape when caught and how to aid other Borribles when in trouble. Knocker insisted that the eight of them should have all this knowledge ready in their minds so it could pop up automatically. There was no telling what they might come across on the long and dangerous journey to Rumbledom; they would have to be prepared for anything and everything.

After the session with the books there was always more physical training. Dodger taught them how to jump from a great height and fall without hurting themselves; how to take punches rolling with the blow, how to duck and weave. He taught them the vulnerable spots of the Rumble anatomy and again how to use the

Rumble-stick. Then, in the latter part of the afternoon, Knocker, who'd had a great deal of experience, more than any other known Borrible, taught them field tactics which was all about crossing commons and parks. He took them into the wildest terrain, like the middle of Clapham Common which was very open and deserted, just the place for Rumbles to burrow in secret and establish themselves unnoticed. Like other Borribles Knocker much preferred crowded streets with markets and shops, but unlike the others he'd been obliged, because of his calling, to do an enormous amount of country work. Somehow he had made himself overcome the basic fear that Borribles have when faced with woods and fields. They hate such things. "Fields", they say, "are always windy and there is nowhere to hide, no crowds to get lost in, and there is nothing to pick up, no lorries for things to fall off. It's not so bad when the sun is hot and a Borrible can lie under the shade of a tree looking at the sky moving between the branches, but even then a Borrible really likes to be up to something, in the street."

In spite of all this Knocker forced his team to undertake many a journey into Battersea Park and he taught them how to listen for the sound underneath the ground that told them a Rumble or a mole or a rat was down there. They learned how to climb trees and how to jump from them and how to crawl through bushes. But, over and above all this, Knocker made them train hour after hour with the Borribles' traditional and preferred weapon. It had been used by them for generations, and had been chosen for its simplicity, its range, its power and its deadliness. It was a weapon that was very ancient but was as efficient as any modern invention. It could be made anywhere and, back in the days of the nineteenth century when Borribles had endured great hardships and had been hounded from place to place, it had become their favourite method of defence because of the cheapness of its manufacture. The weapon was of course that very dangerous one, the catapult.

Every Borrible was born an expert with the catapult but the Eight would have to surpass the usual standards and become boringly accurate, able to hit a Rumble on the snout each time they fired.

"You must never miss," Knocker told them. "You will have a great deal of provisions to carry, but if you all keep ten stones in reserve you should be able to account for eighty of the enemy between you. If you are besieged, always choose somewhere where you can find plenty of ammunition lying about, then you will be invincible." And so each of the Eight became a crack shot; every one of them could take a fly off a park-keeper's nose at a hundred yards and he'd never even notice.

That was how every day was filled. After the daily sortie to the Park they returned to Rowena where they found that the High Street Borribles had provided them with a supper of food taken from the market. They ate with huge appetites and, after talking to each other for a little while, they rolled up in their sleeping-bags and snoozed on the floor of the long, dusty room. The next day they would have to wake early and do the same things again—run a little faster, shoot a little straighter. They would have to tackle difficult questions and find new answers to the problems that Knocker would devise. He would make them go over the expedition route on the street map of London and play war-games where he would imagine them in impossible situations and oblige them to think their way clear as quickly as they could and if Knocker wasn't satisfied they would have to do it again, and then again. They were tired all the time.

About one o'clock on a grey afternoon towards the end of the fortnight, Spiff, with two or three other stewards from the High Street, made an appearance in the store-room of the Rowena Crescent Gym. It was the beginning of the rest period and Spiff walked around the room talking to the Borribles who were stretched out on their sleeping-bags dozing with their eyes only half open. When he'd had a short word with each, he came over to speak to Knocker and Dodger.

"Afternoon, Knocker," said Spiff, nodding his head abruptly at the two stewards by his side. "This is Rasher and this is Ziggy."

Knocker stood up and said, "Those are fine names, certainly, I would like to hear the stories one day."

The two stewards nodded but did not smile. They looked out of humour.

"Yes," said Spiff, "that will have to wait of course. Now, Knocker, you've reached the end of the two weeks. How have you got on?"

Knocker reached for a large book on his desk. It contained a detailed description of each Borrible's training, together with various comments.

Spiff waved it aside. "No, I can look at that later, just a verbal report will do."

"Keep it general, too," said Rasher acidly.

"Well," said Knocker, looking sideways at Dodger, "they are very good, all of them. Some are better at one thing than another, but they are all naturals with the catapult. They could knock off a running cat with their eyes closed, girls as well, in fact Chalotte is better than all of the others, except perhaps Orococco. Hand-to-hand fighting is good, climbing good, running very fast. With the Rumble-stick they vary, but Bingo is fantastic. They aren't so good at scouting work in the countryside, but that takes years of practice and it's unnatural, but they're first-class in the streets and markets, you hardly see their hands come up from beneath a barrow when they takes their dinner. Marvellous. And all of them are dead keen." Knocker hesitated and lowered his voice.

"I'm only worried about one of them, although he'
worked as hard as anyone, harder. But I dunno, there's
something that worries me about Napoleon Boot. He
always seems to be thinking about something else
there's a slimy feel to him, it's . . . well, to tell the truth
Spiff, I dunno, it's just a feeling."

Dodger nodded at the three stewards to substantiate
what Knocker had said.

Spiff looked back down the hall to where the Borribles
were resting. Some were reading the Rumble books
others were just relaxing and looking at the ceiling
Napoleon Boot was scrutinising the road map of Greater
London and memorising street names.

"He never stops," said Knocker. "They all know *The
Borrible Book of Proverbs* by heart, but Napoleon knows
it backwards and sideways as well. He's too good to be
true."

Spiff creased his face. "Well, son, there's nothing we
can do now. They have to have a Wendle with 'em
because they've got to cross the Wandle. You know
how suspicious they are of anybody who wants to cross
their bloody river." He sniffed. "It ought to be all right,
I mean the adventure is in their interest, ain't it? The
Rumbles could easily burrow under Wandsworth Common and move from there down to the streets. The
Wendles are in more danger than we are simply because
they're nearer to Rumbledom, ain't they? It'll work out,
you'll see."

There was silence as if nobody agreed with him, not
even Spiff himself. He changed the subject.

"Well, your blokes must leave soon anyway, the
longer they wait the more dangerous it is. There was a
psychological advantage in letting the Rumbles know
we were on to them, but the longer we take in getting
up there, the more time they will have to prepare their
defences. Our Eight might not be able to get into the
Rumble Burrow. Imagine—all that way for nothing!"

Ziggy, who had been trying to interrupt Spiff's flow, at last got a word in. "I've never liked this idea, you know, Spiff. I think we should have gone up there in force, taken them on, given them a thumping, duffed 'em up."

"Out of your mind," said Spiff impatiently; he was always right and knew it. "We'd have been outnumbered ten to one and they'd have been fighting on their own ground. We stand a much better chance by sending eight professionals like this, and eliminating their leaders, mark my words."

"Oh, it sounds all right on paper," said Ziggy condescendingly, "but I don't think that those eight over there can manage it. They haven't done anything yet. Anyone can fire a catapult at a Woollie and run—but what if it's a Rumble with a Rumble-stick at your throat, eh?"

"Look," said Knocker getting annoyed, "I've trained this lot. If anyone can get inside the Rumble Burrow they can."

"Rubbish," said Rasher, joining the argument, "they don't stand a monkey's."

"They do," said Knocker.

"They don't," said Ziggy.

The stewards frowned at their feet.

Spiff sniffed again. "I've been looking at the map, Knocker. I thought that the Eight ought to go up the Thames, from St Mary's to Wandsworth Reach. I know it's dangerous, but it will save days on the journey, and it means the Eight will be going in from a direction that the Rumbles won't dream of. Even if they've got lookouts deployed as far as Wandsworth Common Railway and Earlsfield, we'll outflank them. What do you say?"

Knocker was angry all over again. "But, Spiff," he cried, grabbing the steward's arm, "the river is a death trap, all those barges and tugs and police launches, they'd be run down or run in without a chance. They've had no training for water. I don't even know if they can row. I thought they were going to march overland, and now you want to throw 'em into the river. It's not on, Spiff."

"How far do you think they'd get then if they went overland," said Ziggy, "with a solid line of Rumbles from Merton to the River Thames?"

Rasher shoved his face up to Knocker's and tilted it sideways. "If your blokes are so good, why are you making excuses? Can't they do it?"

"It's a question of time, training," spluttered Knocker.

Spiff nodded. "Just so, you'll get an extra day for boat training and rowing."

"But we haven't got a boat," said Knocker, looking at all three of the stewards as if they were mad.

"Oh, you'll need a boat," said Spiff, "to row up the river. You'll need one before then to train in, won't yer?"

"Where can we get one?" asked Dodger, looking distraught.

Spiff turned on him angrily. "You're a Borrible, ain't yer? Steal one—this afternoon—instead of kipping."

"Yes," said Ziggy. "Let's see how good this team is. But I tell you, if you can't get over this little problem I shall use all my influence to see that the adventure is cancelled. I've never liked it you know."

Spiff laughed. "Don't take any notice of him. I know you'll manage, Knocker. You just prove to us that your blokes are as good as you say they are, eh?" And with that the three stewards climbed up the wall on the exercise bars and one by one they disappeared through the narrow windows that led to Rowena Crescent.

Knocker was shaking with temper as he watched them go. He had a tendency to take things seriously at the best of times but this criticism of his team and his training of them was a personal insult.

"Just like that, eh?" he said to Dodger. "Get a boat, steal it, launch it, learn to row it, just like that!"

"And only today and tomorrow to do it in," said Dodger soberly.

Knocker walked over to where the Eight were waiting, propped up on their elbows, their interest aroused by the discussion. "Well," he said, "no rest for the wicked. Get your hats on, I'm taking you to the lake in Battersea Park. We're going to steal a boat."

Only one person amongst the Eight registered enthusiasm. Napoleon's dark face became brilliant. He stood up and said, "A boat, eh? That's good, know about boats we do, up the Wandle."

Knocker was relieved. Of course, the Wandsworth Borribles lived on or near water all the time. Napoleon could be a great help. "We're going to have to steal a boat that can make the river trip along the Thames as far as the mouth of the Wandle. Napoleon, can you teach this team how to row and steer?"

"Why, of course, Knocker," said Napoleon, with a slight sneer colouring his voice. "It'll be a pleasure."

One by one they slipped from the gym and went their separate ways to the Park. They reassembled by the huge iron gates and walked along the roadway till they arrived at the boating lake. Each Borrible had his hat well down over his ears, a catapult under his jumper and a few stones ready in a pocket, just in case.

Knocker felt sad, for soon the Eight would be gone. What an adventure it would be for them. What times they would have; but he, Knocker, would be left behind and forgotten. He had worried about it every day but think as he might he could see no way at all by which he could wangle his inclusion in the team that would set off on the perilous journey to Rumbledom. He shook the desire from his mind, it was no use thinking about it.

It was not long before he and the others came in sight

of the small wooden hut where tickets were sold to those who wished to spend an hour boating. The high summer season was nearly over and most of the boats were chained to one of the islands in the middle of the lake out of harm's way. Only about a dozen or so were roped to the little jetty which stood near the ticket-office. Inside the wooden shed was a park-keeper with a brown suit and a dark brown hat. He was licking a pencil and writing with it slowly in a big book. Not one boat moved on the flat surface of the water. Knocker and the others sat down by the edge of a path to watch. After a while Knocker said, "What do you think of the boats, Napoleon?"

"We're a bit far away to judge," said the Wendle, "but you see they've got some metal ones there, by the jetty." His voice changed when he talked about boats. He became excited and his face shone, while his companions looked terrified. Borribles tend to dislike water even more than they dislike woods and fields. "They aren't really any good for a river trip, too short and wide, unstable, and not big enough anyway to take eight of us. Those are the ones we want." He pointed out to the islands and the others could see that amongst the scores of metal boats were a few old long ones, built of wood with seats and cushions and rudders that were worked by two pieces of rope. They were much bigger.

"Lovely, graceful things they are," said Napoleon enthusiastically, "low in the water, they will float over any wave or wash cast up by barges on the river. Four rowlocks, I should think, two teams of rowers . . . if the girls are up to it." He looked behind him at Chalotte and Sydney. Chalotte said, "Get your boat first, Wendle."

"Take it easy," said Knocker, stopping any quarrel before it started. "If we want one of those wooden boats from the island we'll have to get out there. Any ideas?"

"Too far to swim," said Vulgarian, whom they all called Vulge now.

"And he won't hire us one because we're too small," said Sydney, "even if we had the money—which we haven't."

"So we'll have to pinch a metal boat to get out there," added Stonks.

"Yeah—but have you noticed," said Torreycanyon, "that they keep the oars separate, only hand 'em out with the boats, don't they? And worse, the boats tied to the island ain't got no oars at all."

There was silence. Knocker waited; this was all part of their training. He knew what he would have done; the situation obviously called for diversionary tactics of some kind. Someone would have to entice the keeper out of the little shed so that others could dash in and get some oars. Something like that was necessary.

Suddenly Napoleon Boot stood up. "Look," he said, "boats is my speciality why don't you let me do it?"

"All right," said Knocker, "who do you want to take with you?"

"I want to do this one on my own."

"On your own!" cried Vulge. "I'd like to see it."

"You will," answered Napoleon. "You will."

"Well, it better be good," said the chief lookout. "We haven't got time to waste."

"Just after nightfall tonight you will have your pick of the boats," said Napoleon scornfully, "and you'll be able to row this lot of sailors up and down till their arms drop off. How's that?"

"That'll do me fine, Napoleon Boot," said Knocker grimly.

Napoleon left them and went down the path towards the little hut on the jetty. He swaggered as he walked. The others retreated and screened themselves in some bushes. When they were settled Orococco said, "That

Napoleon may smell a little but I betcha there's no flies on him."

They watched the Wendle strut towards the wooden shed. At the end of the jetty he halted, pulled his hat down over his ears and then walked straight on past.

"What's the little bleeder up to now?" asked Dodger of no one in particular, and he got no answer.

When Napoleon was small in the distance he suddenly turned and ran as fast as he could back towards the hut. He dashed to the ticket-office, threw open its door, and jumping up and down he yelled at the keeper inside. What he said the watchers could not imagine but they could see that Napoleon was very agitated. The keeper listened attentively, then he got up quickly from his stool and came out onto the jetty, pausing only to lock the door of his hut.

"That's no good," groaned Bingo, "we can't get in there now."

The keeper threw two oars into the nearest boat, picked up the tiny Napoleon and jumped aboard. The boat rocked and swayed dangerously but it did not capsize, and Napoleon seemed quite happy sitting in the stern as the keeper set the oars in the rowlocks and plyed them expertly. The little craft shot out onto the lake heading for the larger of the two islands where the unused boats were tied along the shore in rows.

Knocker looked at Dodger and shook his head. "Blessed if I know what he's at," he said. Dodger shrugged his shoulders. The boat neared the island but before it touched the shore they could see that Napoleon had got to his feet. Then the boat hit the bank, stopping abruptly, and the Wendle was shot off his feet and into the water.

Torreycanyon roared with laughter. "Cocky little stinker's fallen in," he guffawed. The others laughed too.

"Shuddup," snarled Knocker.

The park-keeper stepped into the water, wetting his trousers to the waist, and rescued Napoleon, placing the Borrible in the boat and wrapping him in a rug that he took from the bench. Then he tied the boat to a branch and wagging his finger at Napoleon he disappeared into the island's vegetation. No sooner had he gone than the watchers were amazed to see Napoleon leap up, untie the painter and row for the shore, and could that boy row! He was small but he made that boat into a living thing and it flew across the lake like a kingfisher. Knocker looked at the faces around him, jaws were open and eyes were wide.

Napoleon jumped onto the jetty and without bothering to moor the boat he ran along the wooden planking to the path and darted into a telephone box that stood empty nearby. The Borribles saw him climb up a couple of the broken window panes to reach the receiver more easily and he made a call. That done he raced off at top speed to be lost amongst some trees about half a mile away. For a while nothing happened and the watchers in the bushes stirred uneasily.

"I think that cocky little so-and-so is out of his mind," said Stonks. "All he's done is stir up trouble."

"I dunno so much," said Sydney. "Let's wait and see."

And so they waited, and they waited, and after what seemed a long while, but in reality was only ten minutes, they heard the "Hoo-haa, hoo-haa, hoo-haa," of a police siren and a patrol car skidded to a halt by the telephone box.

"Oh, lor—here come the Woollies now," said Dodger wearily.

Two policemen threw themselves out of the car, ran down the landing-stage and tried the door to the little hut, but it was firmly locked. Then there was a hallooing and a whistling from the island and, looking up, the policemen saw the keeper jumping up and down and waving his arms and making an awful noise. He must have been quite cold because the Borribles could see that all the bottom half of him was darker than the top half, which meant he was still very wet.

The two policemen poked about in the boats for some oars, but they were all in the hut. The only oars available were in the boat that the keeper and Napoleon had used and that had drifted until it was now about ten yards from land. The policemen tried to hook it in with a long pole, but they couldn't quite reach. Another police car arrived with an Inspector in it and he took control and ordered one of his men to go out and get the boat. One of the constables took off his coat and waded into the lake, but the bottom shelved away fairly rapidly and by the time he got to the boat he was swimming. Spluttering and cursing his luck he got hold of the painter and pulled the boat to the jetty and a dry policeman got in and rowed to the island where it was the work of a minute to rescue the keeper. While the boat was returning to the shore the Head Keeper bowled up on his bicycle and stood joking with the police Inspector. They thought the episode was most hilarious and they threw back their heads and laughed and laughed. Water does that to some people.

Very soon the wet policeman and the damp keeper were together on the jetty and the Inspector sent them off in one of the cars. The Head Keeper unlocked the shed, put the oars away and locked up again. He stood talking and laughing some more with the Inspector, then they shook hands and the keeper got on his bike and pedalled back to his office, and the Inspector drove back to the police station on Lavender Hill.

It was all over. Everything was quiet and dusk began to come down over the Park. The deer, who lived behind the railings, had already disappeared into their wooden shelters. Only a few people were strolling about and all of those were making their way to the gates. Very soon now the bell would ring and Battersea Park would close for the night. The waiting and watching Borribles undid their packs, took out their greatcoats and squatted down, expecting they knew not what.

"I hardly see the point of that operation," said Sydney; she always spoke a little precisely like that. "The hut is locked and there are no oars outside. I think Napoleon has made a miscalculation somewhere."

Just at that moment there was a rustle in the bushes behind them and a very bedraggled Napoleon Boot ran up. He was panting and laughing so much that it looked like he might be sick. His hair was plastered down over his skull, his clothes were soaking and stuck to his body and his skin was steaming from the heat generated by his mad running across the Park. He fell to the ground and the sounds coming from him made his companions think that perhaps he was very ill. Knocker pulled the sodden Borrible over onto his back and peeled off the wet jacket. He then removed his own greatcoat and covered the shaking and shivering body with it.

"It looks bad," said Dodger.

"Man," cried Orococco, "we don't want a casualty before we starts."

The Borribles stood in a glum group, looking down at Napoleon. Knocker rubbed the hands and legs of the Wandsworth Borrible as hard as he could to aid the circulation. Gradually Napoleon got his breath and sat up. "Don't fuss," he said between gasps. "I'm all right, just a bit out of breath, and I can't stop laughing." And as if to prove it he started shaking and shivering again.

"There's nothing to laugh about," said Knocker sternly, relieved now that he knew that Napoleon Boot would survive. "We've wasted the whole afternoon and achieved nothing except for you to have a good giggle."

Napoleon groped into his wet clothes, there was a jangling noise and his hand reappeared clutching a massive bunch of keys.

"Look at that," he chortled. "What's that, eh? Scotch mist?"

There was a stunned silence, then Bingo asked "Well, what is it?"

Napoleon rolled over and over with merriment. "It's the keys to the hut, of course," he spluttered when he had recovered sufficiently, "and to the whole bleeding Park, I shouldn't wonder."

"How'd you do it?" asked Dodger.

"Well," said Napoleon, "I went dashing up to the hut and pretended to cry my eyes out. 'It's my dog,' I said. 'It's my dog.' " He laughed again and the others began to laugh too. " 'He's swum over to the island,' says I, 'and he's such a little frightened lovely dog, he can't swim back.' 'That's all right,' says the keeper, 'soon get him, no trouble.' Then you saw what happened after. He goes and locks the door of the flaming hut so that was Plan A gone, in a trice. When we got near the island I pretends to get all excited about the dog, don't I? I jumps up and down and says there he is, there he is, and so I falls in—splash! Well, the keeper has kittens at that and leaps in to effect a rescue, as you might say. Well, that was the whole crux and point of Plan B. As he's carrying me back to the boat I lifts the keys out of his pocket. Well, he's all for bringing me back right away and never mind the dog. 'No, no,' says I. 'I'll get all hell beaten out of me at home.' Well, you saw the rest, I pinches the boat, gets on the blower to 'Old Bill' and tells them that Keeper 347 has been marooned on a desert island in the middle of Battersea Park while rescuing a dog. Then I takes off in the other direction. Now we've got the keys," and he jangled them in front of Knocker's face, "we can take boats when we like, and practise all night, like I said, Knocker, just like I said." And Napoleon rolled over and laughed so loudly that the others had to put a coat over his head to deaden the noise.

Knocker stood up and shook his head in admiration. The others did the same and they looked at each other in the deepening gloom and chuckled and felt confident.

As soon as they had eaten the rations they had brought with them the Borribles crept down to the hut on the lake where they had no difficulty in opening the door and stealing the oars they needed. They crowded together in one of the small metal craft and Napoleon rowed them out to the centre of the lake and they waited while the Wendle inspected the larger boats. They were fine long comfortable things, possessing four wide seats with cushions and lots of space for stowing gear fore and aft. But they were solid and heavy and would need scientific rowing.

Napoleon chose the best one and came back to report to Knocker. "Number Seventeen," he said, "been well looked after." As the group moved to embark he pulled Knocker aside, grasping his elbow. "I think the boat will be too heavy for just four to row," he said quietly. "There will have to be two of us on each oar. That means when it comes to the actual trip there will be no turn and turn about, we'll have to row all the time."

Knocker thought about it for a second. "You'll have to row by night and hide by day, and keep well away from police launches. They'll run you in, as soon as look at you. Won't take them half a second to suss a bunch of Borribles in a stolen pleasure boat."

But at that moment they didn't worry too much about the future. The novelty of boating occupied and amused them and even Knocker took a hand. Napoleon made them work very hard indeed, for they only had that night in which to learn the art of rowing. Napoleon sat in the stern and steered the boat with the two pieces of rope which were attached to each side of the rudder behind him. Dodger sat up front to make sure they didn't run into anything, though the moon had come up and it was easy to see far out over the silver water.

They sat two to an oar as Napoleon had suggested, for they would need a great deal of power when they were out on the River Thames. Not only would they have to contend with the tide but there would be waves washing outwards from passing barges and tugs, and there would always be the danger of collision. Napoleon gave them their positions in the boat and told them to keep them, except that he would take Knocker's place on the expedition because Knocker wouldn't be going.

"When we're on the river," Napoleon said, "there'll only be eight of us so there'll be no one on the rudder. That means we will have to steer by rowing; listen very carefully to my commands and act on them immediately. Anyone being a bit slow could get us run down, capsized, we could lose all our equipment and worse we could drown." And so Napoleon went on. He taught them the basic rowing commands; how to begin rowing, how to stop, how to feather the oars, and they learnt to pull steadily and hard without wasting too much of their energy. Next time they got into the boat they would be on the wide and thronged waterway of the Thames itself.

All through the night they rowed and listened to Napoleon Boot, Navigator. As the hours wore on they realised what a serious thing the river trip was and they looked at each other with concern. Their minds grew numb with the physical effort and blisters rose on their hands and still Napoleon kept them rowing till they could row as well as any Wendle and could change course at the slightest order from the stern. Only when the sky had paled and dawn climbed over the blocks of flats along Battersea Park Road did Napoleon direct them to the lake-side. Thankfully the Borribles obeyed the command to ship oars and they sighed when they heard the prow of their boat grate on the gravel of the shore. They sat motionless for a while, their heads bowed, their muscles tight. Dodger who had done little all this time stood up in the prow, stretched, then jumped ashore.

"Come on, you lot," he said, "we've got to hide this boat before it's spotted by the keepers."

Nearby was a dense clump of bushes and the Borribles manhandled the heavy boat right into the middle of them. They stumbled and tripped over their own feet so tired were they, having been awake for twenty-four hours without a break. They tore foliage from the bushes and grass from the ground and camouflaged the boat so well that it could hardly be seen, even from a distance of a yard or two. When he was quite satisfied, Knocker ordered the team of Borribles back to base. It was full daylight by the time they reached the Prince's Head and the lines of lady cleaners were already chatting at the bus stops as the Borribles turned into Rowena Crescent. They climbed into the basement gym and crawled under the sleeping-bags and blankets which were laid out on the exercise mats. There were loud groans and sighs of relief as they closed their eyes and stretched their burning limbs but Knocker could not sleep for a while. He kept asking himself the same question over and over again. "Now we've got it, how do we get it from Battersea Park to Battersea Reach?"

Chapter 3

Knocker need not have worried. By the time he awoke later the same day the problem had been solved.

It was not easy waking up; his body felt as stiff as a wire coathanger and he thought he'd never be able to move again. Even to open his eyelids and look at the ceiling took a concentration of all his effort into the necessary muscles. He turned his head and saw that Dodger was coming in through one of the windows with Napoleon. They were carrying steaming jugs and fruit and bread rolls. They had been up to the market for breakfast.

Knocker staggered to his feet, moving like a wooden doll with swollen joints. Napoleon landed gracefully on the floor and he laughed.

"You ought to be fitter than that, Knocker. Just as well you aren't coming on the trip, ain't it?"

Dodger laughed then and that got through to Knocker.

"All right, you two. If that's breakfast, hand it over and wake the others." Knocker sat down on a bench and poured himself a cup of tea and drank it. It was lovely. He poured another and tore at a roll with his teeth. Dodger came and sat next to him and helped himself to some food.

"Bingo's not here," he said conversationally. "He must have gone out."

"Of course he has, if he's not here," said Knocker irritably. "You're not very bright this morning."

"I mean out on a job," said Dodger and he stood up and looked down at Knocker unpleasantly. No Borrible likes to be told that he isn't bright.

"Anyway, it's not the morning. It's the afternoon."

Knocker returned Dodger's gaze. "I'm sorry, Dodger, I didn't mean that. It's these aches and pains. Forget it."

"All right, then." Dodger wasn't frightened of a quarrel, no Borrible is. "Chalotte and Sydney and Stonks and Torreycanyon are out, too," he said, looking straight in front of him.

Knocker jumped up, spilling his tea. "What?" he cried. "Gone off without permission, without saying where?"

"What's wrong, Knocker?" asked Dodger, genuinely surprised. "You can't expect Borribles to act like regular troops. They're not Rumbles. Borribles just can't do it, that's why we are Borribles, isn't it? I think you've been lucky to keep them together this far; most Borribles would have chucked it last night on the lake, but ours didn't, they stuck together. Miraculous really."

Knocker sat down again. "I'm worried," he said.

"I think," said Dodger wisely, "that you're jealous. You wish you were going on this adventure, you'd like to have a second name, even before others have got their first. That's not right, you know."

Knocker looked at his friend and sucked his cheeks in between his teeth to avoid showing emotion, but he showed it all the same. He didn't admit it to Dodger but he felt guilty for having overslept so badly and he was ashamed of having aches and pains when he should have been fitter than any of his companions.

"I'm worried about the Adventure," he insisted. "Will they manage it? Will the Wendles let them through Wandsworth without trouble? How will Napoleon behave? It's all a worry."

"They'll be fine," said Dodger. "Napoleon will turn out all right, even though he is a Wendle."

"He may be all right now, but what will he be like when he's back in Wandsworth?"

"Remember today and forget tomorrow," said Dodger, quoting from the Borrible proverbs. "I shall be glad to see Northcote Road again. Got some things want to get on with."

The conversation was interrupted by the arrival of Chalotte who came in through one of the windows. She crossed the gym and stood in front of Knocker, breathless. Her cheeks bright with running, she shook her hair in that way that Knocker admired.

"Bingo said could we all meet him at St Mary's. He's had a plan," and she tossed her head again and laughed.

"What kind of a plan?" asked Knocker sternly.

"I couldn't tell you that, it would spoil the fun, it's not Borrible."

"I order you," said Knocker.

"You can order as much as you like. You said yourself yesterday that the Adventure had virtually begun. You're not going on the expedition, so you can hardly give orders any more." She turned and marched over to where the others were eating their breakfast, her cheeks no longer shining with exertion, but with anger.

"You ought to remember," said Dodger, "that they are feeling just as tense as you are. They know they are leaving tomorrow night, and they know that they may not be coming back."

"You're right, Dodger," said Knocker, forcing a smile. "I shall miss you when you go back to Northcote, you know."

"Then you'll have to come down there sometime."

When Knocker had finished his breakfast and regained his temper a little he set off with Napoleon, Vulge and Orococco and they followed Chalotte and Dodger through the streets to Battersea churchyard. There, concealed in the long grass which grew between the big square tombs, they found Number Seventeen.

Bingo and his fellow conspirators, dressed as members of the Battersea Sea Scouts, were loafing by the embankment wall.

"How did you manage it?" asked Knocker, unable to keep the admiration from his voice.

"Simple," said Bingo, with pride. "Rescued the uniforms from the Sea Scouts, shoved the boat onto a set of old pram wheels that I also liberated, and pushed the boat through the Park and down the street, as bold as brass. Got stopped by the Woollie on point duty in Parkgate Road but we told him that we were fund raising for the Sea Scouts and would be taking the boat back that very night; had the Head Keeper's permission, didn't we? Decent copper, held the traffic up for us to cross the road."

"That was a good 'un," said Torreycanyon. "I could hardly stop laughing."

The church itself was locked and the churchyard deserted, just the place for the Borribles and their boat. It was the quiet, dusty part of the afternoon and the lunch-time boozers were long gone from the Old Swan pub. The great factories and towering flats loomed around the tiny octagonal steeple of St Mary's like idiots surprised by beauty, and no one watched from the lofty isolation of their smoky windows.

Two high-masted sailing-barges were moored up against the river wall which skirted the graveyard; sturdy boats they were, constructed in polished wood. They had rigging climbing their solid masts and their gangplanks creaked and shifted backwards and forwards on the ground when the waves from mid-stream reached the bank. Napoleon looked at the boats, his greenish face greener with envy.

"I'd love to live on a boat," he said. "Look at them names, *The Raven* from Chester, *The Ethel Ada*, Ipswich, marvellous."

"We ain't got a name for our boat," said Bingo. "I

mean we can't call it Number Seventeen all the time, can we? Not on an Adventure."

"Yeah," agreed Torreycanyon, "Number Seventeen ain't near posh enough."

"What shall we call it?" asked Bingo, looking at the others.

Chalotte, who had been staring about her, suddenly pointed into the sky. "There's your name," she cried delightedly. "Look up there!"

Right behind the church, and dominating it completely, was a huge factory built from the pallid bricks of a dead and unlovely clay. Written across the blank wall in huge white letters they read: "Silver Belle Flour, Mayhew."

"We could call it *The Silver Belle Flower*," said Chalotte. "You know, it sounds just wrong."

"It don't matter what we call it," said Knocker. "I name this boat *The Silver Belle Flower*," and he kicked it by way of ceremony.

The others knew he was upset about not going on the expedition so they ignored him, but they adopted the name because it was the only one they could think of.

They leaned against the embankment wall and looked across the broad sweep of the river to the gasometers and the Chelsea Flour Mills opposite. The surface of the Thames was an alarming greeny-grey colour and only the floating rainbow whorls of diesel oil and petrol brightened the dull water. The horizon was cut out in dirty brown and black against a sky of diluted yellow ochre, and the sun had not shone all day.

They should have been depressed and frightened but somehow the very extent of the sight inspired them all with pride and determination. The shift of the waves nudging clumps of rubbish downstream; the hooting of tugs and barges as they passed; the unmoving blocks of black smoke from Lot's Road Power Station; the smell, like varnish, of the Thames in London, all these things combined to make their hearts swell and they looked at each other and smiled modestly, knowing that whatever was before them, they would be equal to it.

But Knocker could not partake of this sensation. All he could think of was that he would not be going, so he broke the spell, shouting harshly at them. "Well, stop this daydreaming, let's get this boat in the water."

They got one end of *The Silver Belle Flower* onto the river wall, then the other. They lowered her gently down into a scum-covered rectangle of water between *The Ethel Ada* and the embankment. The garbage had become cornered here and looked firm enough to walk over, but the boat pushed its keel through and found enough water to float on.

"She'll be safe there," said Knocker. "We'll tie her up midway between the two boats. *The Ethel Ada* will think she belongs to *The Raven* and *The Raven* will think she belongs to *The Ethel Ada*."

The Silver Belle Flower was firmly tied to a ring in the wall and, with one last look at the dark river, the Borribles turned and went back to the gym for a good meal and an early night. Just over twenty-four hours to wait and the expedition would be under way.

The last day was a day of rest for the Eight but not for Dodger and Knocker. They went first to report to Spiff about the boat and he was delighted. He sat at his desk in his orange dressing-gown, flicking through a huge book of Borrible Rules.

"That Ziggy was always a pessimist," he said. "I knew you would do it. A piece of pudding stealing a boat. He can't stop us now."

He gave them a cup of tea and told them to take it off with them and drink it downstairs in the store-room.

There was plenty to do down there. Knocker had to

make the final selection of gear from the huge piles that the Borribles had collected from various shops. When the choice had been made he and Dodger would pack the items into the eight rucksacks but first they put the gear into eight separate piles and, so they would make no mistakes, they checked and double checked every heap. Each Borrible had a spare pair of boots and there were waterproof khaki trousers and fur-lined combat jackets to keep them warm at night when they would do most of their travelling. There were special woollen Borrible hats which were reversible, camouflaged on one side and luminous reddy-orange on the other, so they could make themselves easy to spot if they wanted to. They would have a life-jacket each for the river trip and sharp long-bladed knives to wear at their belts. There were eight catapults too, with spare rubbers and pouches. Knocker and Dodger fingered the catapults lovingly. They were the best, as used by professional poachers, made out of polished steel and strong and springy. They had a long range and fired stones, marbles or ball-bearings with great power. To carry a supply of ammunition Spiff had acquired some old army money belts which had little pockets stuck on them; each pocket would carry a round and well-balanced stone. These belts could be slung across the shoulders like bandoliers and each of the adventurers was to carry two of them, giving them twenty shots per person. This meant that between them they had a fire power of a hundred and sixty rounds and the bandoliers were to be worn outside the combat jackets so that they would be easy to get at and the rate of fire would be very fast.

Spiff had also seen to it that every Borrible on the expedition had a waterproof watch on one wrist and a compass on the other, and in a pocket of each rucksack would be the A to Z map of the London streets. There were matches for lighting fires and a basic ration of food in case anyone got lost or separated from the others.

Knocker was pleased with the work he and Dodger had done. "Everything," he said, "except money."

At dinner-time Spiff came into the room with some food and he sat with them while they ate. He inspected the haversacks and asked what was in each one, making sure that nothing had been overlooked. He asked about the route, made suggestions, chuckled one moment, was grave the next. He stayed about an hour before he got up to leave.

"Well, life is all a chance anyway, boys," he said. "Our Eight have got a hard time in front of them but they couldn't have been better trained. I'd like to thank you, Dodger, for coming down here from the North-cote. I know you don't like leaving your manor, so thanks again; here's a little memento." He pulled from his pocket one of the waterproof watches that the expedition had been equipped with. "The lads got a bit enthusiastic and got too many of them," he added by way of explanation. "It's engraved on the back."

Dodger turned the watch over and read out loud: "The Great Rumble Hunt. Dodger Borrible, Trainer. Good luck." He was delighted, Knocker could see that. The watch was one of those big army jobs with lots of different faces and hands and knobs on it.

"It's luminous, too," said Spiff. He looked at Knocker then. "Don't you worry, Knocker, there'll be something for you later on. I haven't got it ready yet."

Knocker nodded. "Thanks, Spiff," he said.

Still Spiff didn't pass through the door, though he'd had his hand on the knob for a long while. "I want you to bring the Eight here on the way to the boat," he said. "I'll want to say a last word to them, goodbye and good luck and all that."

Knocker felt tired and empty. All this talk about the final preparations and the leave-taking made him feel as if his life had finished. Everything was beginning for the others, for him all was ending. "Why, oh why," he thought, "do I have a name already!" Then he thought back to his own name adventure, and he shrugged his shoulders. "You have to take a name whenever you have a chance; if you go through life picking and choosing and waiting for what you think is the best occasion, why you'd never get a name at all."

At last Spiff turned to Dodger who was still looking proudly at his engraved watch.

"Look, Dodger," he said, "I'm not trying to get rid of you, but if you'd like to start off to the Northcote now, you can. It's quite a way but you'd make it before dark. You could pop into the gym and say goodbye to the team on your way and tell them to come here tonight, about elevenish."

Dodger stood up and strapped on his watch, saying, "I wouldn't mind, I've got something I want to do."

"Right," said Spiff. "That's settled, thanks again," and he left the room whistling.

When he'd gone Dodger coughed and looked at Knocker. "Hmm," he said after another cough, "I'd better go then. Cheerio, Knocker. Come down the Northcote in a day or two, stay with me. Good market we've got down there. It'll make a change for you, you know."

When Knocker just sighed Dodger said, "Cheer up, it's only right that every Borrible should get a chance."

"I know," said Knocker, "but adventures like this one don't happen every day of the week. Still, I'll be better once they're gone. I'll come down to you in a few days. I've been through the Northcote, never stayed, we'll have a laugh. We had a laugh here, come to think of it."

"We did that," agreed Dodger. "See you soon, eh—and don't get caught." And with that traditional farewell he went.

Knocker had a miserable afternoon and evening. He

checked the haversacks over and over again just to give himself something to do. He meandered and mooched about the store-room until at last he went upstairs and rested on his bed in the room which he shared with Lightfinger. He hadn't seen Lightfinger for ages. How long ago it seemed, that night when they had found the Rumbles in Battersea Park and had captured one. How much had happened since then; now everything was ready. He gazed at the ceiling until he dozed and the noises of the street sounded further and further away.

It was dark when he awoke and he felt very cold, having neglected to creep under his blankets. He sat up and shook himself and rubbed his body vigorously to get the blood running warmly. Getting to his feet he groped for the light switch. What time could it be? Not that the others needed him any more but he would have liked to have seen them off. Hoping they hadn't gone already he made for the stairs and ran down.

On the landing he bumped into Spiff who was coming from his room with some papers in his hand. "Aha, there you are, Knocker," he said and beamed at the chief lookout. He was apt to make obvious remarks, was Spiff, but he only did it when he was feeling very friendly or pleased with himself. "Got your lads downstairs, just going to give them a word or too, can you come down?"

"Course," answered Knocker and followed Spiff to the basement.

The Eight were all present and correct. They too had had a restless time, though they had tried their hardest to sleep ready for the rigours of the night.

They looked very soldier-like, thought Knocker as he examined them. Warmly dressed, their hats cocked jauntily over their ears, they stood tense and straight, glancing occasionally at their watches or compasses. Most impressive and warlike of all were the double bandoliers of stones they wore and the shiny and lethal catapults stuck into their pockets. The Adventurers shone with health, their skins glowing, but they could not conceal their impatience. They wanted Spiff to say what he had to say and then let them get on with it.

Spiff rustled his papers. "You'll be off in a minute, then, so I won't keep you long. Your haversacks are all here ready, everything you need. Before you go, I just want to remind you of the object of your expedition. Whatever happens you must not forget it. It is to knock out the Rumble High Command, eliminate them. We want no more of them in our part of London. They must be shown that they can't come down here whenever they think they will and move on to our manor. Whatever happens to you, and we all know the dangers you face, if you eliminate your target, your name will be confirmed and remembered. You have the luck to be going on the greatest Adventure anyone has ever heard of. I wish I could come with you, but that of course is not possible. Finally, I would like to congratulate you on the way you have put up with the ardours of the training period—and with Knocker."

Everyone laughed politely and Knocker shuffled his feet and wished Spiff would stop making a speech and let everyone go.

But Spiff hadn't finished. "You've a long way to travel, a dangerous way, and a difficult, perhaps impossible task to accomplish and I'm sure I speak for all Borribles when I wish you the best of luck. And don't get caught."

Knocker and Spiff watched as the Eight Adventurers stepped forward with relief to pick up their rucksacks. With a nod for Spiff and a nervous smile for Knocker they left the room one by one. The last to leave was Napoleon. He stood by the open door, looking trim and dangerous, his eyes were bright and excited. His face broke into a cocky and unpleasant smile. "Sorry you ain't coming, Knocker," he said triumphantly, and he slid silently out into the darkness.

Knocker rushed across the room and shoved the door hard with his foot so that it slammed noisily.

Spiff sat down at the table and looked at Knocker's back while he opened the enormous Rule Book he'd been reading in his room that morning. "Come this way, Knocker," he said. "I've got your present over here."

"Stuff the present," said Knocker ungraciously. Then he turned round, came over to the table and sat down opposite Spiff, mumbling a barely audible, "Sorry."

Spiff ignored the apology as he had done the insult. "Well, here it is," he said. "I'm going to read it to you, only once, so you'd better listen, lovely bit of poetry this is." He licked his lips and glanced up at the clouded face that Knocker was presenting to him. "This is from *The Borrible Book of Rules*, para. 34, subsection 3a. I quote, 'No Borrible who is already named may go on any name adventure whatsoever, he may not even go on a non-name adventure if a Borrible who has no name wishes to take precedence. This rule is unalterable and no exceptions may be made at all, ever.' "

Spiff drew a breath and ran his finger to a note at the bottom of the page.

" 'Except for the following exceptions.' " He pursed his lips to stop from smiling as Knocker looked up sharply.

" 'One. A named Borrible may take part in a name adventure when no other un-named Borrible is available. The choosing of the named Borrible in such a case will be by drawing lots.' "

Knocker looked down at the table again.

Spiff went on. " 'A named Borrible may take part in a name adventure when a vacancy occurs through accident or injury at the last moment and there is no time to draw lots.' " Spiff looked up. "That's a very

useful one that is, very useful. Do you know, I've go
five names myself, five adventures I've had, never believe it to look at me, would you? Oh yes, you have to
know yer way round the old rule book, can't break the
rules until you know the rules, but let's get down to
exception 7/2. It's one I haven't used before." He
coughed and put on a special voice. " 'When an expedition is considered to be exceptional and outstanding,
a quorum of elected representatives may choose an
"Observer or Historian" to accompany the expedition
to record its deeds. He may act in an advisory capacity
only, taking no part in the actual adventure, be it fighting or stealing, etc. etc.' ". He paused for effect, " '—
until such time as all members of the adventure have
won their names by performing the tasks allotted to
them. At that time the Observer-Historian becomes
equal with the expedition and may join entirely in the
expedition. It is understood that during the expedition
the Observer keeps a record of the deeds of each of the
expedition's members for entry into the records on
return.' "

Spiff closed the book with a bang and looked at
Knocker who was dying to smile and laugh and shout
all at the same time but didn't want to in case he'd
misunderstood.

Spiff winked and jerked his head in his crafty old
way. "How would you like to be an Observer-Historian,
Knocker? Never been one of those, have you?"

"No," said Knocker breathlessly, his heart thumping.

"Well, we need a quorum to approve the appoint-
ment, that's four in this case." Spiff gave a yell and the
door opened and three stewards from houses further
up the High Street entered the room. Without turning
his head Spiff said, "All in favour say 'Aye.' "

"Aye," said the three Borribles together, then they
did an about turn and left the room, closing the door
behind them.

"Gotta keep it legal," said Spiff, jerking his head yet again.

He rose to his feet. "Right, Knocker, your clothes are in the cupboard, and a knapsack, everything's there, I did it myself. Get changed. Don't want you to miss the boat, eh? Ho, ho!"

Knocker dashed into the cupboard and threw off his every-day clothes and got into the set of expedition gear that was hanging ready behind the door. As he changed in great haste Spiff talked to him, for he had much to say before Knocker left.

"Don't worry," he began with a chuckle, "they don't know you're coming but they won't go without you. I sent Lightfinger down there with some cock-and-bull story. He won't let them away till you arrive." Spiff was silent for a minute or two, watching Knocker's preparation with more attention than the event deserved. "Do you want to know the real reason why you're going?" he asked at last.

Something in Spiff's manner made Knocker stop tying his boot-lace and he listened intently, observing that the steward's voice had lost its normal speechifying tone.

"Real reason?" he queried.

"Yes, the real reason. Look, you will have to be Historian, write it all down when you get back and all that load of old cobblers, but it don't really matter, see, long as it looks like you obey the rules, but as soon as they have won their names or look like winning their names, brother, you move."

"Move?"

"Double fast," Spiff said, his sharp expression getting sharper. "If you read the Rumble manuals really closely, like I have, and do, you find that they hint about some money they've got hidden somewhere, tons of it. We need that money down here, Knocker, and you're the Borrible to get it. You've gone through the same training as the others, you're a first-class shot with the catapult, you can run like a thirty-four tram, and you've got experience and expertise. You won't do anything rash, though you'll do what's needed when it is. Moreover, I know that you want a second name more than anything on earth. That's why you're going, Knocker, that's why I've been going through the Rule Book. Bring that money back here, son, where it belongs, but whatever you do, don't tell anyone what you're up to, especially Wazzisname Boot. He may be all right, he may not. I know that lot along the Wandle. Above all, watch out for one called Flinthead. If you get on the wrong side of him, your life won't be worth a fart."

Knocker's face paled, not with fear but with anticipation. "But this is an Adventure within an Adventure," he said, coming closer to Spiff.

"That's right, Knocker, it is. I'll see you get your second name all right, but it's going to be bleedin' dangerous and don't think it isn't."

As Knocker checked the contents of his haversack, Spiff told him a lot more things, secret things that no one was to know but the two of them, and Spiff emphasised again and again that Knocker was to share these secrets with no other member of the expedition, otherwise disaster would surely follow.

At last Knocker struggled into his haversack straps and stood impatiently by the door.

"A second name, eh? I'd best be away then."

"That's about the size and shape of it," said the steward.

Knocker opened the door and saw outside the dark, exciting night. He looked round one last time. "Goodnight, Spiff, and thanks. Don't get caught."

"Don't you get bloody well caught," said the steward, gruffly, and then Knocker stepped out into the basement area and closed the door behind him.

Once in the street he looked up through a fine rain

o the few stars in the sky and thanked his lucky ones. Then he took a deep breath and ran with a loping stride down the High Street and towards Battersea Church, the knapsack bumping on his back. The streets were empty and shone damply in the reflected light of the street lamps. The sound of his footsteps echoed energetically from the wet walls of the black buildings and Knocker's heart sang and bubbled within him; he could still not believe it. He was going, going on the best expedition he'd ever heard of.

About twenty yards from the churchyard he stopped running and listened carefully. He didn't want any trouble at this stage. Lightfinger rose from behind a dustbin.

"Knocker," he whispered.

"Knocker," answered the chief lookout.

"It's okay, over here."

Knocker went forward and patted Lightfinger on the shoulder. "I'm going," he said.

"I know," answered Lightfinger. "You must have lost your marbles. This expedition is madness."

Knocker crossed the churchyard and climbed onto the wall and looked down at the water. The boat was there, rocking gently in the slight swell that came from midstream; the oars were out and Napoleon was giving gentle commands to keep the boat from banging against *The Raven*. The water lapped at the sides of *The Silver Belle Flower* and the scum and muck on the water grated against the embankment. Seven white faces and one black one looked up as Knocker jumped down into the boat. He saw the amazement there and his heart felt warm inside him. He wondered how they'd take it. He hoped they didn't mind him coming on their Adventure, but he didn't care. It was his Adventure, too, now. Whatever they said, whatever they thought, he was going.

Knocker had boarded at the stern, by the rudder, and

he sat down and faced Napoleon, who was in the strok
seat.

"I'll row, you steer," said Knocker putting his fac
close to Napoleon's.

"What do you mean?" asked the Wandsworth Bor
rible, half rising.

"I mean," said Knocker, "that I'm coming with you.'

Chapter 4

There was no one to see them off but Lightfinger and he watched the boat edge slowly round the stern of *The Ethel Ada* like a huge insect with only four legs. Darkness covered the craft and soon Lightfinger could only hear the voice of Napoleon saying gently, "Paddle, stroke side, ease up, bow. Hands on the gunwale, number five. Forward all." When Lightfinger could hear no more he turned and walked quickly away, glad to have nothing to do with the gloomy and dangerous Thames.

The Silver Belle Flower crept out until she was well clear of the barges moored along the southern bank. Napoleon didn't take her out into midstream; he wanted to be within easy reach of the bank and its complicated blackness, so that if a police launch appeared they could take cover rapidly.

Napoleon let the boat drift round until the bow was pointing just where he wanted it, then he tensed his muscles and gripped the two rudder strings tightly. "Come forward," he whispered. The crew leaned towards him in their seats. "Paddle," said the navigator and the boat sprang up river, eager to be under way.

Nobody spoke except Napoleon, there was too much work to be done to allow conversation. Every rower was concentrating his whole body, every bit of his brain, on handling his oar as cleanly as possible.

The water surged below the boat and lifted it regularly, trying to bear it backwards and down to the sea. Occasionally a dark mass of barges, lashed together into one rigid floating world, slid by them, towed or pushed by a small tug. Mysterious lights coasted by and men with deep voices called out to one another, and from either shore came the distant groan of traffic, trapped in the streets. It was nearly midnight now, but, small and fearful on the Thames, the Borribles soon lost the sense of time and place.

Gradually, as the rowers came more and more together, a feeling of exhilaration passed from one to the other and their handling of the boat improved. Napoleon, who had never been on the river before, let alone in command of his own ship, was bursting with gratification and fulfilment. He could have sailed for ever.

But the swift tide was against them and it took most of their effort to stay in the same place. There was no ornamental pleasure lake beneath them now but a sinuous monster with rolling ropes of muscle that could shatter a boat like a walnut caught in the crook of a navvy's arm.

They clawed their way forward, away from Battersea Church and up to Ransome's Dock, where Eaton House and Archer House stood behind the green of a narrow strip of recreation ground at the end of Battersea High Street. Underneath the grey-painted girders of Battersea Railway Bridge it was blacker than black and they felt insignificant and frightened, but Napoleon kept them rowing, exerting their small muscles to the uttermost. To the north were Chelsea Creek and the LTE Generating Station. Far ahead, glowing crimson in the night sky, at the end of Battersea Reach, was the Fulham Power Station, a beacon for the night's work.

Napoleon watched his crew carefully, determined not to overtire them, and before long he decided to take cover and let the Borribles rest and maybe eat something from the rations that had been stowed aboard the previous day. His instructions came clearly and the boat slipped into the southern shore and came to a halt between two enormous barges.

"Ship your oars," commanded Napoleon and he went bounding over the benches to tie the boat's painter to a cable which ran from one of the barges to a huge buoy. The Borribles broke into the food and began to congratulate each other, pleased with their progress. "Well," said Napoleon, coming back to face Knocker, anger in his voice, "how'd you manage to fiddle it?"

The attention of the others was caught by the question. They too wondered how Knocker had managed to get himself included in the expedition.

"I'm not here as a member," said Knocker, looking behind him at the curious Borribles, and feeling it was only right that he should explain. "There is in the Rules a provision for exceptional Adventures which allows an Observer-Historian to go along and record it all. Spiff asked me to come, at the very last moment, that's all. I couldn't refuse really—not that I wanted to."

Orococco beamed. "I'm glad, pleased to see you with us."

"Yeah," said Vulge, "you know all about parks and countryside and that."

Everyone else nodded and Knocker felt it was going to be all right, but Napoleon said: "We'd better get one thing quite clear, Knocker, your status as instructor is over, you don't give any orders, see. All decisions will be arrived at jointly. You don't change that."

"No, of course not," Knocker assured them all. "I won't even give my opinion unless you ask for it. I can't even take part in the Adventure until you've finished, though I can use my catapult in self-defence."

"All right, that's fair enough," said Napoleon, "long as we've got it quite clear." He thought for a while and when the others were not listening he leaned close to Knocker and whispered into his ear. "Is that all you've come for, Knocker, just to be an observer?"

Knocker pulled his head back and squinted at the Wendle. "I've come for the Adventure, of course, that's all. What other reason could there be?"

"I dunno," said Napoleon, "but there might be something." And he shoved a sandwich into his mouth and still looking at Knocker closely he munched the bread as if he hated it.

They stayed in the dark shadow by the barges for nearly two hours and when they had all eaten and rested and discussed Knocker's arrival Napoleon made them take their places once more, and with gentle sideways strokes they brought the boat out into the river. There was not much of the night left to them and they would need to be well under cover, hidden from inquisitive eyes, before the slighest hint of dawn should appear in the sky.

"We ain't going much further," said Napoleon, "then we'll have to find some more barges to hide amongst, along by Fulham Power Station."

They rowed on. Several large shapes passed dangerously close and *The Silver Belle Flower* rocked badly enough to ship a little water, but nobody noticed the Borribles and not once did they see a police launch. Napoleon peered into the darkness, his eyes keen and narrow, like some mariner of the high seas, searching for a hideout. Just before dawn he spied what he had been waiting for, a cluster of four or five barges, moored below the low tide mark, and in the middle of them, he hoped, a space of calm water, large enough to hide in during the coming day. After that a little more rowing would put them at the mouth of the Wandle where they could conceal the boat and begin their long trek overland.

Napoleon steered the boat across the tide.

"One last good pull," said the navigator, "and then we can rest."

The Borribles worked with a will and they shot across the river, the greasy waves knocking roughly at the boat.

"Keep pulling," shouted Napoleon. "One two, one two." With a sharp tug on the rudder strings he pointed the boat straight at the dark mass, his eyes finding the gap he sought between the barges.

"Ship yer oars."

The rowers obeyed with relief and *The Silver Belle Flower* sailed silently and gracefully into a little haven of steady water and Napoleon secured the boat fore and aft.

"How do you think we've done then?" asked Stonks massaging his biceps.

"Very good," said Napoleon. "We can rest here all day today, and half of tonight. We've only got to get under Wandsworth Bridge and go a bit further along and we'll be there."

It was decided to leave two Borribles as lookouts while the others slept. Knocker volunteered for the first watch, and Orococco stood with him. The rest of the crew unrolled their sleeping-bags and curled up as best they could in the bottom of the boat.

Knocker kept his watch looking down the grey dawn of the river. Orococco stared upstream and hummed a song, a sad song, and Knocker felt wiser and bigger in himself as he listened, even though the song was sad.

> "River, river, the dawn is breakin'
>   On shadow and wave and wharf and wall,
> And the sun'll soon be appearin', river,
>   Like a big red ball.
>
> "River, river, stop fer a minute;
>   I know yer journey never ends,
> but the city is comin' ter life, river,
>   All of yer friends!
>
> "River, river, listen, the yawnin'!
>   Good and bad dreams are nearly gone,
> Bottles are clinkin' on doorsteps, river;
>   The world's movin' on.
>
> "River, river, windin' ferever,

I reckon you've seen it all before.
Wot's night's endin' ter you, river?
Just one daybreak more."

The Thames was busy now. The two lookouts could hear the sound of hooting tugs and the swish and the slap of the wash thrown up by passing barges, low in the water, nearly sinking under the weight of tons and tons of cargo: coal for the power stations and containers bound for the London Docks.

The first hour of the watch soon passed and Knocker was beginning to feel sleepy when he heard a very slight noise above him on the deck of the nearest barge. He tensed his muscles, slid his catapult from his back pocket and loaded it with a stone from his bandolier. Slowly he stood up and pulled the chunky elastic back so that it was half ready. He glanced quickly up the boat but Orococco was facing the other way, his head nodding. He looked asleep; Knocker waited.

The boat rocked and the Borribles slept on. A scrabbling sound, very cautious, came from above. It seemed to Knocker that someone was trying to find a way out from underneath the tarpaulin that covered the lighter which gave them protection on the shore side. Knocker ran his gaze along the iron wall of the barge, along the criss-cross of ropes that held the tarpaulin down. He could see nothing. Again he looked towards the other end of the boat. Orococco's head still nodded.

The scrabbling noises stopped. Then Knocker heard the noise of a knife making a slit in canvas. He pulled the rubber of his catapult tighter, but as yet he had nothing to aim at. Suddenly there was a splitting sound and a small figure dressed in green and brown burst into view on the very edge of the barge right above *The Silve Belle Flower*. Whoever it was had his back towards Knocker, who, aiming for the kidneys, pulled the catapult to its full extent and let fly. He heard a pained intake of breath and the intruder teetered back and forth as if he could not decide which way to fall. At that moment Orococco turned, his catapult in his hand. He had been feigning sleep, only waiting for the unseen enemy to appear. He took in the situation, saw the target and fired, but luckily, as it proved, he missed. As Orococco's stone sped from his catapult the new-comer lost his balance and fell headlong and heavily into the boatload of Borribles, landing in a crumpled heap between Knocker and the first seat. Knocker threw down his catapult and leapt on the interloper, holding him down while Orococco stumbled over the sleeping forms of his companions to give assistance.

In spite of the blow from the stone, and in spite of the fall from the barge the new arrival was putting up a spirited struggle. He shouted in some strange language and twice managed to get to his feet, before finally he was pinioned to the deck by the two guards. By this time Stonks and Torreycanyon were awake and the combined weight of the four of them was too much for the foreigner. With a sigh and a curse he stopped struggling.

"All right, all right, I give no more trouble," he said, and his accent was thick and heavy, though his English was straightforward and easy to understand.

"Get some rope," said Knocker quickly to Napoleon who had now joined the group, "and we'll tie him up while we see what we've caught."

Bingo, too, had winkled his body from his sleeping-bag and suggested that he and Vulge scout round on top of the barges to see if there was anybody else around.

Sydney and Chalotte made a step with their hands and Bingo sprang upwards and pulled himself out of sight. Vulge followed him but they both returned in a minute with the welcome information that all was clear. No one else on the barges, nothing suspicious on the river.

The Borribles looked down at their prisoner.

"Is it a normal—a child?" asked Chalotte.

Napoleon bent over and pulled off the balaclava hat in leather that the captive was wearing. The ears were pointed, very much so. They had captured a Borrible, and moreover a foreign Borrible.

"Could you please rub me here, on the back?" said the foreigner in his strange voice, and gesturing as well as he could with his bound hands. "That stone you catapulted hit me hard."

Stonks, who was kind as well as very strong, propped up the prisoner and massaged his back for a while.

"Oh, thank you, thank you, I feel better now."

"Borrible?" asked Knocker.

"Borrible," affirmed the other.

"All right, I'll ask the questions," said Napoleon. "I'm captain of this ship." He crouched down before the captive. "If you're a Borrible, where do you come from? Not from London, I'll be bound."

"No," said the foreigner, and he actually laughed. "I'm from Hamburg."

"Blimey," said Orococoo, "an immigrant."

"Cut that out, 'Rococco," said Napoleon angrily, "we haven't got time for joking."

"Who's joking?" said the black Borrible, grinning from ear to ear. Chalotte laughed too.

"What's your name?" asked the navigator.

"My name," said the prisoner, trying to draw himself up proudly even though he was bound hand and foot and prostrate, "is Adolf Wolfgang Amadeus."

"Swipe me," said Torreycanyon in disbelief, "three names! Don't they have the same rules in Hamburg?"

"Yes," said Knocker, "Borribles have the same set-up everywhere."

"That means he's had three adventures, and successful ones," said Sydney, and she looked at Adolf with a new interest.

"That's all very well, but he's a nuisance," said

88

Napoleon. "He's in the way. He'll have to swim ashore, and then make his own way back to Hamburg."

Adolf laughed again. "You have got it all wrong, my friends, I am not superfluous, I am extra. I have come along to join you. I am a great fighter, an experienced general, a marvellous shot with the catapult and I have a high rate of survival. My three names prove that, *verdammt*."

"What do you mean—join us?" asked Napoleon. "We're not going anywhere, this is . . . just a kind of outing."

"Outing," scoffed Adolf. "You are the Best of the Borribles, the Magnificent Eight—though indeed I see nine of you—and you are going to Rumbledom to teach those rabbits a lesson." And Adolf guffawed so loudly they had to tell him to be quiet in case they were spotted.

The captors now looked more uncomfortable than the captive. "How do you know all that?" asked Knocker, breaking his silence. He grasped the German by the collar and shook him. "How did you know? Come on, spill the beans, you little kraut."

Adolf didn't look at all perturbed. "Hamburg is a port; often we get English Borribles stowing away on ships for their name adventure. Over there we are hospitable to foreign Borribles. We do not tie them up and slosh them round the head."

"Get on with it," Knocker urged.

"Not so long ago, we had a Battersea Borrible arrive, very tired, very hungry. I took him into my house, gave him food and beer. We became good friends; he lived under the arches by Battersea Park railway station, he said. Perhaps you know him, no? Anyway, he had been at the meeting when Knocker, that's you, ha ha, ho ho," Adolf Wolfgang Amadeus laughed at Knocker's surprise, "you had captured a Rumble and it was decided to send an expedition to Rumbledom. My friend, the name he won by the way is Steamer, good, isn't it? Anyway Steamer told me all about it, and I said, *verdammt*, what an adventure, what a chance for me to get a fourth name, and in England, too, with English Borribles! What a name I shall have then: Adolf Wolfgang Amadeus Winston." He looked round proudly, pleased with himself. "What do you think, is that not a name and another half?"

"No!" said Napoleon, who didn't like the name at all.

"So I came to Battersea High Street to see what you did, but, I thought, they will never let me on the boat there, they will just leave me behind, but I must get on the boat, and to get on the boat I have to get on the river, so at high tide I waited on Battersea Bridge and when there is a barge going under, with a nice soft load in it, I jump and here I am. I meant to watch for you going by and swim out so you couldn't put me ashore, but the bargemen covered me over with canvas—luckily for me you have come here instead."

"We can throw you ashore from here, too," said Napoleon, "quite easily."

"I wouldn't do that," said Adolf, leaning back in his bonds quite relaxed.

"And why not?"

"Oh, you wouldn't want anyone to know which way you were coming, and if you let me go, I might go around chatting about what I saw on the river and it might get to the ears of the Rumbles, and the element of surprise . . . lost . . . A pity? *Stimmt*?"

"We could throw you into the river," said Bingo cheerfully, "tied to a convenient lump of cement."

Adolf hooted. "Anyone else, maybe, but not a friendly Borrible."

There was a silence then and as no one could think of what to say, or do, eventually all eyes turned to Knocker.

"We'd better have a chat about this," he said, "up the other end of the boat."

They made sure that Adolf was securely bound and then moved to the prow where they talked in whispers.

"It seems to me," began Knocker, "that his story is true. I mean he seems the type to want a fourth adventure—I mean mad enough—like. But however you look at it we can't let him go in case he does give us away. We have to take him along and we'll have to watch him all the time, see if he's a spy, if he leaves messages, things like that. If he isn't, then he's an extra catapult and a bloody good punch-up artist, I bet. We'll have to keep our eyes peeled, that's all."

"We've got to watch him like you're watching us," said Napoleon with a sneer.

"Leave it, then," said Knocker quickly. "I was only giving my advice. I'll shut up."

Bingo spoke up quickly to heal the breach. "Let's vote on it, all except Knocker. Shall we keep Adolf or throw him in the river? Who's for keeping him?"

Seven hands went up; only Napoleon abstained, so that if anything went wrong subsequently he would be able to claim that he had told them so.

"I hope you're not making a big mistake," he said sourly. "Make sure you take his catapult away, and keep his hands tied."

Bingo went down the boat to the prisoner and untied his feet. Adolf was searched and a catapult and knife were found in his pockets.

"You can stay for the time being," said Napoleon, "but I'm not keen on it, see, and if you give any trouble on this boat I'll send you to the bottom of the river so fast the fish will think you're an anchor."

"English understatement, eh?" said Adolf and he laughed, and after smiling at everyone he curled up under a seat and was soon snoring.

"I think he'll be fine," said Knocker. "Time for second watch, I'm exhausted."

Torreycanyon and Stonks took second watch and the others followed Adolf's example, wriggling into

sleeping-bags and falling sound asleep, and the boat
rose and fell softly through the morning, afternoon and
evening, helping their slumbers to remain unbroken.

The fog-ridden sun had long since fallen below the red
horizon when the boat came alive again. Napoleon
aroused everyone with a rough shove and told them to
eat up. He wanted to be rowing again as soon as possible. The Wandle wasn't far away but there would be
much to do before daylight.

The Borribles stretched and rubbed each other's backs
and shared the food from their haversacks and poured
the last of the tea from their thermos flasks. Knocker
took his rations and sat by the German.

"There you go, Adolf, me old china," he said. "We
might have thrown you in the river quite happily but
seeing as you're still here, you'd better have some
grub."

Adolf sat up and ate with an appetite. "*Danke*," he
said between mouthfuls. "Excellent."

"How come you got three names, then?" asked
Knocker enviously.

"Aha," said Adolf, "it's a question of knowing the
rules. You must know a few, otherwise you wouldn't
be here, would you?"

"Oh, that was really Spiff, my steward, not me," said
Knocker.

"In Germany," continued the foreigner, "most Borribles are happy enough to stay at home to get their
names in an ordinary way, a burst of good stealing,
something like that, but if you are willing to go abroad
a bit, like me, and the others don't mind, well, you can
get as many names as you like, and I wanted to get an
English name—Winston, you see."

"Where'd you get the others? Wolfgang, Amadeus,
and Adolf, of course."

"Adolf I got at home, Wolfgang I got in Denmark,
Amadeus in Vienna, burgling."

"They are good names," said Knocker, "very good names, and I bet there are good stories behind them."

"Every name has a story," said Adolf philosophically, "but I am glad you like them, and Winston will add something special. Yours is a fine name, too. You will tell me the story sometime? But what are the names of all the others?"

"They haven't got them yet," said Knocker, "but I can tell you what they will be when this adventure is over." And he explained the reason for the Rumble names.

Adolf was very interested. "We have Rumbles at home, too," he said. "We call them *Gormutliks*. They wield great power, and are dangerous and sly."

They could have talked for much longer like this but they were interrupted by orders from Napoleon.

"Come on," he called, "we've more rowing to do, otherwise we'll never get there. This ain't a holiday, you know."

They went to their seats and Napoleon slipped the moorings and the boat drifted from its hiding place. Once more they crossed the river quickly and getting on station they rowed expertly along the southern shore on the last leg of their river journey. At dawn, if Napoleon's navigation was correct, they would land at the mouth of the river Wandle, the muddy stream where only Napoleon Boot's own people knew a way through the treacherous swamps which stretched for miles under the very streets of Wandsworth.

Chapter 5

The wide curve of the river was empty and still. The ripples of the heavy green water were frozen and dirty. On the Fulham shore squatted the oil depots, faceless places waiting on faceless roads that led nowhere and where nobody lived. Just before dawn Wandsworth Bridge passed over the Battersea boat, casting a darker shadow than the night, and all that the rowers saw were the powerful and unmoving waves that stood and gnawed at the stone piers on which the bridge was built.

They were now into Wandsworth Reach and along the southern side stretched a great wasteland, and although the Adventurers saw nothing they could sense the existence of a wild space from the shapeless whistling of the wind. On the northern bank stood the Cement Marketing Factory and the Trinidad Asphalt Company but the Borribles could not see where the buildings touched the sky because the sky was as black as roof-slate.

It was so murky that Napoleon was convinced he would never find the mouth of the Wandle and his companions began to despair. After several fruitless attempts he went to the front of the boat and knelt down to peer into the blackness. There were dozens of barges here, deeply laden with the old lumber of all Wandsworth, for the land around the estuary was a vast rubbish dump and somewhere amongst the hillocks of refuse meandered the slimy river.

An overpowering stench was brewing by the bank, a mixture compounded of rancid sewage, mouldering waste-paper and the rotting flesh of dead sea-birds. The water dripping from the raised and expectant oars of the rowers made no sound, so thick and oily was it. The Borribles coughed and retched, drooping on their benches, only just able to obey Napoleon's commands as he made the boat nose this way and that, his torch stabbing at the fearsome night.

At last he turned and in a whispered shout, sharp with tired excitement, said, "I've got it."

The boat drifted. The rowers twisted on their seats to look and their hearts shrank to the size of peanuts. In the flat wall of the Thames embankment, hidden behind a flotilla of barges, a gap appeared in the feeble light of Napoleon's torch.

"This must be Wandle Creek," said Napoleon. "Anyway, there's only one way to find out, and that's go up the thing." It was obvious to the others that he was tense, that he didn't really know.

The boat swung slowly round until it was knocking against the solid current of the Wandle and as soon as he was on course Napoleon ordered his crew to paddle upstream. He ran quickly down the middle of the boat, freed Adolf's hands and told him to lift out the rudder. "If you try to escape, I'll catapult you right up the back of the bonce."

Adolf looked surprised. "Escape? This is what I came for, I'm not leaving you now."

Napoleon ran back to the bows to direct the progress of the boat in a low voice and the Borribles pulled steadily, only too glad they couldn't see where they were in the fetid gloom.

They had gone only a short distance when the creek forked and after a moment's hesitation and drifting Napoleon steered them to the left and they rowed on, levering their oars with difficulty out of water that seemed as tenacious as treacle. After ten minutes they heard Napoleon swear loudly and then call out urgently for them to stop. He struck the boat in anger. "Dammit, I forgot the weirs."

The boatload of Borribles was utterly dismayed.

Across the quiet of the night came a sound from beyond their experience, a rushing and a roaring of the elements. Swivelling again in their seats they saw a foaming slope of water slanting towards them in the torchlight; racing yellow suds forced themselves up through a black and shiny surface which slid, unstoppable, towards them, like the most precipitous moving staircase in the London Underground. Polythene containers, empty paint-cans and plastic bottles surged and danced around the boat, buffeting against its sides, like evil spirits on the river to hell.

"W-what is it?" asked Bingo, trying to keep his lips steady.

"It's an effin' weir, that's what, too high to get round. We'll have to take the other fork. There's another weir but it's not so steep." Napoleon's voice was dispirited and exhausted. He felt at the end of his tether, worn out by the responsibilities of the river trip and now this at the end of it.

"If we're caught out here in the daylight, we'll be sussed by the rubbish-men and caught by the Woollies for sure." He thought for an instant and the others waited, the boat still staggering under the onslaught of the swirling water.

"Ship yer oars," he said at length, and as soon as the oars were on board he took one of them and began to punt the boat back the way they had come, while his crew sat uselessly on the benches of *The Silver Bell Flower*, squinting hard to right and left but seeing little. It was all too silent and ugly.

"Keep your eyes peeled for that fork in the creek," growled Napoleon, "otherwise I'll miss it and we'll be out on the Thames again. We must be hidden by dawn. This place is lousy with adults in daytime."

His fear was shared by the others. Already the high banks of the Wandle, held in place by slimy green sleepers and sheets of pitted iron, were taking on a shape and the black sky was not so black as it had been.

"The fork, the fork," sang out Adolf.

Napoleon let the boat drift round into the other branch of the Wandle.

"Get those oars going quick," he commanded, wrenching his own from a mud-bank that was reluctant to let it go. There was a nasty squelch as the oar came away and large dollops of sludge rolled begrudgingly down the wood and slunk back into the river.

Napoleon urged his crew on. The flow of the tide was less strong here and they soon went under a railway bridge, the boat bashing through floating atolls of muck like a trawler in pack-ice.

Another fork came up before them but Napoleon did not hesitate this time.

"Bow side paddle," he called, "stroke side rest, one, two, paddle," and the boat veered to the left.

"We went left last time and it was wrong," said Torreycanyon, loudly with some edge to his voice.

"Yeah," said someone else.

Napoleon's face became so white with anger that it glowed phosphorescent in the dark dawn. "Well, we're going left this time and it's right."

Suddenly there was a clang and a boom and Napoleon was knocked forward and thrown down in the scuppers. The boat stopped moving with a jolt and a scraping was heard as the bows made contact with something. Napoleon jumped to his feet rubbing his head.

"Damn you, don't talk to me when I'm navigating," he shouted. "We've gone and run into a pipe, could have drowned us."

Slung low over the water a huge pipe-line spanned the Wandle near a foot-bridge and it was this that had flung Napoleon to the deck.

"You at the stern, row hard," he cried. "This pipe's

so low over the water that we'll have to force the boat under it. Don't fall in any of yer, there's eels in here and will have yer leg off."

Those at the rear of the boat leaned on the oars while those at the front got down on their backs and tugged and shoved *The Silver Belle Flower* under the pipe-line. When they emerged on the far side it was easy enough for them to push the boat through, while those behind ducked under in their turn.

"It's not over yet," said Napoleon, "there's a real waterfall here, ten foot high, right under The Causeway. To get round it we've got to pull this boat up and out and over this bridge."

Above their heads was a high fence that had been made by the rubbish-men, using old bed frames, bedsteads and strips of metal. Napoleon took a pair of wire-cutters from his pocket and got Bingo to give him a leg-up. He clung to the bankside and cut all the springs out of one of the bed frames, making a gap large enough to get the boat through.

"Throw up the painter," he ordered next and when he had the rope in his hands he told the crew to jam their belongings firmly under the seats and then to climb up the bank to join him.

"We've got to get this bleeder up here," explained Napoleon, whose weariness had dropped from him under the excitement of leadership, " and drag it across this island we're on, then we'll be above both weirs, but we've got to hurry."

The Adventurers gathered around the painter and hauled and hauled and slowly *The Silver Belle Flower* came up from the water to hang vertically above the Wandle. Napoleon looped a couple of turns of the rope around a notice board which said, "Wandsworth Borough Council. Danger Keep Out." The others seized the bows of the boat and manhandled her to The Causeway. They puffed and they panted and waited a while to regain their breath.

"Right, four each side," said Napoleon. "I'll pull, the Jerry can push."

"Not half," said Adolf.

They dragged and pushed the boat across a littered roadway where splintered glass and the debris from long abandoned houses made a crunching sound under the keel. Fifty yards they had to go; it was hard work and they slipped and stumbled and cursed, but at last they came to the main branch of the Wandle, well beyond the two dangerous weirs.

It was pale daylight now and the danger of being spotted in this open and desolate country was increasing every minute. Hurriedly they balanced their boat on the river bank and Napoleon grouped them together.

"When I give the word, we've got to push like hell. She should land flat on the water. If she don't, she'll sink."

On his command they all heaved together, and *The Silver Belle Flower* flew out into the air and belly-flopped onto the water, with a sound that reverberated like a gunshot across the no-man's land of the empty estuary. Before she could float away Napoleon dived down after the boat, sprawled between the benches, scrambled to his feet and threw the painter upwards into the hands of Torreycanyon.

"All back in," yelled the Wendle, "quick as yer like."

As the others embarked Knocker looked back the way they had come, and now in the weak light he could see.

Two black steam cranes guarded the mouth of the Wandle, square and ugly, covered in sheets of flimsy metal, and they had iron wheels which ran on iron rails. These machines it was that loaded the barges with rubbish, scratching patiently every day into mountains of garbage that were always replenished, never diminishing. Scattered lorries waited to go scouring across Wandsworth in search of more waste; huge tipper trucks and skip-carriers stood idle between piles of discarded stoves and gutted refrigerators. Far off, between the Wandle and Wandsworth Bridge, was a mile of undulating mud-coloured barrenness, relieved only by the blobs of white that were seagulls, big as swans, tearing at offal with beaks like baling-hooks.

Knocker shivered at the awesome beauty of it. "Strike a light," he said, "what a place."

"Come on," Napoleon's voice was harsh, "get a move on."

Knocker jumped down into the boat and took up his oar.

"Row on," called Napoleon with venom. "This 'ere Wandle's the steepest river in London, like rowing up Lavender Hill it is, with the traffic against yer."

The Adventurers bent forward. Their hands were sore, their backs ached and the tensions of the night had exhausted them. With their eyes closing and their muscles burning they rowed on and on, across a wind-swept landscape with no trees or buildings, until, after Armoury Way, they came by the back-yards of factories to Young's Ram Brewery and at last they heard Napoleon's soft command.

"Hold it steady now, ship yer oars."

They relaxed and the boat came gently to rest. Behind them dawn was lying along the streets of Wandsworth like a tired animal and the straight sides of the buildings, raised up in smoky yellow bricks, towered into a dusty sky. And very high, one bright window of light showed where an early morning bus-driver grumbled his way from a warm bed into a cold kitchen.

Napoleon did not allow the crew to rest for long. "Right, you lot, we're here!" he said, a certain amount of satisfaction in his voice, and the Borribles turned and not one of them didn't gasp in horror. In a cliff-like factory wall a deep hole was visible: a brick culvert, barely large enough to allow the passage of the boat, hardly high enough to clear the heads of the rowers. It dripped with green slime and Napoleon's voice echoed feebly around it, dying weakly, sucked into nothing. The stench was disgusting and solid, rolling out onto the straggling river in misty clouds, like the final gasps of a decaying beast.

"Swipe me, man," said Orococco, his eyes and teeth looking green in the queer light that floated up from the water, "we ain't going in there, I hope."

Napoleon stood up in the prow, his legs spread, his hands on his hips, like a ruffian pirate captain. "This is the River Wandle," he said. "An ordinary little river that flows under the houses."

"It stinks," said Bingo.

"You've had it too easy," retorted Napoleon, "this is Wandsworth where the best Borribles come from."

Knocker grinned to himself in spite of the trepidation he felt in common with his companions. Whatever else he thought about Napoleon Boot he had to admit that the Wendle had guts and style.

"Now, we're taking this boat in," said the navigator, "and anyone who don't like it can swim home in this." He bent and scooped up a handful of the river water and cast it into the gangway of the boat. The eyes of the Borribles were attracted by the evil-looking liquid while their bodies were repelled by it. The water hardly disintegrated at all but green globules of it rolled into the crevices of the woodwork to lie there glowing.

"Right," went on Napoleon, crouching in the prow. "Gently . . . keep your heads down and I'll fend off with my hands."

Under the cautious power of the rowers the boat shoved its nose into the steaming dankness of the sewer and Napoleon shone his torch this way and that, but it did little good, for the rolling clouds of fog swallowed and digested the tiny beam before it could travel a yard.

The rowers leaned back in their seats, digging their oars through the surface of the water. Adolf sat on the stern seat, shining his torch backwards, and in its light the Adventurers could see the dripping roof of the cavern and sometimes the gaping holes of side tunnels where thick water slid slowly out to fasten itself to the main stream. The German hummed gently to keep up their spirits. "Ho, ho, heave ho." Then he repeated it, "Ho, ho, heave ho. Come, my brothers, ho, ho, heave ho."

Napoleon's commands came regularly in a quiet voice. "Slowly bow side, two strokes. Easy stroke side, now one stroke." And so they groped forward, hesitating at times before tunnels that forked to right and left Napoleon sometimes knowing where he was going, sometimes guessing.

After what seemed hours of paddling the oars struck against the walls and they were brought into the boat. "It's too narrow for rowing now," said Napoleon. "Someone will have to get into the water and pull the boat along."

There was silence amongst the Borrible crew. Napoleon bent under a seat and pulled out a pair of rubber waders. He was laughing to himself as the others could see in the light of his torch.

"I knew I'd have to do it," he said. "The best Borribles come from Wandsworth all right."

Adolf chuckled. "Ho, I don't know about that, we've got a lot of dirty water in Hamburg, my friend. Give me the waders, I will pull you, I haven't done any of the rowing." The German bustled down the boat. He took the waders from the astonished Napoleon, slipped them on and jumped into the stream with no hesitation at all. The rowers swivelled in their seats to watch with amazement. Bingo knelt and shone his torch just ahead of the intrepid little German, so that he could see where he was going, but Adolf had his own torch hooked onto a button of his jacket. He grabbed the painter in both hands and with a "Ho, ho, heave ho," he pulled the boat smartly along as if it weighed nothing.

"Well I never," said Sydney.

Napoleon shook his head. "There'll be a kind of pathway by the side of the sewer a little further on," he called, "then you'll be able to get up on that."

This information turned out to be true and soon Adolf was striding out cheerfully along a brick bank that had been built originally for the sewer-men of Wandsworth, the only adults that the Wandsworth Borribles respected.

Suddenly Adolf stopped humming and tugging simultaneously. The rope went slack and *The Silver Belle Flower* bumped into the bank. Those in the boat looked up to discover what had stopped the German and saw, crouching aggressively against the curving wall of the sewer, an armed Wendle.

He was a thin and wiry figure and he was wearing the same kind of rubber waders that Napoleon had lent to Adolf. Instead of the normal woollen Borrible cap this Wendle, like other warriors of his aggressive tribe, wore a metal helmet to cover his ears and guard his head; made from an old beer can, it glowed coppery green in the light of the torches. He wore a thick chunky jacket of wool covered with plastic to keep out the water and the plastic shone orange and luminous, like the coats worn by the men who work on motorways. In fact the material had been stolen from them. The Wendle's face was hard and tough, much tougher than Napoleon's even, and his eyes moved quickly. He was not afraid even though he was one against ten. With a shout he thrust forward with the Rumble-stick he bore in his hands.

It was then that Adolf showed what a redoubtable fighter he could be. Unarmed, he was not one to avoid a good fight; as he had said, he liked fighting. The spear jabbed towards him and he slid gracefully to one side, his body folding into the water. His companions, who had come to like and admire the German, sprang to their feet in dismay. But Adolf was down not out, for as he fell he went under the vicious weapon and caught hold of the Wendle's right foot. As soon as Adolf's feet touched the river bottom he yanked as hard as he could and the Wendle lost balance and landed flat on his back on the edge of the pathway, the spear shaken from his grasp. The German grabbed his opponent's head and pulled it brusquely into the water and shoved it under the filthy surface.

"Ho, ho, ho," he roared, his face bright with triumph and his blue eyes flashing like police beacons revolving.

There was a clatter further along the tunnel and three more Wendles appeared, armed with powerful catapults, raised and ready, aimed at Adolf.

Napoleon waved his arms and his torch. "A Wendle, a Wendle, a Wendle!" he shouted at the top of his voice. "Don't fire! Borrible! Adolf, let him up. Quick or you're as kaput as a kipper."

The German kept his eyes on the strung catapults and cautiously raised the limp body of his assailant from the black water. He held it in front of him like a shield and without being noticed, except by Knocker, who was now in the prow of the boat with Napoleon, he slid a catapult from the unconscious Wendle's pocket and secreted it in his own.

"Good work," said Knocker to himself, "that kraut's a real find."

One of the three Wendles called out in a harsh voice that came grating along the tunnel wall. "You, put that Wendle back on the path, the rest of you keep dead still. There's another fifty of us up round the next bend."

Adolf carried his burden to the bank and unceremoniously dumped it. Then he stood against the prow of the boat. Knocker was right behind him now and it was easy to slip a few catapult stones into the German's right hand which was held behind his back in the hope that someone would know what he wanted.

Napoleon shouted out anxiously, "I'm a Wendle myself, on the Great Rumble Hunt. Flinthead knows about it, hasn't he told you?"

"He's told us," came the answer, "but if you've drowned Halfabar then you're in serious trouble." One of their number now came forward and knelt beside the half-drowned Wendle. He turned the sodden body over and pummelled the water out of it, ascertaining that the warrior would be capable of many more fights in the future. He nodded to the others and they seemed satisfied.

When Halfabar had been placed in *The Silver Belle Flower* to recover, Adolf was permitted to continue pulling the boat.

"Walk in the river and follow us slowly," he was ordered, "and do everything we tell you. If any of you make a move towards a catapult, well . . . you'd better tell them what, you Wendle in the boat. We could starve you out without lifting a finger. There's fifty behind you now, as well as fifty in front."

Knocker glanced round, as did his friends, and figures appeared wading through the water behind them, perhaps more than fifty, all bearing Rumble-sticks. The Adventurers were hopelessly outnumbered, all they could do was obey.

"Who's the Borrible who's been doing all the talking?" Knocker asked Napoleon, who looked worried, as if the Wendles might take it out on him for this incursion.

"He's a two-name Borrible," whispered Napoleon, "but he's just called Tron. If he had a name for all the things he's done he'd be a hundred-name Borrible, I can tell you. Hard as nails he is, and Flinthead, our chief, why, he's just the same. Nobody comes in or out of here without their say-so."

"I thought this had all been cleared by Spiff. I thought we had permission," said Knocker.

"No doubt we have," said Napoleon, turning his face

to Knocker with some astonishment. "If we didn't have permission we'd have been done over by now."

"But you're a Wendle yourself . . ."

"Don't matter. I've been out, away; they've got to be careful. Only right isn't it, when you think about it? I mean you jumped on the Rumbles quick enough when they came down to your patch."

"Where do Wendles get all their blessed Rumble-sticks?" asked Bingo, wide-eyed and amazed.

"We captures some and makes the others," said Napoleon, "but we've got catapults too, you know, and good with 'em we are. Tron can shoot round two corners and still knock a copper's hat off."

The tunnel widened out a little now. There was a path on either side and both of them were crowded with warriors who gazed without friendliness at their brother Borribles in the boat below. Adolf they prodded with their spears and the Adventurers sat quietly, hoping that he would not lose his temper and start another fight. They felt miserable and apprehensive. Borribles, although inclined to argue amongst themselves, were on the whole congenial people. The Adventurers had known that Wendles were the fiercest of all the tribes but hadn't realised that they were quite so military and suspicious. Napoleon tried to explain the situation to his companions as they went along.

The Wendles, he argued, lived in constant fear of the Rumbles; their territory was the nearest to Rumbledom and had a long frontier with it. Along that frontier the Rumbles outnumbered the Wendles by at least five to one and the Borribles of Wandsworth had only kept their freedom by maintaining a warlike stance. Over the years this had made them into warriors, mistrustful, cunning and hard.

"Still, they certainly look like a gross of top quality villains to me," said Vulge, "and I should know, we've got a few over in Stepney."

The conversation was brought to a halt by the

loud voice of Tron shouting down at the exhausted Adolf.

"Stop there, you, mush!"

"I've got a name, you know, Wendle," said Adolf, looking up, his face covered in mud and sweat. "In fact, I've got three names, Adolf Wolfgang Amadeus, and I would never tell you the story of how I got them," and with that insult Adolf swore his favourite oath, "*Verdammt*."

"You probably got the names second-hand," said Tron sneering and beginning to bring out the first in a series of Borrible insults.

"Even that is better than finding your name in a dustbin," said Adolf with spirit. "Fingy is the name that would suit you well if it were not too flattering."

"Cut it out," yelled Knocker, "this can only lead to trouble. Remember we are after the Rumbles, not each other."

Adolf turned his muddy face to Knocker; even under the grime and weariness the blue eyes sparkled mischievously. "Yes, great leader," he said ironically. "Our adventure must come first," and then he whispered in a lower tone so that only Knocker could hear him, "but I hope I get a crack at this lot one day. I'll bash those tin helmets of theirs right down past their teeth."

The Adventurers were ordered to stand on the bank while the boat was made fast and Halfabar lifted out. He had recovered enough to stand now, although he looked a little groggy and his face was greener than usual because of the quantities of stinking water he had swallowed. He looked round until he saw Adolf, a wet and muddy figure who was being hauled ashore by Stonks and Torreycanyon. Halfabar staggered away from the two Wendles who held him upright and pushed roughly through the little knot of Adventurers who waited on the tow-path. He halted in front of Adolf and shoved his green face up to the slime- and sweat-covered one of the German.

"It is not over between you and me," he hissed, his angry and smelly breath enveloping Adolf's head and making him wince. "One day we'll meet again, where you can play no tricks, and I'll kill you."

"A Borrible who has no tricks is no Borrible," said Adolf pleasantly, reciting an old German proverb. "You'd better go and have a good rest; you need more strength, my little girl. Right now you could probably hit me a hundred times before I noticed you were there." And the German turned and followed his companions along a narrow but dry sewer tunnel that led upwards and away from the main river.

The Adventurers were escorted by an armed guard of Wendles and all around they heard the squelching tread of those who had captured them in the river. On their river patrols the Wendles always wear waders and when they walk the noise is strange and makes the hair creep, and when a hundred march together it sounds like a wet centipede on the move.

"Where's Napoleon?" Knocker asked Bingo who was beside him.

"They took him off ahead, on his own," answered Bingo. "I hope he sticks by us."

Knocker was worried but he comforted himself with the thought that however suspicious the Wendles might be of outsiders, it was in their interest that the Great Rumble Hunt should take place. The chances of it succeeding were small but if it did the Wendles would be safe for years to come. After all, they had sent one of their own men to be trained for the mission.

"It'll be all right," said Knocker, loud enough for all his companions to hear, "they've probably just taken Napoleon off to check that we're not trouble-makers. He'll be back."

They marched on and the tunnel rose and twisted and they shone their torches at the floor which was uneven and broken.

"Keep close together," said Knocker. "If there's any trouble we'll form two lines, back to back."

A few minutes later they came into a vast underground cavern with a floor that sloped steeply away from them. It must once have been the central chamber for the Wandsworth sewage system back in the nineteenth century. Now it was dry and its elegant brick arches were beginning to crumble.

Scores of Wendles were present, standing around the side of the cavern, with late-comers emerging from the many corridors that led there from all parts of the huge borough. Each Wendle held a torch and together they spread an eerie light over the scene. Tron's voice sounded from behind. "Keep going, straight in front of you, over there, where you see that platform. You're going to see Flinthead."

On the far side of the hall stood a small podium and on it was one chair and in that chair sat Flinthead himself; by his side stood Napoleon Boot, talking rapidly to his chief, who appeared to be ignoring him.

Flinthead gazed down at the Adventurers as they lined up. His eyes didn't move and though Knocker watched very carefully the Chief Wendle didn't seem to blink. Knocker surmised that this was because he always lived in the dark and never saw the sun, though it was said that he knew exactly what happened everywhere. Flinthead was the most cunning, the most merciless and the most unpredictable of all the Wendles. Every Wendle went in deadly fear of him, yet he commanded a strange loyalty, a loyalty born out of the threat that surrounded the whole community.

Knocker looked across at Napoleon for some hint of what was going to happen but Napoleon could only raise and lower his eyebrows quickly to indicate that they would all have to wait and see what Flinthead would do. Still the Chief of the Wendles said nothing.

Everything that had been in the boat was now

brought forward and exhibited in front of the line of captives and while they waited Knocker continued his scrutiny of the Chief Wendle. His eyes were frosted over like lavatory windows, impenetrable; they didn't gleam or glint and still they didn't move; it was uncanny. His face was rubbery and, in the light of the hundreds of battery torches, seemed streaked with grey and dark green. His nose was like a false plastic one that had been too near the fire and had melted. It was an evil nose, a dangerous nose, a nose that could smell out treachery and deceit even when there was none. On his head he wore a helmet of copper riveted together in sections and it had an extra piece that came between his eyes and attempted to protect, or hide, the nose, but the nose was too big for concealment. His body was small and wiry, like that of other Borribles, and he was clothed in warm wool-lined waders and a plastic jacket painted with bright golden paint.

His head moved at last and his eyes shifted with it as if they had no independent movement. He looked along the line of Adventurers and at their belongings, then his head became immobile again. Napoleon continued to pour his story into Flinthead's ear, pointing out his companions in turn, giving their names and telling what equipment they had brought. Flinthead began to nod as the tale went on.

"What power he has," thought Knocker, looking round the great hall. There must have been hundreds of Wandsworth Borribles in the cavern now, and although they talked amongst themselves there was none of that cheerful anarchy that one normally associated with the general meetings of any of the Borrible tribes he knew.

"Is your lot like this?" he asked Chalotte, who was standing next to him.

"No, they certainly aren't," she replied. "Creepy, isn't it?"

It was amazing to Knocker how Flinthead had acquired this power. A Borrible community as a rule has little organisation above that of the Borrible house, or at the most, and in emergencies only, the street.

Knocker's thoughts were interrupted when Flinthead slowly raised his left hand, stopping all conversation in the great hall immediately. Every Borrible there must have had at least one eye on Flinthead, every Borrible that is except Bingo and Adolf who had been deeply engrossed in cheering each other with tales of what they were going to do to the Wendles when they got half a chance.

"Ja," Adolf's voice boomed over the silent hall. "Starting with Halfabar, I'll obliterate them."

"And I'll see to Flintbonce there, just for starters," yelled Bingo, and then stopped as he realised that maybe two hundred ears had heard him, that one hundred torches now beamed on him and two hundred eyes had seen him and would remember his face. Worst of all, the blank eyes of Flinthead himself now came to rest upon Bingo like the heavy hand of death.

Flinthead waited and the hall became quieter and quieter, every increase in the silence making the atmosphere more difficult to breathe. Then he spoke and when his voice came it came as a shock. It was a friendly voice, warm and solicitous, like a kind uncle asking after a favourite nephew's health. His mouth smiled, but no other part of his face shared in that smile; his mind was elsewhere, wondering perhaps how to injure the health that had been the very point of his question. He addressed the line of Adventurers.

"Welcome, my friends," he said, looking as if he wished Adolf and Bingo six feet deep in Wandle mud. "Welcome to Wandsworth. You must forgive us, fellow Borribles, if we seem so . . . defensive. You live far from these rugged frontiers, whereas we exist under the constant threat of Rumbledom and its rapacious denizens.

It would be so easy for them, you understand, to come pouring down the hillsides and across Southfields and into this Borough where we . . . pick up a poor living. Heaven knows why they covet what is ours, but then greed is a terrible thing, and although the Rumbles seem to us to be rich beyond the dreams of avarice, we find them everywhere, taking more and more. You captured only one Rumble on your frontier and yet you immediately gathered an élite force from all over London to punish them. Think how much more we feel the need to protect ourselves when we have thousands of Warrior Rumbles on our very doorsteps. But let us forget your awkward welcome. Now that we know exactly who you are, and where you are going, we join in common cause with you. Your enemy is our enemy, your fight our fight."

He coughed, thought for a moment and then went on. "Napoleon Boot, a warrior who carries our trust as well as our love, has told me of you and who you are and what you intend to do when once you reach Rumbledom. It is a good plan, though hazardous, and we hope you succeed. For the present our warriors will look after you. Sleep well and tomorrow Tron will set you on your way to Merton Road; there you leave our territory. Eat well, too. We shall give of our best."

Knocker stepped forward and bowed low and then raised his head and looked straight into the cold eyes. "What," he asked, making his voice sound even and mature, "will happen to our boat? We shall need it for the return journey."

A smile lived for a second on Flinthead's face and then died. "We shall guard your boat as carefully as something of our own. After all, you will need it to carry your spoils."

"If indeed there are any," replied Knocker. "Can you, on our return, guarantee us a passage down the Wandle, till we are safe on the Thames?"

112

"My own personal bodyguard shall be with you as you leave here and shall be at your disposition when you return. That shows how important it is to us that your mission succeed and will be a measure of our gratitude if it does. Next time we shall know you and our welcome will be more . . . amiable. For the present Tron will take you all to a comfortable room that has been prepared."

Flinthead gestured and Tron and Halfabar came forward and indicated that the Adventurers should follow them. After bowing in the direction of the podium they turned about and walked across the huge hall in the footsteps of their guides. The Wendle crowds pushed back and made room for them as if frightened of touching their bodies, but they gazed curiously at their cousins for it was rare for them to meet Borribles from another Borough.

Knocker did not follow the others immediately. He moved closer to the platform and looked up at Flinthead once again.

"Does Napoleon come with us, or does he stay here with you?" he asked the Chieftain.

The Chief Wendle smiled like a tombstone. "He had best stay with you, I think, then you can leave together in the morning. He has told me all I want to know, especially about you, Knocker. I think the Adventure might succeed with you at its head."

"I am not its leader, Flinthead," protested Knocker, looking angrily at Napoleon.

"I know," said Flinthead dismissively, "you are a—what is it—Historian? We all know how to bend the rules, especially that Spiff fellow. Well, whatever you are, I hope you win through. I ask only one thing, and this I want you to promise, that you come back to us and recount all the details and dangers of your expedition and adventures. One of the few pleasures I have is listening to the stories of those who set off to earn their names. I want to hear how you fare, including Napoleon here; a fine name he will have."

"It will be only a small recompense for all the hospitality we have received at your hands," said Knocker politely, though he was deeply troubled in his mind by Flinthead's behaviour. He knew from Spiff that the Chief Wendle had a reputation for meanness and double-dealing. But at that moment all Knocker could do was to pretend he believed everything he was told. Knocker looked at Napoleon. He was a Wendle too and in a crisis would stand and fight with the Wendles, that was only natural. It wouldn't do to trust him with any secrets; secrets would only get to the ear of Flinthead and if the secrets were valuable then Knocker's life, and the lives of the others, wouldn't be worth a handful of Wandle mud.

Flinthead stood, ready to leave. "You are too kind," he said and then without another word he raised his hand and the Wendles in the hall began to leave. Flinthead's bodyguard assembled at the rear of the platform and the Chief went down the steps and was lost in the middle of his men. The bodyguard was formed of well-armed and experienced fighting Wendles, about fifty of them. It would be almost impossible to harm the Chieftain without their connivance, and they were probably loyal to a man. Napoleon watched his leader go and then came to the front of the platform and jumped down to stand beside Knocker.

"That is a great Borrible," he said scornfully, "no little Spiff in a dressing-gown, but a warrior who thinks and plans and knows things. He sees what you are thinking even as it comes to your mind."

"Spiff is just as crafty and just as clever in his own way," answered Knocker. "Anyway, let us catch up with the others, I'm starving."

Napoleon shrugged his shoulders and turned to lead the way across the hall which was emptying now of

Wendles. "They should have sent half a dozen of us on this expedition," he said, "we'd have done it easy."

"You may think that Wendles are better than anyone else, but we think we're pretty good, too." Knocker spoke evenly, trying not to argue with Napoleon.

Napoleon drew a deep breath as if going to launch into an angry speech, but he stopped as if he had remembered something. He half smiled. "Yes," he said at length, "we'll just have to put up with what we've got."

They ran along a dry tunnel and soon caught up with their companions who were being escorted by Tron, Halfabar and about twenty other armed Wendles. After a while they were led into a well-furnished and comfortable room which by Borrible standards was luxurious indeed, with carpets on the floor, a few armchairs and an abundance of cushions and blankets for relaxation and sleep.

The haversacks were brought in and the guards hurried away, only Tron and Halfabar stood at the door for a moment, looking at the Adventurers as they threw themselves down to rest. Then they too departed, locking the door behind them.

Orococco stood up quickly. "They've locked the door," he said angrily, looking at Napoleon.

"Yeah," said Bingo. "What's that about, eh? Answer me that."

"It's all right," said Napoleon, "I . . . asked Flinthead to do it, so we could sleep and eat without being disturbed."

"We could get drowned in here if the tide rose," said Vulge, "I don't like it. Us Borribles hate being locked in anywhere."

"You've got a cheek." Napoleon defended himself. "Why, this is part of Flinthead's own apartments that he's gone and let us use."

"He don't exactly trust us, do he?" said Vulge, striding up and down the room. "Don't let us go anywhere on our own, and locks us in for the night. I hates being locked up at all. It's worse than the nick, underground, gives me the creeps."

"It's not natural," continued Bingo. "All this bowing and scraping to Flinthead, shouldn't bow an' scrape to anyone, a Borrible. I don't think your lot are very Borrible, come to that."

"Are you saying that I'm not a Borrible?" cried Napoleon, livid, and he pulled off his hat and pointed to his ears.

"We don't know about you, yet," put in Knocker, quietly.

"And we don't know about you, yet," retorted Napoleon, turning on the Battersea lookout.

"How does a bloke like Flinthead get all that power, eh?" asked Orococco, "that's what I should like to know."

"Because he saw what needed doing and he did it, because he's tougher and brighter than anyone else," answered Napoleon furiously. "You're not at home now. We came on this trip to get the Rumbles, not for a holiday. Why don't you all just have a good meal and a good night's sleep. That's what I am going to do," and with that he began to help himself to the food that was lavishly distributed around the room and he would not be drawn into any further conversation that night.

The others grumbled amongst themselves but then, being just as hungry and as tired as Napoleon, they tucked into the good food, chose a few cushions and blankets and soon they were asleep.

They slept long and deeply and woke late. Fresh food and drink was brought to them and when they were ready to march there was a loud knocking at the door and it was thrown open. In the doorway, and in the high corridor beyond, stood a crowd of about thirty Wendles: the élite guard, bearing torches and armed and dressed for a foray beyond the limits of the underground caverns. Each one carried a Rumble-stick as well as a catapult, and bandoliers were slung over their shoulders. The detachment was again led by Tron and Halfabar.

"Come," called Tron into the room, "we are to take you to King George's Park, then you have only a little way to go before you cross Merton Road and so leave our territory."

The Adventurers checked their catapults and stones, stepped out into the corridor and stood together. The Wendle guards formed up tightly, and the whole group made off down the tunnel, guiding their steps with circles of light from their torches.

After a brisk march they entered the huge hall where they had met with Flinthead. The small stage was still there but now no one sat on it nor was there one Wendle to be seen. They crossed the hall and entered a tunnel which soon joined the Wandle and they followed the tow-path along its edge. They met no one and Tron explained.

"Do not forget that it is night-time, about four in the morning above, and the night-stealers have not returned from their work and the day-stealers are still sleeping. The daytime shift dress as other Borribles dress, like normal children. We have permanent lookouts everywhere along Merton Road; that is the beginning of no-man's land. There is a system for getting messages back here, though we are gradually stealing enough components to build our own early warning relay with radios. We're getting them out of old taxis."

The Adventurers had to admit to themselves that the Wendles seemed much more friendly this morning. Even Halfabar was sorry that he and Adolf had misunderstood each other so much on their first meeting and he hoped that in the future they would be good friends.

"Come back safely so that you can tell me the story

of your adventures," he admonished the German in warm tones.

"So I will, Halfabar," hooted Adolf, "so I will."

Suddenly on a command from Tron the column halted. They had come to the end of the underground section of the River Wandle. All torches were extinguished and the warriors stood motionless in the obscurity, waiting patiently until their eyes had become completely accustomed to the darkness. Only then did Tron make a sign and one of his scouts slipped soundlessly from the tunnel, wading slowly through the mud and water.

Once outside he gave a low whistle which was answered by the guard on duty. Tron lifted his hand again and two more of the bodyguard went into the river. Tron did this several times until half of his command had gone. Then the first Wendle re-appeared and assured Tron and Halfabar that all was well. Guards had spread out down the Wandle and had seen no suspicious activity; it was not quite dawn and they could get their Borribles to King George's Park and be back underground before it was full daylight and people started going to work.

Tron waved the Adventurers forward and one by one they slithered down the steep bank until they were waist deep in clinging sludge. They strode away stiffly, well protected in their borrowed waders, but they could not escape the ghastly odours of the mud which were released in visible clouds as they pushed their legs and feet along. But they did not have far to wade. As soon as they were clear of the tunnel entrance the guards hauled them onto a small path lying on the east side of the river and there the escort awaited them.

"And how do you like Wandsworth, my friend Adolf?" asked Halfabar as he pulled the German to the bank. Adolf spat down into the muddy stream. "Why, it is just as smelly as Hamburg, I feel quite at home," and he grinned.

The column formed up once more, half the body-guard in front with a torch or two to show the way, the Adventurers in the middle, and the rest of the body-guard behind. Tron gave the word and they stepped out in good order. The Wendles sang heartily as they marched, a stirring fighting song which was their favourite.

"We are the Wendles of Wandsworth Town,
We're always up and the others are down.
We're rough and we're tough and we don't give a damn,
We are the élite of the Borrible clan.
Reach for your Rumble-sticks!
Try all your dirty tricks!
Nothing can beat us
And none shall defeat us.
Say a wrong word and we'll hammer you down,
We are the Wendles of Wandsworth Town!

"We are the geezers who live below
The shoppers and coppers and the traffic flow.
We revel in muck and we rollick in mud,
The slime of the sewers enriches our blood.
Call yourself Borribles!
We are the Horribles!
Cruel black-as-inkers,
Cut-throating stinkers!
Say a wrong word and we'll hammer you down,
We are the Wendles of Wandsworth Town!"

Napoleon joined in energetically, showing his companions that he knew the words and was really quite superior to any ordinary Borrible.

They had emerged from the underground stronghold on the south side of Wandsworth High Street and Tron and the others led them along at a fast pace in a south-westerly direction. The sky became lighter and the torches were turned off, as daylight began to show the travellers where to put their feet. They had not marched for long when the green fields of King George's Park came into view of the leaders. Tron raised his right hand and the column halted.

"What's going on?" Bingo asked Napoleon, who was standing just in front of him.

"Wait and see," said Napoleon. "They know what they're doing, it's their manor, you know."

"I'll be glad when we're away on our own," whispered Vulge, who though small was very independent.

As if in answer to their impatience Tron came back down the line and spoke to them. "We have to cross the river here," he said, "but there are some secret stepping-stones, just under the surface of the water, so you shouldn't even get wet. Halfabar will go over first and show you where they are. I must get back underground before it gets much lighter. We're too conspicuous along here, not like the streets."

Halfabar stepped down from the towpath and using his spear to prod out his way he found the stepping stones below the mud. He knew very well where the stones were but he wanted to make them obvious to the Adventurers. Each one of them was lent a spear by a member of the bodyguard and they followed Halfabar across the wide stretch of hard-topped, soft-centred mud. The mud became slimy water eventually and they crossed that too until they came up against the railings of the park. Here Halfabar had tied himself to a spike and he leant right over to pull up each member of the expedition as he or she arrived.

Not one person slipped from the sunken stones and soon Tron joined to give directions for the next stage of their journey. The bodyguard remained on the east bank, squatting on their haunches, obediently waiting for their leaders to return.

"Right," said Tron as soon as he stood amongst them,

"now we must leave you. The next part of your trip will be easy. We have sent messages out during the night and our lookouts know of your passage. You won't see them but they will see you, but as they know what you look like, and how many you are, they won't bother you as long as you keep to the route. If you stray from it, we shall not be responsible for the consequences. You will follow the river through the park until you come to the end of the fields. There the river goes under a bridge. Above you is a road, Mapleton Road. That will take you westward, across another bit of the park, past the bandstand, and at the end of Mapleton turn into Longstaff, right at the end, then left, then right. You will find yourself in Merton Road, where our influence and power to help you ends. Take a southward direction along Merton until you reach Replingham. We have our last outpost in a school there. Take that road westward until you reach the Southfields, which lie under the great hill you will have to climb to reach Rumbledom. Once you have left our last outpost the dangers that wait for you are many. Beyond Southfields there will be a Rumble scout behind every tree. You will have to devise some way of passing their lines unnoticed, or you will never reach Rumbledom alive, let alone achieve your aim. I wish you success and the gaining of a good name and . . . don't get caught."

With this Tron and Halfabar left the Adventurers, taking the spare Rumble-sticks and waders with them. They bounded over the Wandle without hesitation, flitting across the mud of the river as if it had been as solid as the pavement along Wandsworth High Street. On the other side they gathered their bodyguard together and with one wave of the hand only they ran off at a trot, back to the safety of their underground citadel.

When they had gone, Vulge patted Napoleon on the back with a friendly hand. "Lost your playmates, now. Have to put up with us again, won't yer?"

Napoleon looked sad. "He is a fine Borrible that Tron," he said, "and he has given us good advice."

Torreycanyon shouldered his haversack and looked out over the deserted park. "Well, my chinas, I think we'd better get a move on and get as far as we can before too many people are out and about." And without a further word the ten Adventurers moved off through the green silence bearing their burdens with them.

Under Napoleon's guidance and using their street maps they stayed exactly on the route that Tron had indicated and it led them to Merton Road as he had said it would. It was a busy and noisy road, with cars flashing by and adults rushing along with their heads down. Some stood in bus queues, shifting from foot to foot or staring helplessly after the buses that had left them behind.

When the Borribles came to Replingham Road, they gathered together and crossed in a bunch, avoiding the heavy traffic. On a corner stood a large secondary school of five storeys. Groups of pupils stood outside the main gates waiting for the whistle blast that would announce the start of lessons. Just to one side of the group stood two Wendles disguised in the uniform of the school. Napoleon went up to them and asked, "Borribles?" They nodded and waited for the rest of the band to approach, moving away from the school-children before they spoke.

"We are the last outpost. When you leave us you're on your own. You go straight up there. See the twist in the road? Follow it. It's a long walk, they say, lonely, a kind of no-man's land; no Borribles, no Rumbles . . . as far as we know. Things will change when you get to the Southfields and cross over a large windy space into Augustus Road. It will start to climb rapidly; steep, very. Then more trees and lots of posh houses. Some Wendles have won their names up there. The stories say there are no shops, so you won't be able to live off the land, and there will be Rumble patrols in every garden, I should think. I don't know how you'll get through without being sussed—but then that's your problem, isn't it?"

The two Wendle scouts looked at each other as if to say that nobody would get them on such a foolhardy mission. They were being brave enough just guarding this place and likely to "get caught" at any minute.

The Adventurers thanked them and strode on, realising that their Adventure was perhaps a lot more forlorn than they had at first imagined and that they had many perils still between them and the achievement of their goal.

"Now," thought Knocker, "the Adventure begins in earnest, with dangers everywhere, and it will be a long, long while before we return to the safety of Wandsworth."

Chapter 6

As the two Wendle scouts had indicated, the journey up the rising slope of Replingham was long and tiring. The houses looked uninhabited and bored and there was hardly any adult movement. It was past nine-thirty in the morning and children were at their lessons, their parents at work. This was the first day-time trek of the expedition and the Borribles kept closely together, ready to run, hide or fight. Their eyes flickered nervously to right and left; their catapults were grasped in their hands and stones were loaded ready for firing.

They trudged on upwards towards the lower slopes of Rumbledom, the haversacks becoming heavier with every step they took. Occasionally a door opened in the dead front of a house and a woman shook a doormat or came out to whitestone a step. Sometimes a man scurried by, late for work or on some special errand, and he would turn to look at this strange band of earnest children with haversacks and catapults and woollen hats. But although the man was puzzled, he was too late and too busy to think about the bizarre nature of the sight and he would hurry on.

The steady plodding of their march was interrupted when a car passed them, close to the pavement, and screeched to a halt fifty yards further up the road. A policeman, burly in his blue uniform, leaped from the car and stood in the middle of the pavement with his arms and legs spread wide as if he owned the road, the front gardens, the houses and all the world around him. His face was red and glowing with pleasure.

"*Blimey!* A Woollie in a nondescript," said Bingo, who knew a lot of police terminology because he lived in a nick. "There'll be another one behind us."

Glancing over their shoulders the Borribles saw another car parked a hundred yards behind them and a second brawny policeman was getting out of it, a grin on his face.

"*Verdammt*," swore Adolf, "we'd better get out of here."

To their left opened one of the turnings that led from Replingham; it was called Engadine and the Borribles were never to forget the name. Slowly, stretching their catapult rubbers, the Adventurers backed into it. As soon as they were round the corner they took to their heels and put on a burst of speed for twenty or thirty yards.

"Bingo," shouted Knocker, "you know the Woollies, you'd better take charge."

The two policemen appeared on the corner and stood together for a moment looking along the street at the Borribles. They waved the first car back to them, the other flashed on up the hill.

Bingo said, "That second nondescript will have gone round the block to seal off the other end of the road. I think those Woollies know we're Borribles and not just normal. We're going to have to fight this one, and even then there's a good chance of getting caught."

"Oh, I'm glad this has happened," grinned Stonks, flexing the elastic on his catapult. "Walking gets boring on its own."

"Right," said Bingo, "here they come. Pretend to run away; spread across the road. When I give the word, turn and fire. I'll be in the middle. Those of you on my left take the copper on the left, those on the right the copper on the right. Aim for their knees."

The Borribles, pretending to look very frightened, backed away from the advancing policemen, slowly at first, then more quickly until they were running as hard as they could, which was very fast. The policemen put a lot into their running and were gaining when Bingo called out at the top of his voice, "A Borrible!" and the

Adventurers turned, springing into the air and landing with their catapults stretched. They fired and both policemen fell as if their legs had been scythed from underneath them. Five stones arriving with the force of bullets all at once on the knee-caps can be as effective as amputation when it comes to running.

The police driver, at the near end of the street, had been watching the battle from the open window of his car, but when he saw his two colleagues rolling about on the ground and clasping their knees in pain he shoved his motor into gear and charged it down the middle of Engadine to come to their rescue.

Chalotte ran nimbly to the cover of a front garden. As the car came by, she let it have a stone, glancing along the bonnet. It was beautifully done; the windscreen became veined suddenly with a million lines of cold silver and the driver could see nothing. He was driving too fast and he swerved to be sure of avoiding his crippled friends who still lay in the road. The car, completely out of control, bounced across the pavement narrowly missing Stonks and sending Adolf spinning into the gutter. There was a sound of tearing metal and shattering glass as the car buried its nose in the brick coping that protected one of the house-fronts. The driver, who had earlier, and unwisely, unfastened his seat-belt, went through the frail windscreen like a loco-motive and concussed himself on what was left of the wall.

"Yippee," yelled Bingo and, "Yippee," yelled the others, but Vulge called a warning. "He's on the walkie-talkie. There'll be hundreds up here if we don't watch out."

Sure enough, one of the lamed policeman had pulled out his pocket transmitter and was about to speak into it.

Perhaps the quickest loader and firer of the team was Chalotte. A stone had flown from her catapult almost before Vulge had finished shouting. It smashed into the hand radio and knocked it to the ground, broken and useless.

"We'll have to get out of here quick," said Bingo, looking down to the far end of the street. "The other car will be coming round this way soon."

"I don't mind staying here and taking them on," said Torreycanyon. "I enjoyed that. I hope the Rumbles fall over as easily."

"There'll be thousands and thousands of Rumbles," said Orococco, "and they'll keep coming at us like they was starving and we was their favourite cereal."

"We need somewhere to hide," said Sydney sensibly. "The roads will be crawling with John Law in ten minutes' time."

The group went silent. What Sydney had said was true, but where could they hide? All the houses in Engadine looked inhabited and the police would soon be knocking at every door asking if the Borribles had been seen.

It was then that their luck changed.

They were standing on the pavement near the wrecked car, watching the injured policemen crawl away, when at their feet they heard a slight noise, a grating, scratching noise. They halfturned and looked at the metal coal-hole cover that was set into the pavement just behind them; it moved. They glanced along the street. Every house they could see had a similar cover in front of it, circular and made from heavy iron. They were useful these covers, for the local coalmen could lift them out of the way and empty their heavy hundredweight sacks into them and so deliver their coal into the cellars without trampling all their dirt and dust through the houses—but this cover was revolving, on its own.

"Aye, aye," said Vulge, "what's this then, undercover coppers?"

Suddenly the coal-hole cover lifted an inch, balanced on a human head. It hesitated, then up it came another inch, warily. After a second more it tilted to one side and a nose appeared. It was a large nose and crooked, with coal dust on it as well as a heavy dewdrop which looked as if it might leave the nose at any moment, but which didn't.

Vulge bent down quickly. "What's your game, sunshine, eh?"

A voice came out of the hole; it was cracked and petulant but the words it used were friendly enough. "Borribles, ain't yer? He, he, only Borribles could do that to the Woollies. I was watching from my front room. I'm a good friend to the Borribles, always have been. They help me and I help them. Was one myself once, ain't it, till I got caught. Nasty business growing old. You don't ever want to get caught, do you?"

Vulge looked over his shoulder at the others. "I don't know what we've got here," he said, "but he might be able to get us out of this pickle."

"We'd better hurry," said Bingo. "I can see the other car at the far end of the road, getting ready."

"You come down here, mateys," said the voice from the coal-hole and the dewdrop quivered ecstatically, threatening to lose its passionate hold on the nose. "You come down here, ain't it? I won't tell where you are, and in a couple of days you can carry on to wherever you're going."

"We haven't got a lot of choice," said Torreycanyon. "None of us wants to get caught, at least not before we gets to Rumbledom and does what we came to do."

"Okay down there," called Vulge. "Move over, we're coming in." He pushed the coal-hole cover till it slid over to rest on the pavement and he saw a narrow head, covered with a wisp of grey hair, duck back into the darkness.

"Well," asked Vulge, "who's first?"

"Man, if we stands round here nattering all day, we'll spend tonight in the nick with our ears clipped," said Orococco. "I ain't scared of the dark," and he struggled out of his haversack, threw it into the hole and then wriggled through the narrow opening.

The others followed quickly one by one until Knocker was left alone. He looked about him. The car-driver was still unconscious and the two injured policemen had crawled into Replingham out of sight. The street was empty and no one had seen the disappearance of the Borrible Adventurers. The whole battle had taken no longer than two or three minutes and the crash had not yet attracted attention. However, at the far end of Engadine, Knocker could see the other police car in position. It was still too far away to see what had happened, but shortly those policemen would be driving this way. He must get underground.

Knocker lowered himself downwards through the pavement until his feet touched a shifting pile of coal. The light from above got smaller and smaller as he pulled the iron lid into its grooves. There was a clang like the top half of a sepulchre slotting into place and Knocker and the other nine Adventurers were in complete darkness, safe below the long stretches of Engadine in South-West Eighteen.

Knocker slipped and slithered on the heap of coal. He stumbled, regained his balance for a moment, then fell forward. He was caught and the breath was crushed out of him by two wiry adult arms. He struggled but the arms were too strong. He kicked and squirmed but he couldn't free himself. Hot breath scalded his face as his assailant carried him along; the breath was foul and heavy and Knocker twisted away from it.

The breath became words. "Don't you struggle, my little beauty. We're on your side, ain't it? Oh, my little deario, you are in safe hands now, ain't you though?"

Knocker stopped kicking and waited. The voice he heard close to his ear was the voice that had invited them into the coal-hole; it was a sickly whining voice with a creaking edge to it. Knocker felt himself carried into another part of the cellar and not for one second did the strong and stringy hands that clutched him relax their hold. Knocker didn't like this at all. He slid his hand behind him to reach for his catapult but his hand encountered a large adult one in the act of pulling the catapult away, yet he was still held firmly by two other hands. Was there then another adult in the dark cellar, or did the beast that was carrying him have three hands? Knocker shivered; where on earth were the others?

Suddenly his captor shifted his grip and Knocker was grasped by the scruff of the neck and thrown roughly into space. He landed against another body and he heard Torreycanyon yell out, "Ouch, why don't they put a light on?" At that moment there was a clashing sound as someone slammed a steel door. After a moment's silence a light was switched on, revealing the most dismal sight.

Knocker on his hands and knees blinked his eyes, the bright light coming after the darkness almost blinding him. He shook his head. He could not believe what he saw. He and the other nine were imprisoned in a large cage such as one might see at a circus, only this cage had its bars placed very close together, so close that even a Borrible could not get through. In fact, the cage might well have been made especially for Borribles. Outside the cage, in a large cellar room, stood two men, one middle-aged, the other old. The old man, a boney creature, was rubbing his hands, grinning and sniffing with glee at his dewdrop. The younger man, Dewdrop's son, stood nodding his head stupidly and smiling an uneasy smile, as if he had sat in a mess and was not quite sure what to do about it. He was an idiot, squarely built; a monster of great strength.

Knocker got to his feet and looked at his companions. They were motionless, staring at the jeering old man. Their faces were white and hard with fear.

"Oh, no," cried Sydney, turning her head away from the dreadful scene, "a Borrible-Snatcher."

Stonks grabbed at the bars and tried to shake them with all his power. "You dirty old sod," he yelled at the top of his voice. "Let us out of here. I'll kill you, I'll kill you."

The old man only rubbed his hands harder and sniffed more happily. He elbowed his son and nodded his head so vigorously that it seemed that the dewdrop must leave his nose for ever, but it stuck like gum, swinging backwards and forwards clanging against his nostrils.

"Look at the dearios," he chortled. "Ten lovely little Borribles. I've never had such a haul in my own life; we'll be rich, Erbie, so rich that the horse and cart won't be able to carry all our goodies. Oh, my God, ain't it beautiful! A little bit of persuasion and they'll be workin' day and night, ain't it? Best little deario burglars in the whole wide world, ain't it, Erbie?"

Erbie did not change his expression one bit, but he nodded slowly and said, "Yeah, dad, yeah," as ideas swam sightless through his muddy brain, like poisoned fish in the Wandle.

"Blimey, we're in serious trouble now," said Bingo. "A Borrible-Snatcher, Dewdrop and Son. We'll be lucky to get out of this alive, and if we ain't dead, we'll be caught, sure as eggs is poached."

"Keep your heads," said Knocker quietly, though he felt as scared as the others. "Anyone here got a catapult?"

Dewdrop cackled and slapped his son on the back so heartily that the moron staggered forward a step or two and lost his inane smile, but it soon returned, as gormless as before.

"Oh no, me deario, we got all the catapults; dangerous things as can hurt blokes, like those poor constables outside rolling on the ground with their knees cracked, ain't it? And my boy Erbie, he took all the stones too. We're going to look after them for you, don't you worry your little heads . . . and your haversacks, too. I'll look after you real well while you're here, ain't it? And you're going to be here a nice long while, my dearios, and we're going to be real friends, ain't it?"

Napoleon's face was white with anger. He raised his fist and shook it at Dewdrop and his son. "You can't keep us for ever, you stinkin' old goat."

"Not for ever, no," agreed Dewdrop, "but for as long as I, or you, live or until you get caught, eh, my deario," and he smirked and slapped his legs in glee and Erbie's smile increased very slightly.

His mirth was interrupted by a loud knocking on the door upstairs. Dewdrop glanced towards the ceiling. "Come on, Erbie," he said, "we'd better go up and tell those nice peelers that we haven't seen a thing. Wouldn't know a Borrible from an ordinary child, would we?" And he twisted his head on his neck and gloated over the caged Adventurers who hung their heads in despair.

"Come on, Erbie," and he got his son by the collar and began to pull him away. "We'll come back to these pretty children as soon as the coppers have gone and you can persuade 'em about a bit if they don't agree to our little plan, me deario, ain't that just it?" Erbie's smile intensified and his eyes probed the Borribles' bodies like damp fingers and he followed his father docilely out of the door which was locked behind him.

The Adventurers fell silent; no one made any suggestions because no one could think of anything. There was no way out. The cage was solid, not one bar in it would budge. The floor was made of iron and so was its roof. Even if they got out of the cage the two doors to the cellar were locked. It seemed hopeless. It was hopeless.

"Well, damn me," said Orococco at last, "we're supposed to be the best in the world, and we get caught first time out by a Snatcher. That's the end, man, the very end."

"What will he do to us?" asked Sydney, a little tearfully.

"What they always do," answered Napoleon, angry with himself and everyone else. "He'll keep us prisoner, beat us, or hand us over to that crazy son of his, and then he'll divide us into two teams, and he'll let one team out while the other stays here as hostages; and we'll have to steal for him, day after day, night after night. Steal not for grub or things that he needs, but for things he can sell, for money, so he can get richer and richer."

"We'll have to do shops, houses, post offices, banks, anything he can think of, just so as he gets rich," added Bingo, "and if one of the thieving teams doesn't come back, why, he just beats the others near to death and makes them carry on stealing and when we're no good any more he'll hand us over to the Woollies."

"So you've had it either way," said Knocker, finishing off the explanation to the Neasden girl. "You stay here for ever thieving for him, or you carry on stealing till you get caught, or you run away and your mates get handed over. That's it, no way out."

After this summary of their desperate condition the group was silent again. They did not need any further reminder of the seriousness of their plight. Borrible-Snatchers were a rare phenomenon but were the most dangerous enemy that a Borrible could encounter. Snatchers had been very prevalent in the nineteenth century, snatching Borribles off the streets, even from their beds, and then forcing them to steal, not for survival but for riches. Snatchers sometimes kidnapped ordinary children but they preferred Borribles because they ran faster, were brighter and, above all, Borribles did not grow up and could be used for ever to wriggle through small windows. In modern times only a very few Snatchers were known of but their descriptions and their whereabouts were common knowledge to all Borribles and they shunned them always. But in this strange and unknown part of London, below Rumbledom, Dewdrop has made his lair. He had waited patiently and now he had captured more Borribles in one swoop than he could ever have hoped for in his wildest dreams. Soon he would be rich.

"This looks like the end of our Adventure," said Torreycanyon eventually. "We'll never get to Rumbledom now and no one will ever know what happened to us."

"Don't give up hope, *verdammt*," said Adolf, but he didn't hoot and he didn't sound as if he meant it.

"There's one way out," said Knocker, "a way that will save the expedition, but it means a sacrifice."

"You get us out of here," said Napoleon bitterly, "and I'll sacrifice anything, anybody."

"It's like this," said Knocker, and he spoke slowly as if words were hard to come by. "Half of us will be left here always, and five will be out stealing, turn and turn about. One day we could draw lots and the five who are out, well, they just don't come back, but get away. That's all we can do."

The Adventurers looked at each other. It was a solution but a drastic one. Five to go and face the dangers of Rumbledom even more outnumbered than ever; five to be torn apart by Erbie and eventually handed over to the authorities, never to be Borribles again. The thought was horrid. Being caught was an extinguishing of identity, it was death. Worse than death, it was the loss of beauty, of freedom, a descent into ugliness. Look what had happened to Dewdrop, he had been a Borrible and then he had been caught and turned into something normal.

"That's not much of an option," said Stonks. "Two chances we got, a dog's chance and no chance."

"Let us wait," suggested Adolf, "let us wait a while before we decide on such a dire step." He tried to smile. "They will beat us and not give us much food, so Snatchers behave, it says in the old books, but he must let us out to steal. Let us promise always to come back, for the time being at least. Maybe we will find a way."

With heavy hearts they agreed that for the present they would do what Dewdrop ordered. They would bide their time as well they might and hope against hope that their luck would one day turn.

So began a harrowing time for the ten Borrible Adventurers, perhaps the worst of the whole expedition, for although many more dangers were to threaten them, never again would they feel so despondent, so small, so powerless.

Dewdrop and his son Erbie pretended to earn their living by going from street to street with a horse and cart collecting rags and bones and old iron. On the side of the cart was painted in deep red paint, "D. Bunyan and Son, Breakers and Merchants." The poor old horse who did all the work, pulling the cart up the steepest hills with the two men aboard, was called Sam

Dewdrop and Erbie did collect rubbish and old iron when it was positively thrust on them but they never went out of their way to find it. They only rode round the streets looking for things to steal and houses to burgle. Everything they found or stole they sold for money which was put away into a secret hiding-place in the old house in Engadine. Dewdrop Bunyan had snatched Borribles in the past for burgling purposes but he'd only snaffled them in ones and twos. Now here he was with ten all at once and he decided to work them very hard every day and night so that he would become even richer even quicker. He would get them to burgle the big houses on the other side of Southfields and even some on the hills leading towards Rumbledom. He would become the richest man in the whole of London.

Dewdrop had satisfied the policemen investigating the Borrible battle that the assailants had got clean away.

"I saw them," he told the gullible Inspector. "They ran round the corner, down Merton way, miles off by now, I should think, nasty little bleeders." Of course the Inspector believed the tale; there was no reason not to, for Dewdrop Bunyan was a well-known local character.

When the policemen had given up their search and the rag-and-bone man felt quite secure he began to starve the Borribles and encouraged his imbecile son to prod them with a sharp stick through the bars of the cage. Erbie often pulled one of the prisoners round the house on a dog's lead, tormenting the Borrible until he or she could stand no more and would attack the stupid adult. But Erbie was so strong that the attacks of a tiny Borrible just made him snigger, though he beat his attacker unmercifully till the blood flowed. Then he would drag the semi-conscious captive back downstairs and throw the limp body into the cage and Erbie's crazy fixed smile would explode into a strange and blood-curdling laugh.

Dewdrop always joined in the laughter, rubbing his hands and rocking his head sideways on his shoulder so that his dewdrop wagged this way and that in the light of the bare bulb that lit the cellar. Every one of the Adventurers suffered these torments and at the end of a few days all had lost weight and were covered in bruises and sported cuts and black eyes.

"I'm going to kill him one day," Napoleon would walk up and down muttering under his breath. "I'm going to kill that great stupid loon, and then I'll kill his father, and if I don't I hope as how the Wendles hear about them and come up here and take these two and stake them out on the mud flats of the Wandle, and they'll sit round and sing songs while these two maniacs slowly slip below the surface and suffocate, bloody lovely." Napoleon was a real Wendle when roused.

About a week after their capture Dewdrop began to take the Borribles out on raids. Sometimes they went at night to burgle a big house, at other times they went during normal working hours to steal from supermarkets and department stores. The rag-and-bone man always kept at least five of his captives in the cellar under the demented eye of his son, Erbie. So eccentric and sadistic were this oaf's pleasures that it was more of a hardship for the Borribles to be kept in the cage than to be taken out stealing.

They stole well for their master and there were several reasons for this, the main one being that stealing comes naturally to all Borribles, although it is not usual for them to steal stuff they don't need. But they were also well aware that Dewdrop would let Erbie beat them to within an inch of their lives if they didn't do well in house or shop. He could even turn them over to the police for the pleasure of seeing them get their ears clipped.

The key to the cage was kept in Dewdrop's pocket and it was attached by a long chain to his braces and he never let it out of his sight or gave it to his son for one minute, for Dewdrop trusted no one. He was sly and he was cunning.

Weeks went by and still the Adventurers were no nearer escape. They stole and they burgled, returning to Dewdrop after each sortie to find him sitting on the seat of his cart with Sam munching in the nosebag, shaking his head up at the sky to get to the hay. Wearily they loaded their booty onto the back of the cart and clambered in after it, hiding under a piece of canvas so they would not be seen by prying eyes. Then Dewdrop would settle back in his seat, flap the reins and the old horse would lean into the traces and take them home. Home! Back to the dreary house in Engadine and the dreadful cold cellar with a cage in it and in the cage ten desperate and forlorn Borribles.

They became cheerless and they moved like people without minds. They had not one glimmer of hope and they hardly talked to each other, which for Borribles is a sign of mental disintegration. Their spirits got lower and lower until there came a day when they spoke no more. The ten companions lost count of the weeks spent in the cage, and back in Wandsworth the Wendles forgot about the expedition; even the Borribles of Battersea gave the Adventurers up for dead. The imprisonment seemed to go on for ever. Knocker's original suggestion, that they should draw lots and that one team of Borribles should simply disappear when Dewdrop sent them thieving, seemed more and more attractive. Each Adventurer had come to believe in his own heart and mind that this was the only way. All that stopped them taking up the subject again was the bleak thought of being left behind, alone with Dewdrop and Erbie. But then, just when they needed it, luck took a hand. Something happened.

Very late one evening, about eleven o'clock, Knocker and Adolf, Chalotte, Bingo and Torreycanyon were taken out by Dewdrop and driven in the cart almost halfway up the hill beyond Southfields. The five Borribles sat silent beneath the tarpaulin on the back of the cart and listened to the tread of Sam's hooves on the tarmac. It was a cold evening, for winter was coming on, and they shivered all the more because they were hungry. Sam pulled slowly, the hill was long and steep. Occasionally they could hear Dewdrop call out, "Come along you, Sam, my old deario," and then there was the crack of the whip as the rag-and-bone man hit the old horse as hard as he could. Once the Borribles would have said, "Poor old Sam," because Borribles are mighty fond of horses, but now they had no sympathy to spare for Borrible or beast.

Sam tugged the cart up and up the steep hill, past many silent mansions standing in great gardens, until Dewdrop stopped in front of a very large house hidden behind high hedges and surrounded by acres of lawns and flowerbeds. The Borribles heard the brake being pulled on and then the tarpaulin was jerked back and the cold air came rushing in. Dewdrop's dewdrop looked like frozen jelly, green in the pale light of the stars.

"Well, my little dearios," creaked the evil voice, "we're going to have a fine time tonight. Here's a nice big house, what we have here, family gorn away for a second holiday, ain't it? Skiing and somesuch; I hopes they breaks their legs. But that's not why we're here, is it, to look into their health? We're here because they're there, ain't it? This is a family with a lot of money, no doubt they've taken it with them, but you can't take everything, oh no, too cumbersome and heavy. Can't have a skiing holiday with a grand piano up your jumper, eh? I'm going to wait here with Sam, my horse. You three . . . " He suddenly jabbed his boney finger into the tender flesh of Chalotte, Bingo and Torreycanyon one after the other. "You three will concentrate on the downstairs, should be some lovely silver in there, knives and forks, Georgian flower bowls and such. Oh, my dearios, I do like a beautiful thing, it was beauty that put me on this road, ain't it."

He turned and jabbed Adolf and Knocker. "And you two will go upstairs, look into the studies and bed-rooms, nice antique stuff they'll have up there, pottery I should think, and if that don't work out you get into the children's playroom. Rich family, ain't it, spends a fortune on their little spoilt brats, I shouldn't wonder. Well, stealing's a great leveller, ain't it? We'll take some

139

of those rich toys, my dearios, and I'll give 'em to someone else, make 'em happy. Now go on, and don't forget to come back, else you won't see your friends no more."

The Borribles leapt down from the cart and, taking a sack each, they ran nimbly across the grounds of the house to the back garden, out of sight of the road. It was quiet and dark and not a thing moved in the whole world. Knocker soon had a window open and they lost no time in getting inside. Leaving the other three to work the ground floor, Knocker and Adolf raced for the stairs and, in the light of their torches they rifled the bedrooms, snatching up anything they considered worthwhile.

When their sacks were nearly full, they went into a long wide room that was obviously the playroom; there were models and games everywhere. Without a word Adolf and Knocker began to collect some of the smaller and more expensive items.

After a while Adolf said, "I think we've got all we can carry." His voice sounded flat and depressed. "We'd better get back to Dewdrop now, or he'll be beating us again for being too slow."

"And if we don't get enough stuff he'll beat us for that, too," said Knocker, thinking that he couldn't go on living like this much longer. He went to the last of the toy-cupboards and said, "I'll just have a look in here."

Adolf was at the other side of the room when Knocker opened the cupboard. He couldn't see what Knocker saw but he heard a gasp, and then a chuckle and then a whistle of pleasure and happiness with a note of hope in it too. It had been so long since Adolf had heard anything so cheerful that he looked up immediately and scuttled over the room shouting. "What is it, what is it?" and then he saw and he swore his favourite oath. "*Verdammt*," he said and then again, "*verdammt*," and finally, "a million *verdammts*."

In front of the two Borribles, on the second shelf, level with their eyes, were two of the finest steel catapults they had ever seen. The elastic was black and square and powerful and looked new and full of resilience.

Adolf and Knocker looked at each other, their eyes gleaming and shining with a bright spark such as had not glowed there for many weeks.

"How on earth can we get them back to the cage?" asked Adolf. "That dammt Dewdrop maniac searches us every night."

"He does," said Knocker, his mouth curling into a tight-muscled smile, "he does, but he never looks under our feet."

"*Verdammt*," shouted Adolf, "you're right. I saw some sticky tape over there, just the thing, but we must be quick, or he'll think something fishy is going on."

Both Borribles, their hearts throbbing, hastily fixed a catapult to the sole of a boot. With a minimum of luck, they might be able to get the weapons back into the cage.

"Where can we get some stones," said Knocker as he finished fixing his catapult, "and how would we smuggle them in if we had them?"

Adolf struck his forehead with the flat of his hand. "I saw some large marbles in that cupboard over there. I tell you, the kids in this house have everything in the toy line."

It was true enough. In a large cake tin was a fine collection of coloured marbles, all of them as big as a good-sized stone and all of them heavy.

"We can't take more than five," said Knocker counting them out. "We'll carry them in our mouths."

"Long as Dewdrop doesn't make us speak when we get back to Engadine," said the German.

"Well, let's go," said Knocker, "and hope for the best."

They left the house and ran across the starlit lawns to where Dewdrop sat on the cart, his shoulders hunched and his head swivelling at the slightest sound.

"Where've you been?" he snapped. "The others got here hours ago. You're trying to get me caught, ain't it? Well, you remember, my dearios, if I gets caught I'll make damn sure you lot does. Get in the cart with those sacks and cover yourselves up." And when that was done Dewdrop cracked the whip and old Sam leant into the traces, turned the cart round and took them home again.

At the back of the house in Engadine was a large yard where the rag-and-bone man kept his scrap metal and where he stabled his horse. It was approached from the road that ran behind and parallel to Engadine and it was always this entrance that Dewdrop used after one of his forays.

Once Sam had been shut in the stable for the night Dewdrop pushed the Borribles to the house, staggering as they were under the sacks of booty.

"Come along, my beauties, my little stealing wonders," he muttered impatiently. "I want to see how well you have been working for my early retirement. Ho yes, this is my redundancy pay, ain't it, me dearios? Hurry along, you brats, 'fore I brains yer."

The five Borribles said nothing. Each was holding a precious marble in his mouth and dared not speak.

Inside the house they dumped the sacks in the hallway and then filed down the narrow steps to the cellar. Erbie stood there, drooling and smiling and nodding as they went into the room and lined up as they always had to line up.

"Hurry up, Erbie, my ol' darlin'," said Dewdrop as he came into the room. "There's such a lot of stuff tonight we'll be up till morning just looking at it. Get those little dearios locked up safe and sound and give 'em a little bit more bread, just so they knows how much I appreciates 'em."

Erbie came along the line and under the watchful eye of his father he ran his hot and heavy hands over the frail forms of the Borribles. He felt everywhere, grinning and sniggering, making sure they had stolen nothing from the sacks to keep for themselves. The Borribles stood with their mouths firmly closed, the marbles feeling as big as footballs. When Erbie had finished his searching and prodding and fondling, Dewdrop went over to the cage and stood there with a truncheon in his hand. He opened the gate and quickly pushed the Borribles inside. The door clanged and Erbie threw some stale bread through the bars and then both he and his father sped from the room to spend avaricious hours with their swag.

As soon as Dewdrop and Erbie were upstairs the marbles were brought from their hiding places and aroused great interest; but when the catapults appeared, why then there was rejoicing and hope.

"Oh, my," chortled Vulge, as he fingered a catapult lovingly, "I know who's going to get a clout round the ear with this little beauty. Knock his bloody brains out, if he had some—ain't it?" he added in impersonation of his jailer.

"Man, oh man," cried Orococco, jumping up and down and smashing his right fist into his left hand, "this is it. I'll pulverise them, I'll feed 'em to the sparrows."

"How'd it happen?" asked Napoleon. "How'd you do it?"

"Knocker found them," said Chalotte, her eyes alight. "At the house we were turning over, and Adolf found the marbles; there's only five, but that'll be enough." She blushed and added, "Knocker told us all about it in the cart on the way home." Then she smiled at Knocker, apologising in a way for telling his story but showing that she was proud of him.

"That's it," said Knocker throwing his chest out a bit. "It was easy. Look, tomorrow it's you lot who go out.

When you get back, me and Adolf will have our catapults ready. We're out of practice but we should be all right, and we've got five good heavy marbles. This is how we'll do it. When you're lined up and Erbie's waiting for his old man to come and supervise the searching, that's when we strike. We'll shoot to kill," said Knocker, looking sombrely at Adolf who just grinned and flashed his blue eyes. "After what we've put up with nothing else will do." The Adventurers murmured their assent. "We must get Dewdrop, he's got the keys. You others will unlock the cage. Then we'll all get into the back yard, take the horse and cart, and anything else we want. Agreed?" Everyone nodded. For the first time in weeks they were happy and hopeful.

The next day was a long day and there was a longer evening to follow it as Knocker and Adolf waited for the return of Dewdrop. Two catapults and five marbles were all that they had to help them to reach freedom. Knocker walked up and down the cage, flexing his muscles, watched by his four companions.

"They won't be long now," said Chalotte trying to soothe him. "It will be all right, you'll see."

"Adolf," said Knocker at one point, "you have had more adventures than me. We have five stones only; you take three, I will take two. You aim at Dewdrop, I will take Erbie. We fire, without words, as soon as Dewdrop steps into the room."

Adolf said, "You do me a great honour, Knocker my friend, for you are a good shot with the catapult."

"I saw you fire at the policemen," said Knocker. "You did it well."

"Listen," said Bingo, in a whisper, "here they come."

Sure enough there were footsteps upstairs and Erbie came creeping sideways into the cellar like a white crab. He slithered over to the cage and had a prod or two with a pointed stick. The Borribles got as far away from the idiot as they could.

"Better get an aspirin, sonny," murmured Bingo, "because you're going to have an awful headache. You think you're dopey now, but wait till you've had a little bash round the bonce."

There was a slamming of doors above and some heavy thumps as the Borribles came in and dropped their sacks of loot onto the floor. Then they were pushed downstairs by Dewdrop, who could be heard grumbling because it had been a poor night's stealing.

The door to the cellar stood open and the Borribles stumbled in.

"Go'ron, you lazy little fools," shouted Dewdrop. "Nothing, nothing you brought me. How can I make a living like this? Monsters, ungrateful monsters, I'll be working until I'm a failing old man at this rate, never able to retire."

He rushed through the doorway and stopped to look round the cellar. His face was angry red, purple in the tight skin near his mouth. "None of you shall eat tonight, none of you," he snarled.

Adolf and Knocker had their backs to the door, crouching in the cage, catapults firmly gripped, spare marbles in the ready hand of a colleague. They glanced at each other and on the nod they turned unhurriedly, stretching the catapults as far as they would go, a murderous extent, and let fly, each at his target.

Knocker's marble hit Erbie on the left temple, hard. Erbie swayed, his smile petrified, stiff as blancmange, but he did not fall; unconscious, he was kept upright by some trick of gravity.

Adolf did not have the same luck. As he released the elastic Dewdrop moved forward, intending to thrash the Borribles, for he was in a foul temper, and the marble only clipped him on the back of the head, serving but to increase his anger and his vigilance.

He looked towards the cage and reached for the truncheon that always stood just inside the cellar door; the moisture at the end of his nose glowed blue, green and mauve.

"Throwing stones, ain't it?" he roared, then he saw the catapults and was scared.

"Erbie, we'll have to lock the doors on these guttersnipes until they comes to their senses."

But it was too late. Napoleon kicked the truncheon out of Dewdrop's reach. Adolf reloaded and he didn't miss a second time. The projectile crashed and splintered into the middle of the rag-and-bone man's forehead and he staggered back against the wall, sorely hurt, and his dewdrop, that globe of multi-coloured mucus, finally broke off its infatuation with the nose and fell to the floor.

"Oh, Erbie," Dewdrop cried piteously. "Oh, Erbie, help me, my boy, my son, my joy."

But poor Erbie was in no state to help anyone. Chalotte had thrust a second marble into Knocker's hand as soon as he had fired the first. He reloaded and shot at Dewdrop's crazed son, still rocking on his heels. The heavy glass bullet struck Erbie a fatal blow above the heart and he fell backwards, demolished, like an old factory chimney.

Dewdrop could not believe what he saw. He raised a bewildered hand to his bleeding forehead, the blood trickled down into his eyes and confused him. Napoleon picked up the truncheon and stood ready, but he waited for Adolf to fire his last shot.

The German, veteran of many a battle, and survivor from a multitude of tight corners, took his time.

"Oh, my son, my poor little Erbie, what have they done to you, you little darling what wouldn't hurt a fly? Oh, what a cruel world, my boy. Erbie speak up and chat to your father."

Adolf's third marble flew straight as an arrow, and as fatally, to the temple of the Borrible-Snatcher. He lurched and pressed both hands to his head, then, lifeless himself, he fell forward with a mighty crash across the lifeless body of his son.

"So perish all Borrible-Snatchers," said Knocker grandly, and the others looked at each other with a wild delight. They were free.

It was the work of only a few minutes to find the keys and open the door of the cage. They discovered their haversacks in the next cellar room, where they had come into the house of Dewdrop Bunyan and Son so many weeks before; their catapults and bandoliers were there too.

Soon the Adventurers were re-equipped and in marching order. They found food upstairs in the well-stocked kitchen and they ate as they had not eaten for many a day. Then, smiling and almost crying with happiness, they went out into the yard.

Knocker went to the cart and threw his haversack into it; Napoleon, keeping close behind him, did the same.

The others hesitated for a moment and lowered their haversacks to the ground.

"Where," asked Sydney, "are you going with that cart?"

"What do you mean?" said Knocker, his eyes widening, taken aback. "Rumbledom, of course."

"We think," said Chalotte, "that escaping from a Borrible-Snatcher is an Adventure in itself, let alone killing one. We've earned our names already."

"But that is not what we came for." Knocker looked at the ring of faces that surrounded him, searching for some support. The support came immediately, from an unexpected source.

"No," said Napoleon Boot stepping forward, "that is not what we came for. I'm with Knocker."

"I think I have earned my English name," said Adolf. "I understand Chalotte, she is right, we have done enough, but I go with Knocker. That is because I am slightly mad. I have a thing about Adventures."

"We all want to go really," said Bingo, sitting on his haversack, "but . . . I mean . . . we've been so knocked about by Erbie, and we haven't eaten properly for ages."

"We aren't fit for the job, now, are we?" said Torreycanyon. "Perhaps we should rest up for a bit, eh?"

"What are you on about?" snapped Napoleon. "We can't go back now, what would we look like?"

Seven Borribles looked selfconscious and shifted their feet.

"However rotten we feel," insisted Knocker, "we've got to go on. We're free now, that's a tonic in itself. Anyway, you lot can do what you like. The three of us are going. Get the horse, Nap."

Bingo stood up and the others moved a step.

Chalotte said, "If Knocker and Nap can agree for once then something very dodgy is happening, so we'll have to go along, I suppose, to see what they're up to," and she gave Knocker and Napoleon a long and piercing look.

Bingo shrugged his shoulders, threw his haversack into the cart and quoted a proverb at no one in particular, "If you're my friend, follow me round the bend."

The others did as he did and exchanged grim smiles with Knocker. The horse was brought from the stable and Sydney went over and spoke to him affectionately.

"So we're all going to Rumbledom, Sam, after all, and you will come with us. Rumbles don't like horses, but we do, you will be our mascot and mate and we will protect you." And all of them stroked him and gave him lumps of sugar they had taken from the house and they put him between the shafts and made ready. They took a long raincoat from the house too, a good one that Dewdrop had always worn on rainy nights, and Bingo who was the lightest, sat on Stonks's shoulders, for he was the strongest, and Stonks sat on the driving seat of the cart and they put the raincoat round Bingo's shoulders and it looked for all the world as if an adult was driving. The rest of the Adventurers hid under the tarpaulin at the back and with a crack of the whip and with a "Giddeyup, old Sam, me deario, ain't it?" Bingo drove them out of the yard and they began the last lap of their journey to the borders of Rumbledom, South-West Nineteen.

"There's one thing," said Knocker, as they all sat warm and content under the canvas, "we were in Engadine so long that the Rumbles have probably given us up for dead—and if they don't like horses, so much the better. Sam can take us right up to their front door and kick it down."

Chapter 7

It was dark.

It was the darkest part of the night but Sam knew the way to Rumbledom and he pulled the cartload of Borribles joyfully, knowing in his heart that he would be beaten and cursed no more. He took them away from the hateful memories of Engadine, and Bingo, secure on the shoulders of Stonks, sang a rousing Borrible song to himself, a song that told of the dangers past and the dangers to come.

"Sound the fife and beat the drum,
We're riding, we're riding to Rumbledom!
Dewdrop's dead, and Erbie too,
We're going to do what we must do.
Onwards we ride to glorious fame,
To rout the Rumbles and earn a name!
With a fee and a fo and a fie and a fum,
We're riding, we're riding to Rumbledom!

"From Peckham, and Stepney, and Tooting we come!
We're riding, we're riding to Rumbledom!
Wandsworth, Whitechapel and Neasden too, We're
    going to do what we must do.
Ahead lies battle and maybe death,
We'll soldier on as long as we've breath
To rid the world of that snouted scum,
We're riding, we're riding to Rumbledom!

"Armoured in courage from bonce to bum,
We're riding, we're riding to Rumbledom!
Though they are many and we are few,
We're going to do what we must do.

So, giddeyup Sam, and spare no speed!
To triumph, or Hell, or Kingdom Come,
We're riding, we're riding to Rumbledom!"

Bingo's companions joined in the song, their hearts full of a divine excitement, a feeling which mingled strangely with the serene joy they felt at being Borribles, at being alive and together on an adventure of their own, an adventure that would be sung about again and again in the years to come.

Sam took them through many deserted roads and gardens and strange silent streets, heaving the old cart across the steep hills which guarded the borders of Rumbledom. The horse strode out purposefully, head down and legs thrusting hard, the colour of his coat alternating between deep purple and gold as he entered and left the quiet pools of light which fell gracefully from the tall white swan-necks of the concrete street-lamps. Sam pulled them from Brookwood to Elsenham, into Augustus where the slopes began in earnest. Up Albert Drive and Albyn, through Thursley Gardens and along Seymour and Bathgate, up Somerset Road at last and the slopes flattened and the sky lightened and turned blotchy like yesterday's porridge and a cold dark wind came across a boundless open space and numbed the intent of the Adventurers as they peered from beneath the warm canvas. The crisp air lined their lungs with ice, chilling their blood at the heart. Sam hesitated. One last road to cross—Parkside. He shook his head and neighed valiantly and went out into the green and black stillness that was Rumbledom.

Bingo guided the horse and cart to a large clump of trees not far advanced into the wilderness. The wintry light of morning glinted without friendliness on a sheet of water nearby. "Bluegate Gravel Pit, Disused," said the map.

"We'll camp by the water's edge," said Knocker to

Bingo, "then at least we can't be attacked from the rear, and we can post lookouts along the line of trees."

"There's no one about," said Bingo, "it doesn't look like we've been spotted. If we make it to those trees, we'll be safe."

Sam pulled them towards the copse. The cart lurched and jolted and the Borribles, who were standing now, had to hang on with all their strength to avoid being thrown out under the wheels. They looked keenly in every direction to see it there was any sign of their enemies, but not a bird flew overhead and not a dog hunted through the clumps of grass, even on the horizon where the grey sky was brightening.

"Come on, Sam, my old deario," cried Bingo in a tired voice, "nearly there, ain't it? Then we'll rest and eat all day, my little darling."

Sam dragged the cart deep into the copse and halted. His coat was steaming and his legs were trembling after the long uphill flight from Engadine. Bingo pulled on the brake and the Adventurers leapt to the ground. They spread out in all directions to search through the undergrowth, making certain that there were no Rumbles in hiding or, even more dangerous, that there was no entrance here to a Burrow, one of those large underground warrens where Rumbles live in security and comfort.

They found no trace of the enemy and so Napoleon and Vulge prised Bingo up and away from the shoulders of Stonks and stood him on the ground. Bingo stretched and rubbed his legs. "What an empty and gloomy old dump Rumbledom is," he said. "What's on the other side?"

"Not much," said Knocker. "There's no more London, just countryside with separate houses, funny."

"And they lives down below," whispered Vulge, pointing downwards, "right under our very feet, eh?"

"That's right," said Orococco. "They lives in Burrows and we lives in Boroughs. That's the difference!"

"Hey, you lot," called out Napoleon, "come over here and help me with poor old Stonks. He's gone all stiff-solid, carrying Bingo all this way; he's got cramp in all his muscles. Poor sod can't move."

The Borribles gathered round and inspected their rigid companion.

"Don't worry," he said, hardly able to move his mouth, "I'm all right, honest. Keep your eyes open 'stead of fussing about me; they might creep up on you."

"Chalotte and me will go on watch," said Sydney, and the two girls went to the edge of the copse to stare across the rolling fields.

The others lifted Stonks gently from the cart. He came off the seat as stiff as an armchair. They laid him on the grass on his side but his body remained in the sitting position.

"Just give me a rub down." He tried to laugh. "I'll soon be as good as new."

They took turns in rubbing Stonks hard on his legs, arms and back, and when his muscles were loosened a little they covered him with sleeping bags to keep him warm. They then settled down for a council of war.

No noise came across the open spaces of Rumbledom but traffic whined along Parkside now as people began to make their way to work. Only one thing was moving hear them in the dreary landscape, the cool black steam that rose from the surface of the gravel pit.

It was easy to decide what they needed at that moment—food and rest. They opened their haversacks and made a feast of the food they had brought from Dewdrop's house. There were tins of beans, loaves of sliced bread, packets of biscuits, tins of steak-and-kidney pie, rice pudding, slabs of chocolate, both milk and plain, with nuts and raisins. There was cheese and liver-saus-

153

age and bottles of Guinness and cans of ale. Dewdrop and Erbie had lived well and it was a complete banquet, coming as it did after the weeks of privation in the cellars of Engadine.

Then, with two of their number constantly on watch, they slept all morning. In the afternoon they just dozed or sat chatting lazily to one another, firing their catapults at the water as they talked. Some fell asleep again, to wake up later and join in the conversation. They talked about the Rumbles, their adventures so far, and of the training that Knocker and Dodger had given them and would they ever, all of them, get home safe and sound.

"They like staying in the warm," said Knocker of the Rumbles. "It is well into winter now, so they'll spend most of their time in the Burrows. We've been so long in coming that it's probable that they've forgotten about us and won't have many lookout patrols on the go. On the other hand they are no fools and they're sly. They may have seen us already, they may be on the other side of the horizon, gathering their forces."

"Has anyone, apart from a Rumble that is, ever seen the inside of a Burrow?" asked Chalotte.

"No," said Knocker, "but according to Spiff, who knows more about them than any other Borrible, you want to forget the idea of it being a cosy little Burrow, it's really a defensive Bunker, very luxurious though, carpeted, pictures on the wall, separate rooms, beds, blankets and bathrooms, centrally-heated, of course, workshops. They want for nothing and they eat well, though you couldn't eat what they eat, funny stuff, make you sick, it would. The Bunkers are complicated, designed like a spider's web, strong, lots of cement. Rumbles, they know every inch of it. Some of you will get lost, be set on in a cul-de-sac. But remember the place in the middle to which all the tunnels lead, it's called the Central. When you get in the Bunker you'll be on your own, each one of you has to do for your namesake and then hop it. You know what they look like, you did that in training."

"We get in, get our target, and then get out," said Sydney.

"That's it," answered Knocker. "We'll rendezvous back here. If anyone is captured, or wounded, or killed, the others do not wait. The survivors take the horse and cart and they go, night or day. There may be thousands of Rumbles after us and they can fight, too. They could easily over-run us and massacre us by sheer weight of numbers."

"I wish I knew what they were up to," said Vulge, standing up and firing his catapult at a plastic ice-cream cup floating on the gravel pit and sinking it with his first stone. "It's too damn quiet!"

Just then Orococco pushed his head through the trees. "There's a sweet little Rumble comin' this way, sniffin' with his snout and poking about in the grass with a nail on the end of a long stick! I could exterminate the little nuisance from about fifty yards."

"Oh, boy," said Vulge, slipping his bandolier over his shoulder, "if he's alone let's nobble him and ask him a few questions, see what his mates are up to."

Napoleon who had been asleep rolled over and said lazily, "Yeah, someone go and bring the little feller in."

"Don't harm him," said Knocker to Orococco. "We want him alive. Remember, they talk to children. If he doesn't suss you as a Borrible, tell him you've got something you want him to see, here in the trees."

"That might make him run a mile," joked Orococco flashing his teeth.

"Well, in that case, clout him across the head and drag him in by his feet," said Napoleon and went back to sleep.

Those who were awake sprang up and ran through the bushes till they reached the perimeter of the copse.

Across the windswept grass, picking his way slowly through the gorse bushes, they saw the Rumble. He was sniffing about cautiously and a great deal of the time he flicked his eyes around as if fearing attack or discovery. Orococco was already some distance away, skipping, affecting aimless pleasure.

"He's pretending to be a normal," said Knocker, and they all watched.

Orococco kept the gorse bushes between him and the Rumble for as long as he could but eventually the Rumble noticed him. The Rumble stopped and looked about with more nervous twists of the head. But he saw no one, only Orococco hopping happily along like a child playing truant from school. The Rumble sank behind a small gorse bush till only its snout protruded. Orococco pretended that he'd seen nothing and made as if to skip by, but then he stopped and the watchers saw him wave at the Rumble who came out from behind the bushes and stepped hesitantly towards the black Borrible.

Orococco clapped his hands and talked for a while; he pointed towards the copse where his companions were hidden, then he waved again at the Rumble and skipped on.

"Wonder if it'll work?" said Vulge.

"Depends what he told him," said Chalotte.

The Rumble stood where he was for several minutes waiting for Orococco to disappear over the horizon. As soon as he thought he was alone he turned and began to run towards the Borribles.

"*Verdammt*, it has worked," cried Adolf, rubbing his hands.

"Spread out," said Knocker. "Get behind a tree or something and when the little bleeder comes by, jump him."

From their hiding places the Borribles watched the approach of the solitary Rumble. The animal's snout pulsated with suspicion, the small red eyes darted from right to left, probing, trying to see beyond the trees. It raised its Rumble-stick, it could smell something wrong but its greed had been greatly aroused by Orococco's tale. The padded feet brought it nearer and nearer. At the edge of the trees it halted and turned to look over the wild downs. Nothing moved on the surface of the countryside. The Rumble shifted the bag that was thrown across his shoulder, took a deep breath through its snout and plunged into the copse. It did not plunge very far. As it passed between two trees Vulge and Torreycanyon rose from the matted undergrowth like two fast-growing maneating plants, one before and one behind the surprised Rumble.

"Aaaaagh," it squealed, the sound beginning loudly but fading away to a weak and disjointed whimper.

"Aaaaagh," imitated Vulge. Then he grabbed the Rumble by the scruff of its fur and shook it as if trying to dislocate every bone in its body. "You mouldy old eiderdown, we've come a long way to have a chat with you. Gone through endless dangers to engage you in fruitful converse, and all you can do is to go 'Aaaaagh'."

"Yeah," joined in Torreycanyon, slapping the animal gently across the snout, "you're a rat." He did not have the same inventive vocabulary that Vulge was blessed with.

The animal drew itself up. "I'm not a wat," it said, "I'm a Wumble."

"And I'm Towweycanyon, a howwible Bowwible," said Torreycanyon and he seized the Rumble-stick. "Look at this," he said to Vulge, "a very nasty tool."

"Yeah," agreed the Stepney Borrible, "and there's thousands of Rumbles out there and they've all got one. Come on, let's get back to the clearing."

They held the prisoner by his arms and dragged him back to the middle of the trees where the others soon gathered. They sat the Rumble down by the cart and tied him to one of the wheels.

"Oh, my goodness," said the Rumble, looking nervously around, "I weally can smell a horse. Yu can't wealise how dweadful they are."

"Isn't it marvellous how they can't talk properly?" said Vulge, giving the ropes a really good pull and a tug to make sure the prisoner couldn't escape.

The Borribles sat round the prisoner in a semicircle and even those who had been dozing woke up and came over towards the cart to examine the captive.

"Right," said Bingo cheerfully to the Rumble, "we're going to ask you some interesting questions, and you're going to give us some interesting answers. If you don't keep us amused, if we should get in the slightest bit bored, I shall give you to Sam to eat. He likes hay."

"Sam's the horse," said Chalotte in a kindly, menacing way.

"Aaaaagh," groaned the Rumble, weakly.

"Well that's bloody boring for a start," said Vulge. "If he's going to say nothing but 'Aaaaagh' all the time, we might as well give him to Sam straight away."

Sam the horse, hearing his name mentioned so often, ambled across to the group of Borribles and stood contentedly looking over their shoulders, munching. He looked at the furred creature with a certain amount of appetite, for it is a fact that horses enjoy eating the occasional Rumble, finding that they taste like well-matured hay, good and sweet and nourishing. The Rumble shrank back in his bonds. Though normally quite courageous, understandably enough neither he, nor any of his kind, could bear the sight or smell of a horse.

"Don't let him near me," he shrieked. "I'll talk, I'll tell you everything, only don't let him touch me."

Vulge looked round the half-circle of his friends. "Well," he said, "at least that's better than 'Aaaaagh'."

"How many Rumbles in your Bunker?" asked Torreycanyon.

A thin yellow tongue appeared briefly along the slit in the Rumble's snout. "There's hundweds, certainly,

158

maybe more, but we're only one Bunker, there are hundweds of those too, all interconnected."

"And the High Command, the eight top names, where are they?" asked Sydney, her voice cool.

"You know about the Eight?" asked the Rumble, looking at them with a growing terror. "Then you're not ordinawy childwen, you're . . ."

"That's wight, my old china," scoffed Vulge, "we're howwible Bowwibles. You want to listen when we talk to you."

The questioning went on all through the afternoon, with the Rumble gradually realising that this was the Great Rumble Hunt that had been promised.

The Borribles found out many things. The Rumble that Knocker and Lightfinger had captured all that time ago had returned alive to Rumbledom country. His story had struck fear and dismay into the hearts of all Rumbles, young and old, male and female. But that fear had hardened into anger, and the dismay had crystalised into resolution and the Rumbles had looked about them.

At first the High Command, following the general mood, had over-reacted, conscripting all their able-bodied animals into the Warrior Corps. Training had been intensive and Rumble scouts had been sent out regularly as far as Southfields and even to Wandsworth Common. Some had been settled in a continuous line along the railway line over which it was thought the Borrible force would be obliged to advance, for the Rumbles had expected a mass invasion. This impression had been conveyed to them by Timbucktoo, the Rumble that Knocker had treated so roughly in Battersea Park. He had led his compatriots to believe that a vast horde of Borribles was on the march and that all of Borrible London was in a state of war.

But the weeks had gone by and there had been no sign of the enemy. The Borrible threat receded in the mind of the ordinary Rumble. The scouts deserted their posts and returned to the life of comfort and ease to which, to tell the truth, they were well used. Patrols still went out to Southfields and such, but Rumbles dislike the streets as much as Borribles hate the countryside and so the patrols had become less frequent and more inefficient. Most Rumbles completely forgot the menace of the Great Rumble Hunt, others suggested that it had only been a vain threat made in anger, one that the Borribles could never sustain. "Anyway," thought the average Rumble, if he thought about it at all, "those Borribles are mean snivelling little dirty things, they could never make the long and perilous journey to Rumbledom, they don't possess the wherewithal, the knowledge, the brains. They couldn't mount such an expedition with their resources. They live in rotten little streets and barely scrape a living. They have enough to do to stay alive. No," they argued, "the vast domain of Rumbledom, on top of the great hill, on top of the world almost, is safe."

But the Rumble High Command did not see the problem in quite the same way. They had been threatened, and though the threat might only be an idea as yet, it was an idea of their overthrow and a great danger lurked in it. It was a concept that could lead only to disaster if nothing was done. Furthermore, they felt, they had a perfect right to go wherever they wished, beholden to no one, and that right must be defended.

So the High Command had made a plan, emanating from their chief and dictator, Vulgarian. They must strike before they were struck; destroy the Borribles of Battersea before their idea could take root and spread. A large Rumble force of crack regiments would be equipped for a night attack on Battersea High Street, to seek out and destroy any Borribles they found and obliterate the Borrible war-machine that Timbucktoo had assured them was being prepared.

Warriors had been put into special training and were ready to undertake the long journey. They had not the slightest intention of marching those many miles; they already had one motor-car and only awaited the delivery of others before setting out. They intended to strike with speed and in several places at once, causing as much panic and destruction amongst the Borrible population as possible.

In addition to such offensive measures, the Rumbles had seen to their own defences and reviewed the whole situation. There were only two entrances to the main bunker, and both were guarded day and night. Rumbles it was said never let go of anything, and they would hang on to Rumbledom for grim death. What had never occurred to them was that a tiny force of chosen Borribles would infiltrate their territory and attempt to assassinate the High Command and so leave the Rumbles leaderless and ineffective. Thus the Adventurers found that the element of surprise was with them; no one knew of their arrival. That was the good news; the bad news they had already known: they were hopelessly outnumbered and retreat, even if they succeeded in their task, would be impossible.

When the Borribles were satisfied with their interrogation they moved away from their prisoner so they could talk without being overheard. They leant against the trees and discussed matters, scanning the horizon at the same time.

"Well," said Bingo, "how are we going to play it?"

"What our friend forgot to mention," said Knocker, "is that although there are only two entrances to the Bunker, there is in fact a ventilation shaft that comes out above the kitchens. It's in one of the books. I think that's the way we—I mean you—should go in."

"Wait a minute," interrupted Stonks. "My target is the doorkeeper. I'll have to go in through the door, otherwise I might not find him."

"I've got an idea," cried Torreycanyon. "We can make a diversionary attack on both doors, just a couple of us, and the main body can get in through the ventilator."

"Here comes 'Rococco," said Stonks, "running."

"What a mover," said Sydney. "I hope it's not bad news."

Orococco stopped a few yards from the copse, turning to make sure no one was watching before he slipped into the trees.

"Hello," he panted, "everything okay?"

"We're just talking about how to attack," said Napoleon. "Any trouble?"

"Nah," answered the Tooting Borrible, "I've just been for a little runaround, see what I could see. Did you get the Rumble I sent you?"

"Not half," said the Wendle. "What did you find out?"

"Well, I don't think they know we're here," said Orococco. "I saw quite a few of them wandering about with those lance things of theirs, Rumble-sticks, but they didn't look worried, just stooging up and down. I found the two entrances to the place, and I found out where the ventilation comes out, on top of a hill. It will be a piece of duff."

Napoleon turned from listening to the Totter and looked at Knocker, suspicious again. "And what will you be up to during the attack, eh?"

"Adolf and me will help cause as much confusion as possible," answered Knocker, without looking at the Wendle.

"Not half, *verdammt*," agreed the German.

After a little more discussion Torreycanyon's plan was adopted unanimously and the Adventurers went back to the clearing. There, a surprise awaited them. The Rumble had disappeared, even the ropes that had bound him were gone.

"Who tied him up then?" Napoleon shouted at Vulge, anger tightening his face.

Vulge looked guilty. "I made sure he couldn't get free." He glanced at the others. "Really I did."

"Bloody well looks like it, don't it?" said Napoleon. "If he gets back to his Bunker we've had it."

"Don't panic," giggled Sydney, "look at Sam."

The horse was lying down at one side of the clearing with a stupidly contented expression on his long face. From his mouth dangled a little frayed end of rope; it swung gently with the movement of his champing jaws.

"Well, I'll be double *verdammted*," cried Adolf. "Sam's eaten him," and he hooted.

"Would you Adam-and-Eve it?" said Stonks incredulously. "So he has, the sly old rogue."

"That makes one Rumble the less," said Napoleon practically. "I wondered what we were going to do with him."

Sam gave a neigh of pleasure and rolled over on his side, stuck out his legs and promptly went into a deep sleep.

"That's just what I'm going to do, man," said Orococco, "get something to eat and then have a good snooze. After all, tonight's the night, eh?"

That seemed like a good idea to everybody and after a light snack they curled up in their sleeping bags. Knocker, Adolf and Chalotte took the first watch of two hours, two hours to gaze across the chilly greeny-grey expanses of inhospitable Rumbledom.

It was deep winter now and high up on this hill the air was sharp-edged and brittle. "No wonder those Rumbles have fur coats," thought Knocker, as he watched and shivered. Nothing moved out there in the vastness, nothing except a few adults taking dogs for walks or children racing along on bicycles. It was strange, he reflected, how this raid was going to take place and no adults, no policemen would ever know about it—but then there was a lot happened that they never knew about and didn't want to know about, either.

Chalotte came and leaned against a tree nearby. She didn't look at Knocker at first, but kept watch over the green land where the advancing mist of dusk was making it difficult to distinguish between trees and gorse bushes, pathways and grass.

"It's going to be dangerous, isn't it," she said. It wasn't a question.

"We always knew some of us wouldn't survive," answered Knocker.

"I sometimes think," said Chalotte, "that we're not really meant for this kind of Adventure. It would be nice to go back to being just a Borrible, living in our nice broken-down houses. You know the proverb 'Fruit of the barrow is enough for a Borrible'. I mean this Adventure has turned out to be far beyond what we normally do. It's suicide."

"Wait a minute," protested Knocker, surprised. "This is the greatest Adventure we're ever likely to hear of, let alone go on."

"Hmmmm." She sounded unconvinced. "You ought to make it clear to the others that by this time tomorrow they're likely to be dead. Who wants to die for a name? That was never Borrible."

"Fruit of the barrow may be all right, but we've got to have Adventures, too. Look, if you hadn't come on this one you wouldn't have seen Dewdrop and Erbie and learned what happens to us when we get caught. We'd heard about it but now we've seen it, we know."

"Yes, but supposing Spiff got it all wrong, supposing those Rumbles just came down on a spree, just to visit the Park, not take over all of Battersea, like he said. What then, eh? It would be silly, just them scared of us and us scared of them."

"Oh, that's rubbish," said Knocker laughing coldly.

"Old Spiff don't make bloomers like that, he just don't. He has studied the Rumbles for years, he knows them inside out. I mean, do you think the Wendles don't know what they're up against? Flinthead is Flinthead because of the Rumbles, it's all down to them . . . obviously."

"You admire Spiff too much," said Chalotte. "The more I see of expeditions the more I think of getting back to where we belong. I mean how important is a name? You've got one and yet you're going on a suicide mission for another." She shook her head, glanced at Knocker, and then said what was really on her mind. "There's something else, isn't there? Something secret, that you know, and Spiff knows. Ordinary expeditions are fine adventures and funny, but this one is making us like the Wendles. That can't be good, can it? The things we do might look right now but they could turn out wrong in the end."

Knocker became stern; he couldn't manage long and complicated arguments. "You and Sydney have really pulled your weight, all along. I didn't believe you could at the beginning, but you have. Are you going to spoil it all now by being scared?"

Chalotte didn't become angry, in fact she smiled. "I told you at the start we'd be as good as anyone else. As for scared, well, we're all scared of something. You're scared that you won't get another name, and another after that." And she placed her hand ever so lightly on his and took it away again.

Knocker blushed and turned his head to look at her but she was gone through the trees back to her lookout post. Over the sunless fields of Rumbledom the mist lay in pools and there was not a soul to be seen. Soon it would be dark; he would be glad when it started.

The Borribles watched and slept by turns through the evening of that day but by midnight they could rest no more, so they roused themselves for one last meal together. They crowded under the cart and held their feast by the light of torches tied to the spoke of the cart-wheels. They were subdued, but Adolf told them of his travels and how he had got his names, how this was the best adventure he had ever known and how happy and glad he was to be with such a band. He slapped Napoleon on the back and said he "wasn't bad for a Wendle," and even Napoleon had to laugh at that and he gave the German another can of Dewdrop's Guinness.

At the blackest part of the night they began to prepare themselves. They reloaded their double bandoliers with the choicest stones and they replaced the used rubbers of their catapults. Adolf and Knocker even took with them the spare catapults they had used for their escape from Dewdrop's house. They removed all shiny things from their jackets and they tucked their trousers into their socks and tied the laces of their combat boots tightly and well so that nothing could get caught on nails and doors and things. They put Sam back between the shafts and loaded their haversacks onto the cart so they should be ready to run for it if they ever managed to get clear of the Bunker. When all was done they shovelled up a huge pile of stones from the gravelly shore of the lake and threw them into the cart as well. If they had to make a running retreat it would be an advantage to have a good supply of ammunition with them. At the very last, Knocker took a tin from his pocket, opened it, and began smearing his face with the contents. It was black greasepaint, used so that his white skin would not be spied by the enemy in the frosty starlight. Orococco laughed as the others fol-lowed suit.

"Man, oh man, I've seen everything now. If we has a daylight attack, will you fellas get me some white paint so my face don't stick out?"

His friends, feeling a little foolish, told him to

"Shuddup", but he only laughed again, and at odd moments through the night he chuckled to himself whenever he saw the others with their black faces.

When they were ready to leave they stood together and very tough and determined they looked. One by one they went to the horse and patted him and asked him to be patient, standing in the traces like that, and Sam neighed like a war-charger and stamped a hoof. Then they synchronised their watches and took a compass bearing on the copse and finally, without a light to guide them, they moved off in single file. Orococco led them out, for as he said, not only did he know the way, but he was still the blackest of them all.

Chapter 8

It was a cold and clear night and a ground frost made their footsteps crunch loudly as they walked over the stiff white grass. They did not speak but there was not one of them who did not yearn at that moment for the crowded and friendly streets of his Borough. After a walk of about a mile Orococco stopped and the Adventurers gathered in a circle. The Borrible from Tooting could not resist a joke even then. "Why, friends," he laughed, "we looks like a Black and White Minstrel Show."

"Get on with it," snapped Stonks, who like everybody else was very tense and eager to begin.

"Okay, Mr Bones," said Orococco, "you see that mound beginning to rise a little, over there, against the sky? That's the Bunker, only it looks like a hill. There's a couple of saplings and a few bushes to the right; they screens the Great Door. If we climbs the hill and walks over it in a straight line, we'll come to the exit hole of the ventilation network, and on in a straight line from that, 'bout half a mile, is the back door, smaller, not so well made. Don't stamp your feet when you're on the hill, you'll wake up all the rats in Rumbledom if you do."

"Right then," said Stonks, "I get off here. My target's just the other side of that door."

"With a hundred thousand friends," added Napoleon, sardonically.

"Kind of odds that keep a Borrible alert," answered Stonks, not to be put down even by a friendly jest . . . and you never knew with a Wendle.

"Who do you want to go with you?" asked Knocker. "We must get on, we've got to be out by dawn."

"Torreycanyon, if he'll come," said Stonks turning to his friend.

"Course I will," said Torreycanyon in answer and he began to creep quietly away. "We'll give you ten minutes, then we go in."

The remainder went on, moving at a jogging trot up the side of the hill that rose over the Bunker. Sure enough, at the top, hidden by thick gorse bushes, was the main outlet for the air conditioning system of the whole Bunker city. It was covered by a large iron grille, solid and heavy, painted green to camouflage its appearance. Orococco said, "There she is. Now, who's coming with me to the other door? I can recommend it, very frail and only five hundred and fifty Rumbles guarding it. Any offers?"

Bingo sprang up. "Battersea and Tooting together," he cried, "what a team! I'll pick you up by the legs, you old Totter, and bash them to smithereens with your head bone."

Orococco turned to Knocker. "Give us five minutes," he said, "and by the time you've got the kettle boiled for tea we'll be in there with you," and he and Bingo ran off.

There were six of them left round the vent now; Chalotte, Sydney, Adolf, Napoleon, Vulge and Knocker himself. They squatted and waited.

"Friends," said Vulge after a while, "those five minutes have gone into eternity. Shall we dance?"

Napoleon forced his knife under the edge of the ventilation grille and pushed it in as far as it would go. Then he exerted all his strength and levered and twisted; the grille shifted in its sockets just a little.

"It's coming," said Sydney, and shoved a stone into the gap so that the grille could not fall back to its grooves. Adolf and Knocker seized the edge of it and pulled together to upend the square of heavy iron before lowering it to the ground. Chalotte bent over the dark aperture and peered in. "It looks a long way down," she said.

Napoleon risked a quick beam of light from his torch. The ventilation shaft dropped vertically for about ten feet then turned a right-angled corner.

"There's only one way to find out where it goes," said Vulge, "and that's to go."

They had all brought a length of strong rope with them, wound round their waists, and Vulge took his and tied it firmly to the foot of a nearby growth of gorse.

"I'll go first," he said. "I'll give you the whistle if it looks all right." He tested the rope and looked closely at the face of his fellow Adventurers. "'Erewego—and don't let's get caught."

And he slipped over the edge and was gone. One moment he had been standing there smiling and wagging his head, the next nothing was to be seen but a section of tightened rope. A minute later the rope became slack and they heard the familiar Borrible whistle.

"I'll go next," cried Chalotte excitedly, and she took the cord firmly between her hands and stepped backwards into space, walking casually down the side of the shaft.

"*Verdammt*," said Adolf, nudging Knocker, "she is very good that girl."

Napoleon decided that Sydney should follow Chalotte and then he himself would go down. To Knocker and Adolf he simply said, "You two come afterwards, and remember the Adventure has really come to its climax now. You are not to interfere with any of us unless we ask. This is our Adventure, see."

Adolf watched the Wendle slither down the rope, leaving him and Knocker standing alone on the windy hill. "He doesn't like you very much, you know," he said to Knocker. "He thinks you are up to something."

Knocker grinned and whispered to the German, "I

am up to something, mate, and you're going to be up to it with me. As for Napoleon it's in his nature to be suspicious, Wendles always are."

"Ho ho," hooted Adolf, "never mind all that. Something is what I like to be up to. Let's hurry."

Stonks and Torreycanyon sneaked through the gorse bushes on their bellies and approached the Great Door with caution. A premature alarm would alert the defences and change the task of the Borrible attackers from a difficult to an impossible one. The grass and bushes were damp with the threat of the coming dew and soon the two attackers and their clothes were drenched.

"We'll soon dry off when we get inside," said Torreycanyon. "I'll use my Rumble as a towel."

"It's funny in a way, isn't it?" said Stonks. He stopped crawling and faced his companion. "Going after a bloke with the same name. It's like going after yourself. I mean, the names we've got aren't our names, they're really theirs, and when we've eliminated them, why then the names will be ours for ever, and the Adventure we've had, even if we've been killed, can never be taken away."

"It'll be taken away if we're all killed and nobody gets back to tell the story. If it's never written down, then it's gone for ever, have you thought of that?"

"Yeah, maybe Knocker shouldn't have come this far. He can't be Historian if he's captured or killed."

Torreycanyon held Stonks by the arm for a moment. "Ah," he said, "but if he hadn't have come this far he would have had no story to tell."

About ten yards from the door they stopped side by side and checked their watches.

"Another five minutes."

"Look at that door," said Stonks, with respect in his voice, "im-bloody-pregnable." It was true. Although not large, for Rumbles are about the same size as Borribles, it was stoutly built in oak, with iron bars reinforcing it. Its hinges were massive and heavy, designed to withstand a great deal of battering. By the time it was vanquished, that door, all the Rumbles in Rumbledom could be behind it.

"This is the time for guile," said Torreycanyon wisely, "but what kind of guile, I do not know."

Stonks looked at his watch. "Come on," he said, "I have an idea. Let's unwind our ropes."

Stonks joined the two pieces of cord together, then crouching, he made for the trees that grew a short distance from the Bunker door. Torreycanyon followed. At the foot of a stout sapling Stonks said, "You're going to climb this tree, so as it'll bend down with your weight. Here's the rope, tie the middle of it round the top of the tree and drop both ends down. Got it?"

"Yeah," said Torreycanyon, "course I got it," and he scrambled up the tree which dropped more and more as he climbed higher.

The tree swooped and bobbed as Torreycanyon tied the rope to the slim trunk and threw the loose ends to Stonks, whose shape he could make out only dimly in the darkness below. Then Torreycanyon felt himself drawn nearer and nearer to the ground, as the strongest of the Borribles pulled on the rope until the topmost twigs of the tree touched the grass.

"Stay where you are, Torrey," said Stonks breathlessly, "keep your weight on while I tie it down to this root over here."

It took Stonks but a moment to secure the sapling and when he had finished he allowed Torreycanyon to step from his perch.

"Whatever it is you're going to do, Stonksie, you'd better do it now, because the others are going in at this very moment."

As Torreycanyon said this someone stirred behind

the Great Door. Stonks winked at his companion and took up the spare piece of rope that dangled from the tree-top. He went over to the Great Door, knocked and then spoke up firmly in a Rumble voice. "Sowwy to twouble you, old bean, but I've something splendid here and I thought you might like it, I mean it could do wonders for your weputation. Come on, Stonks, open up there's a good sort."

There was a second's hesitation on the far side of the door and then Stonks and Torreycanyon heard the bolts being slid and a key being turned in the massive lock.

"Torrey," whispered Stonks," when I tip you the wink, do that rope," and Stonks made a gesture with his hand.

Torreycanyon crouched and Stonks stood behind the door as it swung slowly open.

Then Stonks the Borrible spoke to Stonks the Rumble, both of them the strongest of their tribe.

"I wealise you're vewy stwong, Stonksie, but even I don't think you can keep hold of this," and the Borrible put the rope's end around the door and thrust it into the greedy hand of the Rumble. "Hang on," said the Borrible, "wemember we Wumbles never let go," and he made a gesture to Torreycanyon who severed the restraining cord with one sweep of his knife. The sapling was released and it sprang upright with enormous power and speed, dragging the short end of rope with it. The Rumble door-keeper at the end of the rope, true to his breeding and upbringing, held on tightly and shot through the doorway like the first Rumble rocket to the moon, knocking the Great Door open with such force that it would have killed Stonks had he not jumped away from the danger.

The Rumble whizzed over the Borrible's head at escape velocity and was swung away in a wide arc. Still he held on and if he could have strengthened his grip he might have lived for ever, but when the sapling reached its apogee it suddenly and treacherously reversed its direction. So there came a moment when the Rumble was travelling away from the door at a speed that was much faster than safe, and the top of the sapling was travelling at the same speed but back towards the door. The rope became taut and even the remarkable strength of Stonks the Rumble could not hold onto it and it was torn from his grasp. He disappeared into the black night, a fast-moving silhouette against the starry sky.

"He'll be burned to a frazzle on re-entry," said Stonks with a sniff and a spit. They waited a long while in silence.

"He's been ages up there," said Torreycanyon with irritation.

Just then there came a scream and a crashing of branches from about three hundred yards away. Then there was a dull crump and the ground where the Borribles stood shook and shivered.

"Ah, that sounds like a satisfactory abort," said Torreycanyon, rising from his crouching position and sheathing his knife at last. He stepped over to Stonks and took his hand and shook it. "I'd like to be the first," he said, "to congratulate you on being the first of us to win a name. Well done, Stonks, no other's name but yours now."

The Great Door to the Bunker now stood open and undefended. The two Borribles tip-toed towards it and peered in. An electric light showed an entrance hallway with a comfortable armchair for the guard on duty. There were some blankets and nearby a little table with food and books to sustain the watcher during the long night. On the other side of the hallway a lighted tunnel led off to the heart of the Burrow. Both the hallway and the tunnel were lined with bricks and there was carpet on the floor and pictures on the walls. It looked very warm and comfortable, homely.

"Nobody about," said Stonks and they entered the hallway and pulled the massive door shut behind them.

"What a smashing place," said Torreycanyon. "Don't stint themselves, do they?"

"They have no need to, mate, no need," said Stonks and he shot the bolts and turned the key in the lock. "Look," he went on, "I've done my bloke so I'll stay here and watch the exit, that way we've got a line of retreat." He picked up the Rumble-stick which had belonged to the guard who had left his post so precipitately and he hefted it in his hand. "Any Rumble who tries to get the door from me will have four inches of nail in him. You can tell the others when you see them. I'll also pull some bricks from the wall and make a couple of barricades across the tunnel. If you come back this way you'll have to give the whistle and I'll let you over."

"It's a good idea," said Torreycanyon. "I'll tell anybody I see." Then he said, "I'd better get going. Goodbye, Stonks—don't get caught, eh?" And there was a catch to his voice as he spoke.

Stonks caught hold of his friend and embraced him. "Take care, my old china. Win your name well. Don't you get caught now, I'd miss you."

And Torreycanyon turned abruptly, a tear in his eye, and he ran down the lighted, twisting, dangerous tunnel as fast as he could go, eager for his name.

Orococco and Bingo slid down the bumpy hillside, getting wet where they sat and slithered on the soaking grass. The slope ended in a small cliff and they fell together, all of a heap, into a little open space at the bottom of the hill.

"Quiet, Bingo," whispered Orococco, "we've landed right on their doorstep."

"Saves walking," said the Battersea-ite.

They crept on all fours till they came up against the

Small Door. As its name indicated it was less important than the Great Door on the other side of the hill; even a Borrible would have to crawl through this one. There was a judas in the door so that the guard could see outside without having to open the barricade. Still kneeling the two Borribles looked at each other, then back at the peephole.

"I suppose this calls for guile," said Bingo.

"That's all we got, man," said Orococco. He knocked at the door. There was no answer.

"He's sleeping," said Bingo and he knocked, this time with the butt of his catapult, very loudly indeed.

There was a sudden and muffled snort from behind the door. Orococco shook his head. "Sleepin' on duty, they deserves to get duffed up!" He put his face close up to the judas. It was very dark there under the bank where the door was concealed.

The flap in the door flew open and a sleepy voice said, "Who goes there, Wumble or foe?"

"A weal Wumble," said Orococco, flashing his teeth.

"No such thing as a black Wumble," said the guard, his snout coming up close to the opening and quivering distrustfully. "What's your name?"

"My name's Owococco," said Orococco, winking at Bingo who was close to the door but out of sight of the person within.

There was a shocked silence from the Rumble, then he said, "Wait a minute, that can't be your name, it's my name."

"Tewwibly sowwy," said Orococco, "you must be mistaken, old boy. Owococco is posalutely my name, always has been, don't yer know."

"I have no wish to be offensive," said the voice behind the door, "but I ought to know my own name. I'm fwightfully sowwy but I am Owococco," and the snout came nearer the little opening and sniffed and sniffed. "You don't even smell like a Wumble," said the snout.

176

"Well," said the Totter from Tooting, "all I can say is open the door and have a look, and you will absotively wecognise me as one of your vewy own."

"I can't do that," said the guardian, "it's against the wules, and according to my list evewyone is in tonight."

"All wight then," said the black Borrible, "stick your nose wight out and take a weally good sniff and wecognise me and let me in. I'm exhausted, and I have important news for the High Command."

"I'm one of the High Command," said the Rumble, suddenly intrigued, "you may tell me all."

"I'll tell you nothing until you let me in," insisted Orococco. The snout came further out and attempted to sniff round the Borrible's face but he fell back half a step and the snout was obliged to push itself a little further and again a little further, still snuffling and vibrating. It was then that Bingo rose and seized the snout in both hands and held on with all his might. Orococco slipped the strong cord from his waist and wound it several times round the snout and, tying it very tightly, he fastened the free end to the root of a strong growing bush. The Rumble could hardly breathe but Bingo did not let go, nor did the rope slacken, for all the animal's struggles behind the door. Orococco got close to the snout. "Shuddup," he whispered, "if you don't stop that wriggling I'll beat your nose till it looks like a limp wind-sock."

The struggling abated, then stopped altogether.

"Now, listen," went on the black Totter, "you can reach the bolts, and you can reach the lock. Open up. We have an ultimatum for your mates, and they're going to get it one way or the other, whether you have a snout or not."

Orococco Rumble hesitated, there was a little more kicking of padded feet and a flailing of arms, but the snout did not move an inch from its imprisonment. Then the two Borribles heard the bolts slide and the

177

key grate in the lock and Orococco threw his body at the door with such force that the cord holding the snout broke with a loud twang and nearly pulled the Rumble's head through the small aperture. This fierce assault slammed the body of the guardian back against the wall of the passage and there was a sickening thud.

Bingo vaulted into the corridor, rolled over and came to his feet holding his catapult at the ready, but he did not fire for this was Orococco's game. Orococco seized the Rumble-stick that leant inside the doorway and used the point to fling aside the door. The Totter drew back his arm, ready to thrust the deadly sticker into the furry breast of his namesake, but before his muscles could act the Rumble fell forward onto the floor, the weight of his body banging the Small Door shut.

Bingo sprang to his feet and turned the body over. "Strewth," he said, "you must've broke his neck when you opened the door."

"Never stand behind a door when there's someone coming through the other side," said Orococco. "That's an old Tooting proverb which ain't in the book but ought to be."

"Hey," said Bingo, coming over to stand before his comrade, "you've got your name already. That's great, congratulations," and he slapped the Totter on the shoulder.

"Thanks, man," said Orococco, "now we'd better see about getting yours." And he turned and locked and bolted the foor before slipping the key into his pocket. "Remember I got the key, Bingo, just in case I don't make it. Now let's go see if the others got the kettle on yet." And holding the sticker across his body he ran as fast as he could down the tunnel and Bingo sped along close behind him.

Vulge lay full length in the narrow ventilation shaft and inched his body along with his elbows; the top of the tunnel scraped his back. Behind him he could hear the others breathing hard as they followed. After a few yards, which seemed like miles, he came to a greasy grating set in the floor. He reached behind him with an effort and pulled his torch from a pocket of his combat jacket. He masked the beam with his hand and saw that he was at the end of the tunnel. Something bumped against his feet.

"Chalotte," he heard her say.

He shone his torch on the grating and saw that it was held down by four screws. He reached for his knife and slowly began to unscrew them.

"What's up?" asked Chalotte.

Vulge twisted his head as far as he was able. "Grating to the kitchens, four screws," he whispered and then went back to his work. It took a long while but at last the grating came free and he slid it below his body and stuck his head down to look into the kitchens.

It was an enormous modern installation, equipped with long stainless-steel ranges and endless working surfaces, for it had to cater for the hundreds of Rumbles who lived in the Bunker and on its smooth running would depend their health and well-being. The management and ordering of such a place would demand complex skills and the Rumble commissariat could only be controlled by members of the High Command.

At that moment only three Rumbles of any importance were visible to Vulge, two females and one male, and they had not been in the kitchens long for they were rubbing their eyes and yawning. The two female Rumbles began bellowing orders, and skivvies and scullions, about a dozen of them, rushed to their duties. Huge saucepans were sent clanging and spinning onto the stoves, and hot-plates glowed red and herbs and plants were washed and shredded and the morning gruel soon simmered in the pots.

With a start that nearly gave him away Vulge recognised the male Rumble; it was the chief, the main one, his very own target. Vulge withdrew his head quickly and scrambled over the opening into the end section of the shaft, allowing Chalotte to move up a little. He shone his torch behind her and saw Sydney. He popped his head down through the hole again and watched. The High Rumbles stood in the middle of the kitchen urging their minions on, smelling the soups and supervising the baking of the Rumble bread. Vulge pulled out his catapult and was easing a stone from his bandolier when the Chief Rumble, Vulgarian himself, spoke to the women. He sounded irritable and short-tempered.

"I wish you'd huwwy, you two. When I say an early bweakfast, I mean an early bweakfast. I've got a nasty feeling something's afoot. Last night, one of our Wumbles didn't weturn, and I'm wowwied. Come on, huwwy it up."

"It's no good," snapped Chalotte Rumble, "it can't be weady for another half-hour at least," and she jerked her snout up an inch to indicate the end of the discussion.

"Hmm," said Vulgarian, "then I'll go and have a bath. Send me my bweakfast on a tway as soon as it's weady," and he pulled his dressing-gown tight about him and stalked off without another word.

"What a bully," said the Chief of the Commissariat to her companion. "Who does he think he is? We wun this department."

"Don't take any notice," said Sydney Rumble, "he's due for a nasty shock one day."

"Yeah and today's the day," said Vulge to himself grimly. "I missed a chance there, dammit." He pulled his head back into the darkness of the tunnel where Chalotte waited.

"Mine's gone to have a bath," said Vulge, "but yours is right below you, and Sydney's. All you got to do is thump 'em."

Chalotte twisted and spoke to Sydney, then she crouched over the hole and looked down. Below her was a good ten foot drop, enormous for a Borrible, to the top of a wide kitchen table, white with scrubbing. She took her catapult from her back pocket, wrapped the elastic carefully round the butt and clenched the weapon between her teeth, then with a nod at Vulge, she let herself fall from his sight. Immediately Chalotte had gone Sydney wriggled forward, her catapult already prepared, and sprang, eager as a cat, through the opening. Napoleon was still some distance away but inching nearer. Vulge did not wait for him. He sat on the edge of the hatch, lowered himself by his arms till his body was at full extent, and then let go.

His feet hit the wooden surface and, following the precepts of Dodger's paratroop training, he allowed his legs to crumble and he rolled over curving his shoulder to take the force of the fall. He came off the edge of the table and fell easily into a crouching position on the kitchen floor. From there he witnessed a fight that made his eyes twinkle.

Chalotte and Sydney had arrived in the kitchen perhaps ten seconds before Vulge, but they had wasted no time. The two Rumbles of the High Command had been caught flat-footed by Chalotte's inexplicable appearance but they had soon rallied. They each seized a Rumblestick from a rack which stood against the wall and shouted to the kitchen-hands to arm themselves and give the alarm. But Chalotte was a magician with the catapult. She had loaded and fired her weapon twice before the two Rumbles could cast their spears and they retreated down the kitchen towards the hot stoves and steaming ranges. The sound of Chalotte's stones as they sliced through the air unnerved the Rumbles, and their lances, when they were thrown, skeetered harmlessly along the tiled floor.

Now Sydney's catapult was ready and, ignoring the shouts of the scullions and the possible threat of a flying

Rumble-stick, she stood and drew the heavy-duty elastic right back to her ear and a well-aimed stone flew to strike her foe in the centre of the forehead. Sydney Rumble fell lifeless to the floor, bringing down a pile of soup bowls with her.

Chalotte's enemy was to meet a more grisly fate. At the noise of the crashing crockery the High Rumble took fright, for she was now outnumbered three to one, and pushing and kicking the terrified menials from her path she ran quickly to the far end of the kitchen where huge cauldrons boiled quietly on deep square stoves, warming the day's broth. Against the largest of the containers leant a step-ladder, placed there so that ingredients could be added without difficulty and so that the soup could be inspected from time to time by the chief cooks. But now Chalotte Rumble wanted only to get away. If she were to climb that ladder and take one step across the cauldron she could squeeze through a large vent that led into a different part of the Bunker, escaping to raise the alarm and fight another day. But Chalotte the Borrible, her blood pounding with the heat of battle, was a fast and nimble runner and she pursued her namesake closely. As the Rumble reached the top of the step-ladder, Chalotte reached the bottom, seized the whole contraption and lifted it up with all her energy. There was the briefest of silences as the poor Rumble spun in space, weightless for a second, then a scream split the steamy air and the scream wailed on long and loud until, with a splash, it was submerged deep in the hot and lump soup, but even then the scream went on, freighted up to the surface of the stew in rippling bubbles, like a fart in bath-water.

Vulge ran across the room and covered the saucepan with a huge and heavy lid. "Blimey," he crowed, "she's really in the soup now, ain't she?"

Napoleon's legs appeared through the opening in the ceiling and he dropped to the table and jumped to the floor. He ran to a corner and grabbed a Rumble-stick. He felt the weight of it and looked at the group of kitchen-hands who cowered together in a corner.

"Okay, you bunch of bunnies," he snarled, "you move and I'll tear yer ears off."

Sydney pulled her target's body into a broom-cupboard, closed the door and locked it. "Cripes," she gasped, "that was over too fast, don't seem right."

"Getting in was easy," agreed Chalotte, "it's the getting out."

"What are we going to do with the skivvies?" asked Vulge.

"Lock 'em in the pantry," suggested Sydney, "they won't give us any trouble."

"You do that," said Napoleon making for the door. "Me and Vulge better get going, we've still got work to do. Before you leave here turn the electrics up; let it all burn dry so it'll smoke and fuse and catch fire. Hungry Rumbles can't fight."

"That's it." Vulge crossed the room to leave with Napoleon. "When you've done you'd better try to make your way to the Great Door and see if you can meet up with Stonks and Torrey."

"We might see you again at the Central," said Napoleon, "and then again we might not. Don't wait for anybody. As from now we each take our chance." With this he and Vulge slipped through the door and were gone.

Sydney and Chalotte herded the kitchen-hands into the larder, using sharp spears to encourage them. Once the Rumbles had been disposed of the two girls ran around the kitchen switching all the stoves and ovens to full on, and then, propped against their lances, they looked at each other and a slow smile crept from their eyes to their lips and became a grin.

"Here, we've got our names," said Sydney. "Fancy that."

*

Torreycanyon made his way down the main tunnel. It felt strange to be alone after so long in the company of the others, but there was no stopping now. Somewhere ahead of him would be the main hallway with the corridors running out from it like a spider's web. The Bunker was deserted, for the Rumbles were still sleeping, but in a very short while they would be coming from their bedrooms and making for the refectory to enjoy a copious breakfast.

Occasionally Torreycanyon saw a signpost which, he supposed, was to direct the younger Rumbles until they had learnt their way around. There weren't enough indications for his taste and he realised what a task the Borrible team had taken on. He understood suddenly that he was going to need a lot of luck to find his target, and a lot more to get out of this labyrinth alive. He gripped his catapult tightly, a stone ready for firing, and he stepped bravely forward. Best to press on and meet the dangers as they came, no point in worrying about them prematurely. Good old Stonks was behind, guarding the Great Door, and it would take an avalanche of Rumbles to move him.

Torreycanyon crept past several doors leading from the corridor. On each was a notice saying, "Dormitory"; he listened but heard no noises coming from within. So far so good. He went on, halting and listening at every branch corridor, peeping around every corner before going on and then peering back to make sure he was not being followed.

"Cripes," he said, often. "I wish I could find my target and then get out of here, it's creepy being on your own."

At last luck was with him. He nearly passed a narrow passage leading off to his left but his foot slipped and looking down he saw a patch of oil on the floor. He moved into the passage and shone his torch on the wall, for it was darker there. At eye level words had been daubed in blue paint, and although faded and difficult to decipher, they were still legible. "Garage and Workshops. Keep Out. signed TORREYCANYON RUMBLE."

"Oh boy, oh boy," said Torreycanyon, "I've done it right. I'll get in the garage and wait for him." He knew from his reading of the Rumble histories that the workshops were a vital nerve centre of this underground complex and it was part of the Borrible plan, once they had eliminated their targets, to cause as much confusion as possible. Torreycanyon hoped that possession of the workshops would enable him to wreak great damage throughout the Bunker, merely by pulling a few switches. If he could break in before the Rumbles awoke, he would be in a strong position.

The dark corridor sloped downwards beneath the Rumbledom hillsides. It was slippery and oily underfoot because so much machinery had passed that way but Torreycanyon moved forward only when he had verified with his torch that it was safe to do so. At last he came up against a heavy wooden door, sagging on its hinges. It was scarred and battered where sharp metal edges had been bashed against it. To Torreycanyon's amazement the door was open and a light shone inside.

He pushed his torch back into his pocket and flexed the rubber on his catapult. He was ready. However many Rumbles were in the workshops he would take them on and then destroy their equipment before they destroyed him. But he must be sure to get his target; not one of the Rumble High Command must be left to organise pursuit or retaliation. Torreycanyon took a deep breath, thought briefly of the others and wondered where they were, then he shoved the door with a vigorous thrust of his foot and jumped into the room in the style of the adventure stories he had read or of the spy films he had seen when bunking-in at the Imperial Cinema, Clapham Junction. The door swung back and banged into the wall. Torreycanyon burst through the doorway and landed in the crouched position. His eyes raced over the workshops, his head turned, searching, but there was not one enemy to fire at. Torreycanyon relaxed.

He was in a large rectangular room. It was lined with shelves on which was stowed every tool that might be needed in the underground stronghold and, in addition, there was row upon row of spare parts for the machinery that kept the Bunker ticking over. There were work-benches and power-points, electric drills and lathes, winches and a conveyor belt. It was an extremely well-equipped and functional place and Torreycanyon liked it.

"Blimey," he said, looking round in wonder and respect, "what couldn't we do with this little lot," but then he remembered why he was there and he shook the feeling of awe from his mind. He bolted the door and made a tour of inspection, making sure that no unseen Rumble lurked behind the shelves, or between the work-benches. The more he saw of the place the more impressed he became. He had a practical turn of mind himself, and when he saw all those shining tools, laid out in perfect order, and those handy work-benches, the wood, the carpentry, the work in progress and the projects nearly finished, he felt that it was a great pity to destroy such order. Why, oh why, did he not have such a workshop back in Hoxton? He knew he could have done it justice.

He sighed and came to a corner where he thought the shop ended, but he had discovered another section of the room and he could see at a glance that this was the garage. He remembered that the Rumbles had built a car and had in fact used it for their trip to Battersea, that time when Knocker had captured one of their number. And here it was, he had discovered that car. He lowered his catapult; this place seemed empty too. The car itself was long and sleek and powerful-looking, but what struck Torreycanyon as he inspected it were the changes being made to the bodywork. Someone was converting it into an armoured troop-carrier, a weapon of war. There were little slits in the side of it, so that missiles could be fired from inside while the occupants remained protected. And on the steel panelling, not yet painted, some Rumble had scrawled in chalk, "Death to the Borribles". Torreycanyon glanced back down the long workshops. So that was it; those workshops did not look beautiful now, they looked sinister, and compassion drained from his heart.

His thinking was interrupted by the clink of a spanner falling to the concrete floor and Torreycanyon heard a Rumble oath. He raised his catapult, crouched and looked towards the armoured car, all in one movement. Protruding from underneath the rear axle were two padded feet. A Rumble was doing an early morning stint on the mechanics and the car had been jacked up high at the back to enable the fitter to move comfortably about his business.

Torreycanyon thought quickly. If that Rumble was the only one present, then all well and good, but was there another entrance, and were there more Rumbles to come? He stepped towards the car.

"I say," he said politely, "any twouble?"

"Who's that? What are you doing here? Hand me that Fourteen Whitworth," said the mechanic, rapidly and without waiting for answers.

"It's Bingo," said Torreycanyon, using the first Rumble name that came into his head.

"Bingo," cried the voice attached to the two feet. "Look, if you give me a hand for a couple of hours, we can do the test wun tonight. This car will be invincible; it'll take us down to Battersea High Street in half an hour, give those Bowwibles a beating and bwing us back in time for bweakfast."

The Borrible tensed his muscles and was just about to drag the Rumble out from underneath the car when he had a thought. "Who is that under there, anyway?" he asked. "I can't wecognise you by your feet, they're not vewy distinctive."

"Towweycanyon, of course—who else would be here at thwee in the morning when evewy other Wumble is still in bed? We of the High Command have got a sense of wesponsibility, a devotion to duty."

Torreycanyon stood up and smiled to himself. What a stroke of luck. Unbelievably his target was right there with him, and they were all alone.

The voice below the car said, "Go wound the back and pass me the working light, it's wolled out of my weach. Time is of the essence. The sooner we can teach those Bowwibles a lesson the better. We'll give them a twouncing all wight."

"All wight," said Torreycanyon, and he began to walk round the car hoping Torreycanyon Rumble wouldn't notice that his feet were not padded as they should be. But the Rumble said nothing and he continued to talk as he struggled with spanners and nuts.

"Now, when you get wound the back, be vewy careful, the handle of the jack is sticking out, just don't touch it at all, do you hear that, Bingo? It's vewy dangewous, cars and jacks and that, specially if you're underneath them. Nice things motors, but not seen fwom this angle, like a lot of things weally, all depends on the angle and that."

Torreycanyon moved stealthily to the rear of the garage. Here was the enormous jack, here tools littered the floor, and there was the working light, up against the second entrance to the workshop—a sliding door of steel, large enough to allow the passage of the armoured car. No doubt, thought Torreycanyon, the door was concealed on the other side; camouflaged to look like a grassy bank behind gorse bushes or trees.

The voice under the car went on. "If I stwetch out my hand you can put the working light underneath, there, just by the nearside fwont wheel and then I can. . ." The voice trailed off, and then, falteringly, it started again. "Bingo . . . you've got shoes, feet, weal feet. You can't be Bingo. You're human . . . or . . ."

"A Borrible," cried Torreycanyon. He leapt for the car jack, knocked off the safety catch and triggered the mechanism that released its power. The mighty car, the massive tool of destruction, sank slowly and relentlessly to the oily floor, crushing the small life out of the Rumble who had tended it so lovingly. There was a scream, then quiet, and Torreycanyon slipped his catapult into his back pocket. He spoke out loud to himself and his voice echoed round the hard walls of the garage. "Congratulations to you, Torreycanyon," he said, "on achieving your name. Now you may construct a little mayhem out of the materials that lie about you."

Knocker dropped down into the kitchen as the others had done. Adolf followed him and they both seized Rumble-sticks from the corner of the room.

"Aha," said Adolf, "good weapons for close work." The door opened and they stiffened but it was Chalotte and Sydney returning from the corridor.

"It's all quiet outside," said Chalotte, "but we don't know for how long."

"What's all this nasty steam and stink?" asked Knocker, peering round the room. Sydney gestured to the huge pots still boiling and bubbling on the stoves. "Chalotte shoved her namesake into the porridge," she said.

Adolf hooted. "So we have to felicitate you on your first name. I'm sure you will have many in the future."

"I got mine as well," said Sydney, "in the cupboard."

"You certainly wasted no time," said Knocker. "What about the others?"

The two girls told them that Napoleon and Vulge had set off already, suggesting before they left a rendezvous in the heart of the Bunker, where most of the tunnels met.

"That sounds all right," agreed Knocker. "Adolf and I will try to stir things up a bit; some alarm and despondency is what we want. Meanwhile, you girls could start preparing a line of retreat."

When Chalotte and Sydney had gone, Adolf leant on his Rumble-stick and looked at Knocker from under his brow. "Well, my Battersea friend," he asked with the bright light burning in his blue eyes, "what is it we are up to?"

Knocker laughed with happy excitement. "I'm going to get a second name out of this, and you can help Adolf. Somewhere in this maze of tunnels and corridors is a chest of treasure, money. My job is to get it back to Battersea High Street, so that it can be shared amongst all Borribles."

"A fine Historian and Observer you are," said Adolf. "Where is it?"

"I don't know," said Knocker, making his catapult ready and inspecting the nail on the end of his lance. "The Head Rumble's office seems a likely place, and that's where I am going."

"Excuse." Adolf held up his hand. "That is where we are going."

"Come on then," yelled Knocker and they dashed from the room.

Vulge came to a halt at a place where the corridor divided. A notice showed him which way to go, it said, "Headquarters." He turned to Napoleon.

"See you back at the Central, or at the Great Door."

"Or not at all," said the Wendle, with an ironic smile.

"It is sad to pass through life without one good Adventure," said Vulge, quoting one of the oldest of

Borrible proverbs, and plunged forward with a mad eagerness.

"And remember," said Napoleon to himself as he watched the energetic figure recede, "it is foolish to run faster than what you chase." Then he settled the bandoliers on his shoulders and marched away down the other corridor.

Vulge had not far to go. He rounded a bend in the tunnel and came upon a well-lit and spacious hallway. It was more luxuriously carpeted than any other part of the Bunker. Rows of armchairs were there for lesser Rumbles who might wait to see their chieftain, and opposite Vulge was a stout oaken door. It was guarded by two stalwart Rumbles, armed with lances.

Vulge gave no warning, his catapult was loaded and the first shot stunned one of the guards. He fell to the floor, his soft body making no sound on the carpet. Vulge reloaded quickly but not before the second guard had thrown his Rumble-stick with all his force. It struck the Borrible in his left shoulder and he fell back, staggering against the wall. He could feel blood running down his arm and the pain made him blink his eyes.

"Dammit," he said, but pulled back the elastic of his catapult as far as his wound and the pain would let him.

His antagonist reached for another spear and lifted it above his shoulder; he was a mighty thrower but he was not to throw again. The second stone from Vulge's catapult struck him fairly on the temple, he fell forward and the lance dropped from his hand.

Vulge stuck his catapult into his belt and, with an effort, he pulled the four-inch barb from his shoulder and threw the lance to the ground.

"I hope the bleeder weren't rusty," he said to himself, crossing the room, "and I hope there aren't too many guards inside."

He rapped on the oak door with the butt of a dead guard's lance.

"Who's there?" asked a rich and plummy voice from the other side.

"I've come with the bweakfast," said Vulge, whose imitation of a Rumble was perfect.

The door popped open and Vulge saw the Chieftain's major-domo standing before him. A haughty sneer was stretched along his snout and his rich beige fur was decorated with a green, white and gold sash; these were the colours of Rumbledom.

"Here's your bweakfast," said Vulge, and prodded the regal domestic in the solar plexus with the sharp end of his lance. The butler doubled up, clutching at his stomach, and Vulge clouted him hard across the head with the shaft of the spear. The Rumble collapsed to the floor and rolled over on his back, his snout crashing open like an unhinged drawbridge.

"That's sorted you out, weasel-chops," said Vulge.

He stepped over the body and entered a magnificent and luxurious sitting-room. The carpet was a spotless white and a huge sofa in cream leather was matched with armchairs of the same material and on the misty green walls were original paintings in good taste. There was a colour television set, telephones in brass with ivory mouth-pieces and copies of the national newspapers and magazines resting aristocratically on small leather-covered tables.

Vulge jerked a linen runner from one of the tables, spilling a majolica vase to the floor, where it broke. He folded the material and shoved it inside his combat jacket to pad his wound and stop the bleeding.

"The sooner I get this over with, the better," he muttered, "otherwise this arm will go as stiff as a Rumble's snout."

He opened another door and saw that he had come to the Chief Rumble's office. Here he found a huge desk, meant to impress visitors with its top of dark green morocco, a map of the world on the wall, bookshelves, electric typewriters, Xerox machines and, once more, everything was furnished in white and misty green. It was an expensive and oppressive room, but what Vulge wanted was not there.

Next he entered a circular bedroom, furnished as if for some great pop-star. A huge round bed stood in the centre of white goat-skin carpets, its coverlet made from green silk, the colour of gorse bushes at dawn. The lighting was concealed and gentle.

"Blimey," said Vulge between his teeth, "I'd like to put a match to this lot." He winced with pain, for his wound troubled him. He walked round the bed and blood dropped from him and stained the floor. On the far side of the room, a door stood open and perfume-laden steam floated through it. "The bathroom," thought Vulge, and he stepped inside.

Through the clouds of sweet-smelling vapour Vulge saw his namesake and enemy, Vulgarian Rumble. The Chieftain reclined in an oval bath of green marble which was big enough to swim in. The taps were gold and shaped like Rumble snouts, and scented water poured through them to wash across the furred body and out through an over-flow grating, also of gold. The floor, where it was not covered with absorbent carpets, was covered with Italian tiles of a warm southern tint. Near the bath were several telephones on articulated arms that could be pulled in any direction. Two enormous electric fires faced the marble steps that led down from the magnificent pool so that Vulgarian could warm himself the moment he emerged from the water. Right by the two fires stood a hot air blower on a stand, ready to dry the Chieftain's magnificent coat.

Vulge stepped across the room, trailing the bloody lance point noisily behind him on the tiled floor. The Rumble's snout turned, there was a flurry in his bath-water.

"I twust you've got my bweakfast at last," he began

angrily, and then he saw, not the obsequious butler, or even one of his guards. He saw a Borrible.

Vulge was no reassuring sight at that moment. He face was still smeared black from Knocker's greasepaint. His combat jacket was filthy and torn from the scuffling and climbing about in the ventilation shaft and, even more dramatically, blood was spreading out to stain his shoulder. The Borrible cap was jaunty on his head however and there was a gleam of triumph in his eye. Vulgarian Rumble slid down into the water until only his snout was visible. His small red eyes, intelligent and cunning, fluttered over the room, but he saw no escape. For a while the only sound was the gurgling of the bath-water.

"A Borrible?" asked the Rumble at last.

"A Borrible," said Vulge, "all the way from Stepney, bloody miles."

"Don't swear," said the Rumble.

"Knickers," answered Vulge and gobbed into the bath-water. "This is the great Rumble Hunt, mate. You've got everything you need up here, you should have stayed out of Battersea."

Vulgarian raised himself a little. "As if we would want your stinking markets and rubbishy old houses, but, I'll tell you this, we'll go where we like and . . ."

"Don't want it, eh? What about all that digging down there in Battersea Park, eh? What about that, then? You started this, Rumble."

"We started it! I know Timbucktoo is a trifle over-enthusiastic at times, always wants to be digging and that, but he's harmless. No, it won't do. This trouble is all your fault, Borrible."

"Cobblers," said Vulge, moving nearer the bath.

"How many of you here?" asked the Chieftain.

"There's only eight of us, but that's enough of us to wreck the place." Vulge stood between the two electric fires and let them warm the pain in his shoulder. He was getting weaker and stiffer by the minute. He knew he must finish the task quickly; he felt in no state to defend himself if reinforcements arrived on the scene.

Vulgarian suddenly stood up and the water cascaded from his fur. He was the tallest of all the Rumbles, impressive and commanding. He looked down his snout imperiously at the grimy little Borrible.

"Eight of you!" he cried. "Why, you impudent little whippersnappers, you insignificant hobbledehoys. I tell you that Rumbles will go wherever I say, from Hampton Wick to Arnos Park, and from Ealing Golf Course to Bexley Heath. We won't be stopped by a handful of ignorant street urchins, thieves who live in slimy slums and damp cellars, who cannot afford a bar of soap and would eat it if they could, who smell, whose ears are pointed by the effect of cheap peasant cunning and who are fit only to be our slaves. You Battersea brat, I have only to press that alarm bell and my bodyguard will make a pin-cushion of you with their Rumble-sticks. Hand me that towel, you scrubby little serf. Hand me that towel I say, Borrible!"

Vulge smiled and did not move for a moment. Then he pushed the end of his Rumble-stick through the handle of one of the electric fires and he raised the sticker and the fire pivoted on the end of it. He slid his feet up the steps, his eyes remaining steady on Vulgarian's face and he held his spear forward so that the fire was above the water and near to the Chief Rumble's fur. There was a smell of singeing and Vulgarian took a step backwards, horror replacing the expression of disdain on his snout.

Vulge smiled ironically at the Rumble. "Don't worry about the towel," he said pleasantly, "I'll soon have your fur dry," and he allowed the lance to slant down to the water and the fire plopped into the bath and hissed. The electric current sprang from the fire and arced across the water, and from the water it raced through the flesh of the Rumble Chieftain. It burnt through his heart and demolished it like an old fuse-box and Vulgarian Rumble's voice cried out, but he never heard the sound. His body jerked upright, his dead eyes stared in amazement, then, as stiff as a scaffolding plank, he fell forward into the bath-water and a tidal wave washed over the rim of the beautiful bath and gushed down the veined green of the marble steps.

Vulge sniffed and prodded the body with the point of his spear. It bobbed lifelessly in the tinted foam.

"Well, there you are, me ol' Rumble," said Vulge reflectively. "That's 'ow you singe your fur at both ends. Kilowatts will kill a weasel any day. So," he added, "I've got my name. Mind you, the way I feel, I shan't have it long . . . alive."

He descended the steps and pulled the cables from the remaining electric fire and from the hair-drier. Next he trailed the flex across the room to the door, which he shut, and then he wound the bare wires around the metal door handles. He looked at his work and went on talking to himself. "I don't think I could fight my way out of here with this wound, so I might as well have a scrap here; saves time."

He crossed the room once more and pressed the red alarm bell by the bath. "That should bring the body-guard at a run," he said and he pulled a couple of chairs and cushions across the bottom of the bath steps to form a rough barricade and squatted behind it. The dead Vulgarian floated behind him.

Vulge removed his bandoliers and placed them near to hand. He took out his knife and placed that ready, and he laid his lance on the barricade. He leant back then on a cushion, waiting, favouring his injured shoulder, which was very stiff now though it pained him less. He wagged his head and thought of a few old Borrible proverbs to while away the time.

"It is better to die young than to be caught," he

quoted from memory and he smiled and hoped the others were getting on all right.

Knocker and Adolf ran together from the end of the tunnel and into the hallway that led to the Head Rumble's apartments. Alarm bells were ringing and lights were flashing in the ceiling. In the distance a siren howled and a recorded voice called all Rumbles to their battle stations. Knocker and Adolf stretched their catapults but they need not have bothered. The bodies of the two Rumble guards in the doorway did not move. Knocker put his catapult away and picked up a lance. "Look," he said, showing the point to Adolf, "blood."

"Vulge?" said Adolf with a worried expression. "*Verdammt*, I hope he is still alive."

"Let's see," said Knocker. Inside the doorway they found the body of the major-domo. Blood stained the whiteness of the carpet, blood already turning brown.

"Wait a minute," Knocker whistled through his teeth. "Look!"

In the sitting-room of the Headquarters lay several Rumbles, their bodies contorted, their fur singed. Both Borribles sniffed the air and looked at each other.

"Electrics," said Adolf, "nasty dangerous stuff."

"Don't touch the bodies," said Knocker and he went to the door. Here he and Adolf found more Rumbles, all scorched and twisted and all of them dead.

"This must be the élite guard," said Knocker, "look at their uniforms, their weapons."

"They lead to that door over there," said Adolf, gesturing with his catapult.

"Do you notice how they are all touching each other?" said Knocker, and with the butt end of his lance he bashed the door free from the charred paw of the first in the line of electrocuted bodyguards. Inside the bathroom the wires attached to the handle told their own story. The first warrior to arrive on the scene had tried the door and died. Another had attempted to pull his comrade from the handle and he had died. Many had perished in this manner, their bodies soldered together, their fur crisp. Then the door had been broken down, but there were dozens more bodies in the bathroom, electrocuted on the threshold, knocked down by stones as they crossed the room, or stabbed as they had attempted to storm Vulge's little barricade. The room was a shambles.

"Oh *verdammt*," said Adolf reverently, "what a scrapper, that Vulge. Who would have guessed that such a little Borrible had so much courage in him?"

The trail of bodies led across the room and up to the very edge of the bath. At the bottom of the steps half a dozen of the bodyguard lay in a heap. There had been a terrific battle waged in this bathroom but there was no sign of the Stepney Borrible.

Knocker scrambled over the bodies and the barricade and discovered the half-submerged form of the Rumble Chieftain.

"He got him," he shouted. "Vulge got his name."

"Posthumously, I should think," said the German sadly.

"Wait," said Knocker, "I can see his foot." And it was true. Sticking out from under the pile of Rumble bodies was a Borrible foot. Knocker and Adolf pulled the corpses aside and underneath everything lay a pathetically frail Borrible holding a knife in one hand and the broken barb of a lance in the other. They knelt beside him.

"Has he gone?" asked Knocker.

Adolf put his head to Vulge's chest. "No," he said. "I can hear his heart."

Tenderly they raised the Stepney Borrible into a sitting position and rubbed his hands and his cheeks. Vulge's eyes flickered and then opened weakly. He was covered in blood, though most of it was not his own.

He licked his lips. "Trust you to get here when it was all over," he said and he tried to grin. "Get me something to drink."

Adolf returned in an instant with a jade tooth-mug full of cold water and Vulge drank it greedily. "That's better," he said, looking round the room. "Pretty good fight it was," he added, "but you'd better get out of here. With those bells and alarms going the tunnels will be solid with Rumbles."

"Okay," said Knocker, "we're going. I've just got something to do first. Adolf, watch the door."

Vulge grabbed Knocker's arm. "Give me one of your bandoliers," he said, "I feel lonely without a few stones."

Knocker slipped a bandolier over his head, retrieved a catapult from the floor and handed them to Vulge. "There you are," he said. "Leave some Rumbles for us, won't you."

Knocker left the bathroom and passed into a large study. It was an inner sanctum, different from the main office, more private and intimate. Here there was just a bare desk, some books and a watercolour of the Rumbledom countryside on the wall. Knocker flung the picture to the floor and found what he had been hoping to find—a large safe. He looked at it, baffled. The safe was firmly closed and there was a complicated combination lock on the outside. He fiddled with it, listened to it, pulled the large brass handle, but the safe door would not budge. He ran back to the bathroom and shouted desperately to Adolf. "Dammit, I can't get the safe open. We're snookered."

The German bobbed his head round the door he was guarding. "A safe," he cried, "is that all? Did I not tell you how I got my third name, Amadeus? By stealing diamonds from the most renowned burglar in all of Austria. You come and watch. I will persuade your safe to be friendly."

In a moment Adolf had his ear pressed against the door of the safe and his nimble fingers were twiddling with the lock. There was a click, then another and another until there was a click that sounded more definite than all the rest and Adolf's eyes glowed like the jackpot lights on a fruit-machine. He seized the handle with both hands and pulled open the massive steel door.

"Bull's-eye," he cried. "Oh, *verdammt!* I haven't lost my touch."

Knocker gazed into the safe and saw a large brass-bound box. "You must be the best safe-cracker in the whole world," he said, "Adolf Wolfgang Amadeus *Winston!*"

"*Danke,*" said the German, "I am proud of my new name and will enjoy telling how I earned it—if we ever get out of here."

They pulled the box from the safe and it thumped to the floor. Knocker flung back the lid and sat back on his heels in amazement. It was full to the top with crisp notes of the realm.

"I'll be jiggered," he said, "there's a fortune here."

"No good if you can't get it out," said Adolf.

"Wait," said Knocker, seizing the German's shoulder, "it will need two of us to carry this. We'll have to leave Vulge behind."

Adolf stood up, his face angry. "You may do what you wish," he said. "I am taking Vulge."

Knocker faced his friend, his mouth tight. "The whole point of the expedition is that money. I have strict orders to get the box out. Vulge has taken his chances like the rest of us. Why, he's half dead already."

"And half of him is worth all of you, Knocker, and the money too," cried Adolf and he kicked the lid of the box so that it closed with a crash.

"This money," said Knocker, lowering his voice, "could change life for thousands of Borribles. It's important, more important than any one of us, that's why Spiff wanted me to get it home, no matter what."

"Who cares about your Spiff. I don't want my life changed," said Adolf passionately, "nor do other Borribles. The lives I care about at this moment are my life and Vulge's life, and yours if you will stop being stupid."

Knocker hesitated. He knew that what the German said made sense, but there were other considerations.

"Vulge got his name by a valiant battle," he argued. "You were destined to open the safe, my part is to take this money out of here and win my name that way. Can't you see that?"

"I see it," said Adolf, "but it doesn't mean I have to look at it. You carry the money if you can, I will carry Vulge if I can; the rest is chance. Let us remain friends though we differ. I like stealing too you know, but sometimes other things come first."

Just then there was a yell from Vulge in the bathroom. Both Borribles grasped their catapults and loading them as they moved they dashed through the door.

Two Rumbles armed with stickers were coming into the room, a third lay stunned in the entrance. Vulge was reloading his catapult. A Rumble threw his sticker at Adolf who side-stepped it with ease and the spear thudded into the wall. Knocker fired, Adolf fired and both Rumbles fell. It became quiet and Adolf went to the door to look out. "Only those three," he said, "but others will be coming. Let's go." He crossed the room and knelt beside Vulge. "You're coming with me, my friend," he said. "I will give you a fireman's lift. It will be painful but safer than staying here."

"You can't take me," grimaced the wounded Borrible. "Leave me another bandolier, and I'll do for a few more."

"Rubbish," laughed the German, "are you content to die with only one name?"

Vulge wagged his head in the old way of his. "Go on then, idiot. 'It is madness to quarrel with a madman'."

Adolf ignored the proverb, hoisted his wounded comrade up and carried him towards the door. Knocker meanwhile ran back into the inner sanctum and lifted the box onto his shoulders with a supreme effort. "With both of us laden like this," thought Knocker, "there is very little chance of us getting out. Adolf was right, but then so am I. We will just have to play it by ear."

Their progress was slow and awkward. They stopped frequently to rest and Vulge was in great pain, though he said nothing.

The lighting system had obviously suffered serious damage, for the lights often went out. Bells and sirens clanged and wailed as the general alarm spread through the maze of corridors, and shouts and calls could be heard echoing from side tunnels. Something somewhere was burning and smoke was beginning to drift by, sucked along by the ventilation fans. Steam from the cauldrons left boiling in the kitchens lent an acrid smell to the atmosphere, and the temperature in the Bunker was rising fast.

The fugitives encountered several dazed and panic-stricken bands of Rumbles but they were not trained warriors and a show of belligerence was enough to make them sheer off. But everytime they passed a branch corridor Rumbles issued from it noiselessly on their padded feet and followed at a safe distance, waiting for the right moment to pounce and bear down upon the Adventurers.

"I must rest," said Knocker for the fifth time. "Money weighs you down."

"I too could rest," said Adolf panting, and he lowered Vulge to the floor.

"How are you, my friend?" asked the German.

Vulge was near to fainting with pain but he said, "Mustn't grumble. Got to keep going till you can't go any more, isn't it?"

They had stopped by the entrance to a dark branch corridor and suddenly two figures leapt out with a cry, brandishing lances. Adolf and Knocker stepped back and reached for their weapons but then held their hands. Before them stood Bingo and Orococco, fresh and alert.

"Well, hello sailor," said Orococco. "What's a nice Borrible like you doing in a place like this?"

Knocker smiled with relief. He gestured towards Vulge and the box. "We're trying to get Vulge out. He's done for the Chief, but the bodyguard nearly did for him."

"He knocked them about beautifully," laughed Adolf. "He deserves twenty names."

"He doesn't look too good," said Bingo, "that's for sure."

"How have you got on?" asked Knocker, sitting down on the box of money.

Bingo knelt by Vulge and felt his pulse, saying, " 'Rococco's got his, at the door. He came along to keep me company. I've been running all over the place but I'm damned if I can find mine anywhere. I hope someone else hasn't done him. I'll be stuck without a name if they have."

The lights in the corridor flickered off and the Borribles grasped their lances and stood back to back. They heard the snuffling sound of Rumbles moving nearer but then the lights snapped on again and the Adventurers saw their foes scrambling to get beyond the range of the Borrible weapons.

Knocker came to a decision. "You could come along with us, then, give me a hand with this box and help carry Vulge."

"I don't mind that," agreed Bingo, "as long as I am free to take off after my bloke at any time."

The five Borribles moved on, pausing at every intersection. They were followed, sniffed and snuffled at but not attacked. The hazards would increase when they reached the open space of the Central. There hosts of angry Rumbles could trample them down, no matter how well they defended themselves.

At length Bingo, who was leading, stopped and held up a hand. "It's the Central," he whispered.

They gathered at the end of the corridor and looked out into the wide cavern from which radiated the main arteries of the Bunker. A fearful sight met their eyes. Hundreds of Rumbles ran backwards and forwards across the immense hallway. Blue lights flashed in the ceiling and the alarm bells rang. The roadway leading to the Great Door was crammed with Warrior Rumbles, struggling to enter the tunnel and do battle with whoever was at the other end; thick smoke issued from a corridor above which was written "Kitchens". Some Rumbles were disappearing into a tunnel marked "Infirmary", bearing wounded comrades on stretchers.

Bingo took in the scene and turned to the others. "I've got an idea," he said. "There's a tunnel over there with no one in it, or so it seems, the one that says 'Library'. I'll run across the hall, throw a few spears and some of those warriors will chase after me. You'll have to fight the rest. Not much of an idea but it's Hobson's, isn't it?"

Knocker spoke for them all. "It's the only way."

Bingo took extra stickers from his companions and with no goodbyes he ran light-footed into the hall. So sudden was his appearance that he got three-quarters of the way across before he was noticed by some non-combatant Rumbles, who shouted out to the Warriors who were crowded round the Great Door tunnel.

Bingo planted his feet firmly on the floor and threw sticker after sticker at the enemy. He threw well and he threw hard, each of his lances struck a mark and half a dozen Rumbles fell dead or sorely wounded. The others fell back and hesitated, so Bingo drew his catapult and two more Rumbles fell stunned before he turned and with a remarkable burst of speed vanished into the Library tunnel yelling defiantly, "A Borrible, a Borrible." Scores of Warrior Rumbles raced after Bingo, shouting fiercely in their turn, and in a few seconds the entrance to the Great Door corridor was left deserted.

"Vulge," said Knocker, kneeling, "can you make it across the Central? We'll need all hands to fight our way over."

"Get me to my feet," said Vulge, sitting up, "and give me a sticker to lean on. I'll waltz it over there."

They pulled him upright and thrust a lance into his hand. He tucked the butt of it under his good armpit and used it like a crutch. "There you go," he wheezed, "nice as ninepence."

Knocker got the box onto his back once more and Orococco and Adolf formed up on either side of him. They had few Rumblesticks left but here there would be room for catapult work.

"You lead the way, Vulge," said Knocker. "We'll take your pace."

Because of the terrible confusion and panic that had followed Bingo's exit the retreating Borribles got a good way into the Central before being seen, and when they were, the Rumbles were at a loss, for they had no troops of their own present to deal with this unexpected situation. They knew that Borribles were loose in the tunnels but they had no idea how large the invading force was. Above all they had not expected a band of Borrible fighters to appear suddenly like that right in their midst. They shouted and squealed and their stomachs turned to water. They ran in every direction, except towards their enemies; they knocked each other down and exchanged blows, anything to get away from the deadly stones that flew so rapidly from the Borrible catapults. They screamed out for Warriors, but their Warriors were engaged deep in the tunnels, or were chasing phantoms or other Rumbles in the belief that they were Borribles.

Smoke made pursuit and identification difficult and confusion was spreading into the very outposts of the Rumble Bunker.

Slowly the Borribles moved over the dangerous open area. Vulge hobbled and stumbled manfully, gritting his teeth to keep back his pain, willing himself not to fall and ruin the escape. The Rumbles held back still and made no attempt to attack until, suddenly, a party of their Warriors burst from a tunnel on the Borrible flank.

"We've been rumbled," said Orococco.

"This is no time for bad jokes, panted Knocker, sweating under the weight of his box and wishing he had his hands free.

"The proverb says," hissed Orococco as he fired and reloaded his catapult, " 'Bad times need jokes though never so bad'."

A flight of lances whistled over from the Rumbles but the catapult fire, rapid and sustained, detracted from their aim and the stickers missed their targets and fell harmlessly to the floor: all save one, which struck, the box that Knocker carried and pierced the lid and stayed there quivering. The force of the blow staggered Knocker and he went down to one knee and had to be helped back to his feet.

The Rumbles searched round for more lances but the flying Borrible stones still hampered them and one by one they were hit and retreated to the safety of the tunnels. But there was one Rumble, braver and quicker than the rest, who exhorted his comrades to come out again and he began to organise the non-Warriors into a compact mass, ready to charge the little band of Borribles. If he could them them to act together, all would be over with the retreating Adventurers—but Orococco had other ideas.

Snatching a lance from the floor, he ran forward, one Borrible charging a hundred Rumbles. About twenty yards away from the brave but offending Rumble, Or-ococco threw his lance like a javelin. It left his hand with the power of a bullet and the four-inch nail buried itself deep in the thick fur of the Warrior. A groan went up from the enemy ranks and scores of stickers clattered about the head of Orococco, but he bobbed and ducked and returned to his friends unscathed and they gained the temporary safety of the Great Door tunnel.

Vulge fell to the floor in a dead faint. Knocker flung down his box, tugged the lance free of the lid and threw the weapon back into the Great Hall.

"And work it," he shouted, trembling with anger.

Adolf knelt to inspect Vulge's injury, lifting the jacket aside to reveal the blood-soaked bandage.

"Our Vulge has lost lots of his strength," he said, "but the wound had stopped bleeding. He may be all right, if he can rest." He refolded the cloth and replaced it.

Orococco, watching from the mouth of the corridor, called a warning. "There's a lot of those Warrior boys getting together out there. They're coming our way."

Knocker looked at the others and said, "Rest, just a minute or two. We've not finished. I can hear fighting up ahead; we ain't out of this holiday camp yet."

"It's a lovely place," said Vulge, who was becoming delirious. "Lots and lots of Rumbles in it."

Bingo ran like the wind along the corridor. As far as he could see it was empty of Rumbles ahead, but from behind came the noise of shouting as the Warriors from the Central gave chase.

Bingo ran easily, keeping plenty of strength in reserve. Wherever it was this Library it seemed a long way. He ran on, outdistancing his pursuers until at length he could hear them no more. He slowed his pace and jogged along, a sticker swinging loosely in his right hand, his catapult in his belt. He was in the furthest reaches of the Bunker here and it was strangely quiet; there was no smoke or acrid steam on the air, either.

After what seemed miles Bingo came to a green baize-covered door that was hanging crazily on one hinge. Several stickers stood embedded in it and two Rumble Warriors, with their throats slit, lay dead across the threshold.

"Wendle work," said Bingo, and he went past the bodies and slipped into the room that lay beyond. It was indeed the Library but it had been badly mauled. It was a high room with massively tall bookcases soaring up to an embossed oaken ceiling, which was painted in bright colours with the coats-of-arms of the richest and most ancient Rumble families. Little wooden balconies ran round the walls and beautifully carved staircases led down from ceiling height at each corner. Quiet alcoves with comfortable desks were situated between the bookshelves and little green shaded lamps gave a friendly and academic glow. It was a place for rest and study, richly decorated in the Rumble colours, and it had obviously cost a great deal of money and labour to establish and build up over long years. Here was assembled all the knowledge and wisdom and power that the Rumbles had amassed over many centuries, and now it was being dismantled by a very busy Borrible. Napoleon Boot was hard at work with the cool ferocity of a Wendie with a grudge.

Bingo glanced round the room to see that there was no enemy, and there wasn't, alive. The bodies of a dozen or so vanquished Rumble Warriors littered the dark green carpet, all but covered in mounds of heavy books. Napoleon carried on with his work, unperturbed by Bingo's arrival, which he acknowledged with a curt nod. The Wendle had already pushed or levered over two or three of the huge bookcases and spilled the enormous volumes out across the floor. At the far end of the room one of the long library ladders was propped up to a grating of the ventilation system. Napoleon had prepared his retreat, but was not going to leave before he had caused the maximum amount of damage. The Wendle was nobody's fool.

Bingo watched as Napoleon pushed over a few more bookcases and the tomes cascaded down, covering more of the Rumble dead. He advanced, climbing across the treacherous surface of jumbled books.

"How are you getting on?" he asked.

"Nicely, thanks," said the Wendle, tersely, preoccupied, "and you?"

"I can't find mine anywhere. Where's yours?"

"Under that pile of encyclopaedias. Nice little fellow, didn't cause any trouble."

"How?" asked Bingo, adopting the same terse speech as the Wendle.

"He was at the top of a long ladder," explained Napoleon, pleased to tell the story of his name for the very first time. "I came to the bottom of it and said, very politely, 'Excuse me, are you Napoleon Boot Rumble?' and he said, 'Yes, I am.' So I says, 'Could you come down please, I have a word to say to you.' Bloke didn't even look at me, toffee-nosed little twit. 'Oh, no,' he says, 'I'm too busy. You'll have to wait. I'm looking for a book on Bowwible fighting methods, for the High Command—of which I am a member, I'll have you know. So be off.' So I says, 'You're coming down one way or the other, mate. Gravity is stronger than you are.' That was a remark that caught his fancy, must have, cos he looked at me then. 'Aaaaaagh,' he says, like they do, and drops his book, nearly hit me on the head, bloody dangerous, and he grabs hold of the top of the bookcase. At the same time I kicked the ladder away, so he's got nothing to stand on, has he? Well, the sudden increase of weight at the top of the bookcase made it wobble violently, so that gave me an idea. I runs round the back, up another ladder on the next bookcase and pushes with me sticker, and over went the whole lot, bookcase, books, Rumble and all. Goodnight, Napoleon Rumble. Splat!"

Bingo shook his head. "What a way to go."

"Overcome by the weight of his studies, you might say," said Napoleon and he smirked like a cold draught. "Got any matches on you?" he asked suddenly.

"What for?" asked Bingo.

"Don't be slow," said Napoleon, sighing. "Start a fire, of course, bit of mayhem, cover our retreat. Seen the others?"

Bingo told him what he knew.

"Aha," crowed the Wendle, nodding his head, "I knew that Knocker was up to something. Got a box, eh? That is money, that is. Well, we'll have to see about that, won't we?"

"We haven't got away yet," pointed out Bingo, reasonably.

"I'm getting out, mate," said Napoleon, indicating the ladder. "I'm getting into that ventilation shaft and no Rumble in the world is going to stop me leaving for home. Only two Rumbles can get at you at once up there, one in front, one behind. Any Borrible ought to be a match for a score of Rumbles and a Wendle can deal with twice that number."

"You do for these?" asked Bingo, indicating the prone Rumble Warriors.

"Well, they didn't commit suicide," said Napoleon. "Mind you, they only came into the place in fives and sixes. It was easy really, like falling off a . . . bookcase."

Bingo took a box of matches from his pocket and handed them to Napoleon. "It's a shame about the books. Are there any good adventure stories there?"

Napoleon gave him an old-fashioned look. "I haven't had a lot of time for reading in the last half-hour," he said, and he went over to a stack of books. He put a match to them and, dusty and dry, they burst into flames on the instant.

"What I mean," persisted Bingo, "is that it's a shame; they're sort of nice things, books."

"Nice things! You sound like a bloody Rumble. Can't have no half-measures in an attack like this, Bingo, got to go the whole hog or it don't work. What would happen if we left these books up here untouched? I'll tell you what, there'd be another Rumble High Command on the go in five minutes. This is what it's all about, sonny, power!" And he threw another book on the fire.

"I suppose you're right," said Bingo. "I never thought of it like that."

"Course I'm right," said Napoleon. "Now then, it's time for me to go home. Can't stand fires, water's my element. Are you coming?"

"Can't," said Bingo miserably. "I told you, I haven't found my bloke."

"Tough, but I'm off. I want to see that Knocker; that money's not all his." Napoleon winked mysteriously and made his way from the fire, which was now burning well, and began to climb his ladder. "You could come with me, Bingo, and drop down through the ventilation system somewhere else. It's going to get very hot in this library very shortly."

"It's going to be hotter than you think," said Bingo. "There were two million Rumble Warriors chasing me down the corridor out there. They don't run very fast, do they—but they ought to be here at any moment."

Napoleon became immobilised on the ladder and looked down. "How many? You can't have that lot to yourself, that's greedy," and he came back down the ladder and threw a few more books on the fire.

They waited and the fire crept along the mounds of books and began to rise towards the high ceiling. Soon there was a noise of shouting from the tunnel beyond the green baize door and Bingo and Napoleon placed themselves within sticker-throwing range of the entrance.

"We'll let the first ones have it with these stickers," said Napoleon, "then we'll get behind that pile of books, there beyond the fire, and then let them have it with the catapults as they try to get in. When we're out of ammo, we'll scarper up the ladder, okay?"

"Right," said Bingo. He picked up a couple of lances from the floor and hefted one ready in his right hand. Two breathless Rumbles burst into the room together and Bingo and Napoleon threw their weapons as one man and the two Warriors fell.

Other Rumbles crowded into the room in a compact mass, urged and pushed on by their eager companions behind, and the two Borribles continued to throw spears until they had exhausted their meagre supply. Several Rumbles had been accounted for, but so great were their numbers, it was impossible to prevent them from spilling into the Library and taking cover behind desks and bookcases.

Napoleon and Bingo fell back and crouched behind an enormous pile of books, their catapults stretched.

"I've hardly fired a stone yet," said Bingo. "It's all been lance work."

Napoleon peered through the smoke that was rising from the energetic fire that lay between them and the enemy. "This smoke is going to help them to creep up on us," he said to Bingo. "That's not good." He broke off and fired a shot towards the door. "Look," he said, "there's scores of them coming."

Bingo saw that many more Warrior Rumbles were rushing into the room. They were led by a slim but powerful-looking Rumble, covered in sleek brown fur and with a hard expression on his dangerous-looking snout. He carried three or four lances and wore a sash of gold, green and white to denote his position as Commander of the Warriors. He looked proud and impatient and Bingo knew that at last he had found his target.

The Commander ran this way and that at the far end of the Library, gathering his forces and making them emerge from their hiding places between the fallen bookshelves. He shouted and waved his arms and slowly the Rumbles came forward, throwing lances at the two Borribles who crouched behind the pile of books, only standing up every now and then to a fire stone. Things would have gone very badly with the two Borribles if the Rumbles had been in possession of any reasonable number of lances, but most of their missiles had been thrown in a panicky fashion at the beginning of the skirmish. Now there was a great pile of spears on the Borribles' side of the room and there soon came a moment when Napoleon and Bingo could stand up in full view of their enemy because the Rumbles had no stickers left to throw.

With a sign, the Rumble Commander sent some of his troops off into the corridor to bring more weapons and the rest of his Warriors took up defensive positions amongst the bookcases and the piles of burning books. It was hard to breathe in the room now as the fire gradually gained a firmer hold and the smoke grew thicker. Some Rumbles tried to stamp or beat out the fire, but more often than not their fur was singed or caught fire and their friends had to come to their rescue and save them from being scorched to death.

Napoleon checked his bandoliers. "Not many stones left," he said. "How about you?"

"I've got a lot still, but they won't last for ever," said Bingo, and he fired a stone at a Rumble who was trying to creep along the side of the room to get at a stray lance. "But I can't leave now, I've got to have a crack at my target, and I'd better do it before his mates get back with a new load of stickers."

Bingo reached behind and picked up two sharp Rumble lances. He put his catapult carefully into his back pocket and went slowly down the long slope of books. The Warrior Rumble with the sash stood by the Library door, waiting for his men to return with more lances, for even he was weaponless.

Bingo leant backwards, arcing his body, and threw one of his spears with all his might. His name would have been won there and then had the High Rumble not chosen that moment to step into the corridor to see if his men were returning.

The sticker plunged deep into the green baize of the Library door and it hung there—humming. Bingo swore and grasped his second lance securely, but did not throw it, for there are two ways of fighting with the Rumble-stick. The first is simply to throw it from a distance; the second is to wield it like a quarter-staff until the fighter finds a moment to use the point and slay his stunned or unconscious foe. Bingo moved nearer to the door and the Rumbles fell back. He glanced over his shoulder to see that Napoleon had followed him, his catapult eager to dissuade anyone who thought they could intervene in the fight between Bingo the Borrible and Bingo the Rumble.

The High Rumble leapt back into the room, saw the advance of the two Borribles and saw too the lance, still singing in the door. He pulled it free with both hands and moved towards Bingo. They said no word these two, and no Rumble attempted to interfere; they watched from the safety of their hiding places, their snouts and eyes only just visible through the red smoke.

Bingo held his lance with a hand at each end, using the long haft to ward off blows from his adversary who began the contest by working his weapon like a two-handed sword, hoping to stun the Borrible and then spear him. But Bingo had learned his Rumble-stick fighting well all that time ago in Rowena Gym and he protected his head and shoulders and was content to defend himself, while he measured the style of his enemy, conserving his strength.

It was treacherous underfoot; the books slipped and tripped and burnt the feet. Whoever fell first during this fight would be hard put to it to rise again. Suddenly the Rumble changed his tactics and began jabbing consistently and forcefully, making Bingo avoid the blows like a fencer. The Rumble was an expert, perhaps the best lancer of his tribe.

"Just my luck," thought Bingo, and redoubled his efforts, but backwards and backwards his opponent forced him. The other Rumbles emerged from their hiding-places and hurrahed and some climbed up onto the bookcases and, holding on with one arm, they waved the other and jeered at the two Borribles so lonely and outnumbered.

Sweat was pouring down Bingo's face and into his eyes, and his arms were aching and his hands were bruised and bleeding. He dodged, he weaved, he ducked. He tried to remember all he had ever learnt about fighting with the Rumble-stick, but it didn't seem to be enough. He had managed to ward off most swipes and stabs so far but had not struck a blow yet and his antagonist looked fresh and powerful and was smiling grimly down his snout, his red eyes shining with triumph as he bore down on the Borrible from Lavender Hill.

The battle passed far beyond Napoleon but the Wendle kept his position, holding the spectators at bay with his catapult, though he realised that if the Rumble did for Bingo he himself would have little chance of escape. Bingo too was aware of that eventuality and he strove all the harder, and he thought of his other friends and their long quest and all they had been through together. He had a brief mental picture of them being torn and rent to death by the sharp teeth of the Rumbles and the notion angered him and he stopped retreating. He stooped suddenly and allowed the Rumble's sticker to whistle over his head. He jabbed at his foe and at last wounded him in the knee.

The Rumble staggered and it was his turn to go on the defensive. Bingo thrust and fenced and fought, holding the lance now one-handed, now two-handed. They circled and struggled and still the fight went on and still Bingo found it impossible to get through his adversary's guard. But Bingo had had time to think; only cunning would win him this battle. So, still on the attack, pressing his namesake slowly back down the hill of books, Bingo tried a stratagem. He pretended to stumble. He slithered a step, and, keeping a wary eye all the time on his opponent, he fell backwards, crying in pain for an imagined twisted foot.

The watching Rumbles cheered anew and Napoleon cursed his luck and moved nearer the ladder. He only had one chance, to climb out of the Library as quickly as possible while the Rumbles celebrated their victory. But Napoleon was sure of one thing: if that Rumble did for Bingo, he wouldn't live long to brag about it. He, Napoleon Boot, would make certain that a stone was rattling round inside the warrior's skull before his brain registered the triumph.

Bingo lay on the books, groaning and writhing, but his eyes kept still, watching the Rumble who, in his excitement, had not noticed that the Borrible, in spite of all his pain, had not relinquished his grip on the lance.

The Rumble stepped forward, a smirk spreading over the whole length of his snout. Quickly he raised his spear, ready to pierce Bingo's breast. He plunged it down hard, leaning on it like a man pushing a shovel. At that moment Bingo rolled over with a thrust from legs and hands. He came to his knees and, as the point of the Rumble's weapon embedded itself in the closed pages of some solid volume, he swung the shaft of his sticker and clouted the Rumble behind the ear. The animal fell back, his legs buckling. He half turned, as if to run, but Bingo's lance, still twirling above his head, struck the Rumble again and he fell to his knees. Then Bingo, slipping his grasp along the haft of his spear so that he could hold it like a sword, leapt upon the swaying figure of his enemy and bore him to the ground, and the four inches of steel found the warrior's heart.

The fire crackled in the room and the Rumbles groaned, hope gone with their greatest Warrior slain. The smoke swirled redder and redder in the draught between the door and the open ventilation shaft. Napoleon twisted his head and saw that his comrade, who he had imagined dead, was in fact rising from the prostrate body of the Rumble. Bingo swayed, his face was grimy and his clothes were torn. Blood was pouring down his left arm and down the side of his face where the Rumble spear had grazed his head, taken off his hat and cut his pointed ear. He was a sorry sight, blackened by soot, smoke and sweat.

"Are you all right?" called the Wendle, not taking his eyes from the Rumbles who stood motionless and saddened.

"Yes," lied Bingo, "fine, but I think we've outstayed our welcome."

Napoleon did not reply but went over to the body of the Rumble, removed the sash and placed it over Bingo's shoulders.

"There, Bingo," he said with a smile, "when you get home you can hang it on the wall and write underneath, 'Souvenir of Happy Days in Rumbledom'."

Bingo looked down at the trophy. "Here," he said proudly, "I've got my name. I hope everyone else has. . . ."

They backed slowly up the mountainous pile of books, and the Rumbles made no attempt to stop them; they were leaderless and weaponless for the time being.

The danger would come when the two Borribles mounted the ladder and the Rumbles could charge forward and repossess the lances they had thrown earlier. They would be able to pick the Borribles off as they climbed, or, more likely, they would overturn the ladder and spike their falling enemies on the raised barbs of their spears.

At the bottom of the ladder Napoleon and Bingo considered their situation. "Best thing would be to have one of us at the top first," said Bingo, "then he can cover the other while he climbs."

The Battersea Borrible had been greatly weakened by his battle and Napoleon could see that he was in no condition to sustain another fight should the need arise, so he sent Bingo to the top of the ladder first.

Bingo climbed slowly, like an injured snail. His head ached and there was only a faint grip left in his hands. The hole in the ceiling seemed to get no nearer but he went on, taking care all the way. A fall from that height would be fatal. Looking down on the Library he saw a scene of chaos. The great bookcases were cast down and the once carefully classified books were strewn across the floor or had been built into redoubts by the Rumbles. The smoke was dense and lay across the floor in dirty wraiths and had crept up the walls towards the ventilation shaft. Bingo could see, from his high vantage point, scores of Rumbles looking at him from their barricades and from under the tables in the little alcoves. Their snouts were pointed upwards, greedily twitching for his blood. All that held them in check was the steady gaze of Napoleon Boot.

When Bingo neared the opening in the ceiling he stopped climbing and shoved his left arm over and under a rung. He took his catapult from his back pocket with his right hand, loaded a stone and stretched the thick black rubber, ready to fire at any Rumble that moved.

"All right, Nap," he called and the Wendle, with a last threatening look around the room, began to climb, fast, his catapult between his teeth. He had climbed barely a dozen rungs when there was a commotion in the corridor leading to the Library. Rumble Warriors, sent on the errand by their Chief, were returning, their arms loaded with lances. Their companions in the Library aroused themselves and emerged from their hiding-places and surged towards the ladder, calling loudly for vengeance.

Bingo shot his catapult as rapidly as he could, but hanging by one arm made it tedious work, and he was becoming terribly feeble. Rumbles were near to Napoleon now and lances struck the ladder by the Wendle's hands, one took a chunk of flesh from his leg. He slipped and almost fell. The Rumbles shouted but Napoleon gritted his teeth and pulled his body upwards even faster, and Bingo fired his catapult past his friend's head and broke many a Rumble's skull with stones from the banks of the Bluegate Gravel Pit.

But at last Bingo was forced to retreat into the ventilation shaft in order to give Napoleon a clear run through the trap. No longer worried by missiles from above, the Rumbles swarmed forward and they seized the ladder and yanked at it. The ladder shook and trembled and began to tilt, and it seemed that Napoleon would soon fall onto the deadly spearheads below. Bingo seized the top rung and pulled against the dozen or so Rumbles who were tugging with might and main from the Library floor, but, as Napoleon had said earlier, gravity was a force to be reckoned with and now it was on the side of the Rumbles.

Inside the shaft Bingo struggled and swore, bumping his head and knocking his wounds till the blood ran. Napoleon scurried upwards, hand over hand, not looking at the shining spears beneath him.

When the Wendle was a few rungs only from safety,

the exhausted Bingo was almost lugged out of the shaft by a violent heave on the part of the Rumbles. Bingo managed to hold fast but he was now protruding, half in and half out of the trap-door. He wrestled with the ladder which was gyrating resolutely in an effort to shake Napoleon into space. A great shout went up from the Rumbles and the Wendle only stuck to the ladder by clinging with legs and arms together, but he still found time to spit directly downwards.

"You cross-eyed bunch of weasels," he yelled. "You swivel-eyed moles."

The Rumbles only pulled the harder, determined to drag the wretched Bingo back into the Library. The top rung was torn from his bleeding hands and Napoleon seemed about to sway away from his friend for ever. But Bingo held his arms out to Napoleon and, as the Rumbles threw the ladder down with a fearsome roar, the Wendle thrust his feet into space, floated on air for a split second and then grabbed Bingo's right arm with both his hands. He swung there, lances falling about him, and he looked up into the pained and desperate face of his fellow Adventurer.

"Don't faint now, Bingo," he cried. "I'll be skewered up like a pork joint if you do."

Bingo slipped and slithered in the narrow space, lucky that it was so narrow. Had the shaft been any wider the weight of Napoleon, dangling and trying to work his way up to the lip of the trapdoor, would have pulled them both down. Bingo wedged himself across the opening and, although the pain pierced his shoulder terribly, he allowed Napoleon to climb up his arm. When the Wendle had one hand on the trap-door Bingo shifted his grip a fraction and hauled Napoleon up and in and they fell together in a heap.

It took a long while for them to recover. They gulped deep breaths, though each lungful had more smoke than air in it, and they coughed and retched in dreadful spasms. At last Napoleon got to his hands and knees and peered cautiously from the hole. A dozen or so of the Rumbles were grappling with the ladder, attempting to get it upright. Others raced from the fiercely burning Library, instructing their comrades to run from room to room and along the corridors to guard against the escape of the two Borribles.

Napoleon roused the flagging Bingo. "Come on," he said tenderly, the first time that Bingo, or anyone else, had heard him talk in such a manner. "We've got to get you out of here."

"You'd better leave me," said Bingo, raising his head with an effort. "I can knock them off the top of the ladder as they come up. Give you time to get away."

"I'm not leaving you anywhere," said Napoleon firmly, "and I don't like it here, the air's bad. All you've got to do is crawl."

Bingo got to his hands and knees. "All right, I'll have a go. Which way?"

That was a problem. The shaft stretched away darkly on either side of the trap-door. Which way lay safety, if at all, they could not guess.

"Let's go the way the smoke is going," suggested Napoleon, "it might lead us out. If it don't, we'll suffocate."

So, coughing and spitting, their eyes smarting and running with tears, they moved along the metal tunnel, banging their heads from side to side, like ping-pong balls in a drainpipe.

Torreycanyon leant back against the armoured car and felt pleased with himself. He had caused enough mayhem to account for three adventures. The engine of the armoured car lay smashed to smithereens by the blows of an iron bar he had found amongst the tools. He had emptied dozens of petrol cans all over the workshops, saturating the work-benches and the shelves where the tools and spare parts were kept. Into the petrol tank of the car he had lowered a long length of rag and the petrol had soaked its way up and out. All he needed was a match and the whole place would go up like a bonfire and retard the Rumble war effort by a dozen years. But a match he did not have, his box must have fallen from his pocket somewhere.

During his work he had been interrupted by the Rumbles many times. The Warriors had forced the door and chivvied him back along the workshop with their lances, but Torreycanyon had taken a lid from a dustbin and used it as a shield. Not one lance had hit him, though he was cut in several places from near misses. He had defended himself like a lion in the garage area, just in front of the armoured car, and had beaten off many attacks. Scores of unconscious Rumbles littered the battle ground, others had crawled away to lick their wounds. Torreycanyon was almost content, all he wanted was one match so that he could add to the smoke that had drifted to him from the fires in the kitchens and in the Library.

He leant against the car, liking the solidity of it behind him. He was tired. Twenty yards away stood the Rumble Warriors, waiting for help, and more spears. It was only a question of time before they wore him out and captured or killed him, but all he could think of was his match; he wanted to go out blazing, like a firework. One match to that rag in the car and a touch of it to the floor and fire would spurt down the workshops quicker than a Borrible could run. He wouldn't care what happened to him then; perhaps he would be able to get away through the garage door. There was a red button marked, "Push once", but there might be more Rumbles on the outside, waiting. It would be dawn over Rumbledom, he reckoned; time to be going.

"One of you Rumbles nip off and get a match, will you? I want to pick my teeth." He leant on his iron bar and shifted the grip on the dustbin lid. He laughed aloud at his own stupidity. He hoped the others were safe out of it by now and not wasting time by joking with the enemy.

A sudden noise above his head made him spring into action. So that was why the Rumbles had been so quiet, they'd found a way to outflank him through the roof. If they came at him from two directions at once he wouldn't last long. He clambered onto the car and looked closely at the ceiling. A square flap was being lifted away. Torreycanyon glanced at the group of Rumbles standing by the workshop entrance. They hadn't moved. He swung the iron bar over his shoulder; if any Rumble put so much as a snout through the trap-door, he would swipe it flatter than a dead cat on a motorway.

The trap-door lifted and a hand appeared and took a grip on the underside and pulled it open to reveal a black hole from which thick smoke drifted. There was a coughing and spitting from the shaft and somebody was taking in large gulps of air. Torreycanyon prepared to strike.

"I'll give you cough and spit, you myxomatosed rabbit," he said, "you snouty old stoat."

The hand came out again and Torreycanyon lowered the bar. It was a small human hand, not a paw at all. On the other end of that hand must be a Borrible.

A begrimed and bloody face appeared. Its red-rimmed eyes blinked and the mouth was open, taking in as much air as it could, and then, very nearly suffocated and lifeless, the small body of Bingo flopped out like a filleted fish, and fell into Torreycanyon's arms.

Torreycanyon placed his comrade on one of the seats of the car and looked at the enemy. They were sidling nearer, so with a mighty and blood-curdling bellow he threw his iron bar and it skeetered and bounced across the concrete, sweeping the Rumbles' legs from underneath them. They retreated; they had had enough of this mad Borrible, and they did not want to take him on again until he was dropping with fatigue.

Bingo fluttered his eyelids and looked up. "Oh, Torrey," he groaned, "I'm so glad it's you. I couldn't go a step further, my knees are worn raw and my lungs feel like two smoked haddocks." And poor Bingo started coughing again.

There was another scrabbling noise above Torreycanyon's head and he drew his catapult and seized a stone from Bingo's bandolier. But he saw another hand and the head of Napoleon Boot soon followed it. He was in no better state than Bingo. His eyes were streaming and cuts from a dozen lance wounds had covered him in blood which in turn was covered in grime and grease and soot. His clothes were torn all over and his scuffed knees stuck out through large holes in his trousers. Torreycanyon helped him down and rested him on a seat alongside Bingo.

"Looks like you done all the fighting yourselves," said Torreycanyon, "and you're going to have some more to do, soon as you get your breath back."

Napoleon said nothing but lay gasping. Bingo, breathing a little easier, raised himself to a sitting position and looked over the twenty yards of body-strewn no-man's land to where the Rumbles stood.

"What are they waiting for, Torrey?" he asked.

"More ammo and more friends," answered Torreycanyon. "They've gone right off me."

"Have you any kind of a plan?" asked Bingo, a little dazed.

"Not half," said Torreycanyon. "'Get out!" And in answer to Bingo's puzzled shake of the head he said, "There's a garage door here but I don't know if it opens; I suppose so. The trouble is I don't know what's on the other side. More Rumbles most like. It must be daylight, you know—very dodgy."

"It's the only chance we've got," said Napoleon, coming to himself and standing up, although he staggered violently. "There's no point in going back into the shaft, that would be certain death."

"Well, in that case," said Torreycanyon, "watch the bunnies while I get down and try the door. If they move, let them have it with your catapults. You're lucky to have a stone or two left, I haven't."

He jumped down onto the floor of the garage near to the huge sliding door. He approached the red button, licked his lips and looked at it as if trying to cast a spell. As his hand hovered in the air he turned suddenly to look up at Bingo and Napoleon.

"Here," he said sharply, "either of you Borribles got a match?"

Knocker stumbled on down the Great Door corridor, the weight of the box of money boring deep into his back. His muscles ached, the sweat poured from underneath his Borrible hat and down into his eyes, and the pungent smoke chafed at his lungs. Orococco led the way, scouting round every bend and corner and beckoning the others on. Vulge limped and staggered behind, supported by Adolf when the German was not fighting a rearguard action against the Rumbles who followed along the tunnel. When the lights went out they could feel their enemies come nearer and strike at them in the dark with the sharp points of their lances. Furry bodies brushed past and tried to separate them and bring them down, but they kept together and counter-attacked with such ferocity that the Rumbles suffered many casualties.

Without warning, Orococco stopped at a sharp bend in the tunnel and beckoned to Knocker. What Knocker saw made him drop his precious box and bound forward. About twenty yards further along the tunnel Sydney and Chalotte stood ringed by enemy warriors. They were backed into a kind of alcove in the corridor and a circle of steel-pointed lances held them in check. Their bandoliers were empty and they were fighting with captured Rumble-sticks against ten of their enemies and were obviously on their last legs. Their hats were gone and their hair was grimy with soot, hanging in stiffened strands over their lined faces. Chalotte's lance was broken and she used it like a dagger, flailing it about with a desperate fury.

Orococco and Knocker arrived together on the scene and struck the Rumbles from behind with lances they had scooped from the floor. They yelled and they shouted and the Rumbles fled into a side tunnel, thinking that the whole Borrible nation was at their heels. Three of their number lay on the ground and would fight no more.

Chalotte and Sydney leant against the wall and wiped the sweat from their eyes.

"One minute later would have been one minute too late," said Chalotte, breathless and shaking.

"I thought I'd never see the sky again," said Sydney. "How many of us left?"

"Just us," said Knocker, "and we aren't in good shape. The others have probably had it."

"Let's get on," said Adolf. "There's as many Rumbles behind as in front."

Sydney took up the rearguard with the German, Chalotte marched up front with Orococco and the little procession moved on, fighting its way slowly towards the Great Door. Rumbles came thick and fast from the side tunnels as soon as the Borribles had passed and crowded along behind, just waiting for a favourable moment to attack. What lay ahead the Borribles dared not imagine. Even if Stonks was still guarding the way out there would be hundreds of Rumbles, all well armed, lying in ambush for them in the cold green grass of Rumbledom.

At last they came to one of the brick barriers that Stonks had built just inside the Great Door when he had captured it. Nothing of the barrier could be seen now. Most of it had been trampled and beaten down in some great fight. What remained was covered with the bodies of fallen Rumbles, piled one upon the other and reaching halfway to the roof of the tunnel. It was strangely quiet too and the Borribles stopped a few yards from the battlefield. Nothing moved before them and they looked at each other with wonder.

"I wonder if Stonksie is under that lot?" said Chalotte.

"He couldn't possibly have survived," said Knocker, dropping his box again. "He must have seen off hundreds of Rumbles. What an artist!"

"Well they don't look exactly lively," said Orococco, "so perhaps there isn't one between here and the door."

At that moment an enormous Rumble bounded over the broken barricade and scrambled towards them. He had a spear in each hand and hallooed and shouted in a muffled way.

"Anyone got any stones?" asked Knocker urgently, drawing his useless catapult. There was no answer.

"Those with spears up front," said Knocker, throwing the lance he held at the oncoming monster. He grabbed another spear from the floor and formed a line with Orococco and Chalotte. The great shambling Rumble came on with a strange lolloping gait. He was the largest they had ever seen and probably the strongest. Perhaps, thought Knocker, Stonks had done for these Rumbles they saw about them, and then this powerful creature had taken him from behind as he fought in the tunnel. But whatever had happened the mighty shape still bore down on them, fearlessly, gleefully.

At some distance from the line of Borribles, the giant Rumble stopped and waved the spears in his hands and danced from one foot to the other, then he turned in a circle and shouted happily. The muffled voice became a little clearer.

"A Borrible, a Borrible," shouted the Rumble. "Don't worry, it's me, Stonks. Stonks, you fools, I've kept the Great Door, oh, come on."

"Careful," said Knocker, "it must be a trick."

"It's no trick, Knocker," said the shaggy figure. "Look." And the great Rumble threw down his two spears and lifting two hands—and they were hands—reached behind his neck and fiddled with something. Then the hands got hold of the snout and pulled hard and the whole furry cloak fell away to reveal none other than Stonks, the Borrible. "There," he cried, dancing some more, "it's only me."

Astonished, the Borribles lowered their weapons and crowded up to their friend, all of them asking questions at once.

"Take it easy," said Stonks, delighted by their amazement. "I'll explain."

And he told them how he had captured the door with the sapling trick and they liked that. And how Torreycanyon had gone off into the tunnels alone while he, Stonks, thought it a good idea to stay and guard the door to secure a line of retreat, but before he did, he'd gone to find the Rumble door-keeper to make sure that he didn't recover and come back again. When he'd gone about three hundred yards he'd found the remains of the door-keeper all right but all that he could discover was the Rumble's skin. "A big coat with nothing inside, can't imagine what happened to the rest of him," he said to the others. "Perhaps there isn't anything inside them, who knows?" Anyway it had seemed to Stonks that it might help his defence of the Great Door, at least for a while, if he pretended to be a Rumble, and so he had donned the skin and it had worked very well, as they could see by the numbers of Rumbles lying about.

"I got so used to wearing the skin," continued

Stonks, "that I forgot I had it on when you lot appeared. It was only when Knocker threw his sticker at me that I remembered. Anyway the door's in our possession, but I should think there's twenty Rumble Brigades on the other side of it."

Weary as they were the Borribles congratulated Stonks and patted him on the back and laughed again and again at his tale. Though their position was hopeless, it certainly helped to be told a cheerful story. Even Vulge limped forward, leant against the wall, wagged his head till it nearly fell off, and said, "Take the skin home and use it as a mat. It will look like one of those tiger rugs they have in posh houses sometimes."

They marched on over the barricades that Stonks had defended so valiantly and with so much cunning and came at last to the Great Door. Here they rested for a while and took stock of their situation. Behind the nearest barricade were gathering the hordes of Rumbles who had snuffled along behind them in the tunnels. They did not attack for they did not have to. They knew that sooner or later the Borribles would have to open the door and the Rumbles also knew that on the other side were hundreds more of their Warriors from other Bunkers, fresh and eager to fight. The Borribles would be caught between two fires and one by one they would perish, or be captured. Then would the Rumbles take their revenge. Knocker looked at his sorry and exhausted band. All of them were wounded to some degree, most of them had dried blood mixed into the dirt of their faces. There was no ammunition left for their catapults, so there was no chance of them carving their way through the Rumbles with well-aimed stones. They had as many lances as they could carry, for lances covered the floor all around the Great Door where Stonks had fought. But a lance could be thrown but once, or used at close quarters, and at close quarters they would be swamped by the sheer weight of numbers and they would be captured alive. Knocker shuddered to think what would happen to them. Furthermore, they had no food and nothing to drink. The longer they stayed where they were the weaker they would become. Their plight was grim.

From beyond the barricade the red eyes of the Rumbles watched, glowing, burning into the Borribles, hating them and yearning for their deaths. They began a low chant which rose louder and louder and was taken up by hundreds more beyond them, pouring down the tunnels, united and organised now for the final battle.

"Bite up the Bowwibles," they chanted. "Bite up the Bowwibles." And then there came a beating on the door and it trembled in its frame and the same chant was taken up outside and the door was smashed regularly now with some kind of battering ram, probably an old tree trunk rolled in from the fields of Rumbledom.

"Rest until they batter down the door," said Knocker, "then we'll have to fight."

"Well," said Vulge who was a little more rested and whose wound had been bound up again by Adolf. "At least we did it. We've taken five of their names—probably the whole eight, if we could hear the others tell their stories."

"Torreycanyon, Bingo and Napoleon," said Stonks. "I hope they're all right."

"Well, man," said Orococco, "we never expected to get right through the Adventure without losing someone."

The thumping on the door continued.

"It looks like we're going to lose everyone," said Vulge, leaning against the wall and feeling his shoulder with stiff fingers.

"Isn't it funny," said Chalotte, she was sitting on the floor with her legs stretched out in front of her, "isn't it funny, only a little while ago, we were doing our best to get into this place. Now we're inside and they are bashing the door down to get at us. Things do change round, don't they?"

The Great Door was beginning to loosen on its massive hinges; it wouldn't be long now before the door fell open and Rumbles mustered around the entrance to throw in their lances. The Borribles would have to fight back to back until they fell.

It was decided that Stonks and Knocker and Chalotte would defend the door while Adolf, Sydney and Orococco would man the barricade. Vulge would keep them supplied with weapons, lances or bricks. They all decided not be taken alive, to endure the ignominy of capture, to be beaten, tortured perhaps, and worked to death as slaves with their ears clipped.

At length, when the door could stand no more attacks, Stonks quickly slid the bolts and undid the lock. The next blow from the battering ram encountered no resistance and the door toppled to the ground and six Rumbles and a tree-trunk fell through the opening. Three Borribles, sprang upon them with lances and dispatched them before they could rise. So far so good, but looking beyond the doorway they saw a sight to shrink the heart of the bravest Borrible.

Dawn, grey and bleak, had spread across the dark green wetness of Rumbledom. The trees were black and leafless and their branches stirred roughly in a gusty and damp wind. Rain fell heavily and swirled in the stormy air like shreds of cloud come down to earth, but it was not the weather that caught Knocker's eye as he looked out. As far as he could see, across the foul morning, stood rank upon serried rank of Rumbles, the steel of their lances reflecting the cold light. They stood there, compact and unmoving, their fur plastered to their bodies by the rain, their snouts raised to a warlike angle. They neither shouted nor shook their weapons. They waited patiently for the Borribles to emerge and meet their end.

The Rumble troops were formed into sections, and as the battering-ram detail was conquered, the first section detached itself from the mass of the army and moved forward to attack the Great Door. Beyond them every Rumble was ready to advance, determined to win this battle, however pluckily the Borribles fought, and however long it might take.

Knocker swallowed hard, the biggest lump he'd ever swallowed.

"Swipe me," he said to Stonks. "Rumbles for ever, and all armed."

"Tonight's 'Goodnight', all right," said Stonks. "They've brought all their aunts and uncles this time."

The first Rumble section was within range now and it threw its missiles and retired. Another section ran forward immediately and threw their stickers. Knocker, Stonks and Chalotte pressed their bodies up against the side of the door and waited until the lances fell, then they ran out and cast two spears each at the departing warriors. Many of the enemy perished, but the Rumbles could ignore these reverses, the next platoon was already speeding forward, their lances poised. With their advantage in numbers, the Rumbles could fight in this fashion for days, if need be; eventually the spears would take their toll and the defenders would be wounded and weakened. Then would the Rumbles sweep over them.

The Borribles retreated and took cover. Behind him Knocker could hear Adolf and Orococco and Sydney fighting for their lives; he saw the injured Vulge hobbling backwards and forwards between the two groups, gathering up as many lances as he could. On and on the battle raged, and more and more exhausted the Borribles became and still the Rumbles attacked. Before long all the defenders had been wounded at least superficially and Stonks received a lance thrust full in his thigh, and could no longer run in and out of the

door, but threw his spears from the shelter of the hallway.

"Oh, for some stones," he kept muttering. "Oh, for
a pile of stones as bag as a house. I'd soon have my
catapult twanging away like a banjo."

The Rumbles were nearer now. Their Warriors did
not even bother to charge section by section, but stood
their ground, throwing lances until they were
wounded. Then another Rumble would step forward to
take his fallen comrade's place. They fought with a
silent hatred, and they did not lack courage. Knocker's
arm was weary; he knew at last that he could not lift
another spear, let alone throw it with any force.

"Knives out, lads," he said, and he and Stonks and
Chalotte retreated into the hallway and found themselves back to back with Adolf, Sydney and Orococco.
Beyond them Knocker saw hundreds of Rumbles,
pushed along the corridor from behind by their blood-
thirsty mates.

Vulge wedged himself into a little corner and wiped
the long blade of his knife across his sleeve. "I like close
work," he said and winced as the pain surged through
his shoulder.

Then the Rumbles were all amongst them and there
was a dreadful scrimmage in the hallway, but the attackers were not used to the kind of frenzied resistance
put up by the desperate Borribles and under the cut
and thrust of the knives they fell back momentarily.

"Oh, ho," yelled Adolf at the top of his voice. "This
is cold steel and too close for comfort, eh? Adolf Wolfgang Amadeus Winston will account for at least a
hundred of you. Come on! Come on!" And he shouted
and hooted and the others shouted and hooted with
him, although their muscles ached and their eyelids
smarted and the blood ran down their arms and legs
from a thousand cuts.

But the Rumbles did not come again. Outside, where

there had been a calm and cool dedication, was now all panic and shouts for help. Simultaneously, from the corridors came a surging waft of heavy air, followed by the muffled crump of a great explosion deep in the Bunker. A sheet of flame licked out of the tunnel, killing all that stood in its way. It touched but did not burn the battle-weary Borribles, but the blast of a solid wave of gas raised them from their feet and tossed them violently to the floor. The Rumbles in the Bunker had been silenced and the smell of singed fur and flesh floated over everything.

Stonks recovered first and getting to his hands and knees he crawled to the door. The Rumbles were still outside but a mighty swathe had been cut right through their ranks and the thing that had cut that swathe was a horse and cart. Sam was charging right through the massed Rumbles, and their fear of horses, their loathing of being munched up like a succulent truss of hay, had overcome their hatred of the Borribles and they had fallen back in panic.

"It's Sam," shouted Stonks to the others. "It's good old Sam."

Who knows what goes through the mind of a horse when he is left alone and is not working? Sam had spent the night dozing between the shafts of his cart and, when he had woken in the morning, he had missed the company and affection of the Borribles who had befriended him. There had not been a great deal of love in his life, none at all with Dewdrop, and he did not want to lose his new friends. He had munched a little grass but had found it dull and boring after the delicate flavour of the Rumble he had eaten, so he had pulled his cart to the edge of the copse and there he had gazed wistfully over the dank fields and sniffed. He hadn't smelt Borrible or even adult human but he had smelt Rumble. Sam had been tempted and had set off over the grass, he couldn't resist it. The smell had been so strong that he had imagined a whole meadow full of Rumbles and his imagination had been right. He saw the Rumbles, thousands of them, and with a snort and a stamp he had charged; the cart behind him had felt as nothing and the Rumbles melted away on his right and left. Then he heard a voice he recognised calling his name, calling it with thankfulness and love. Then more voices called out, and looking before him he saw his friends, penned into some kind of a hole set in the hillside, and all that lay between him and those friends were a few hundred Rumbles, so he charged again.

Knocker and the others crawled and dragged themselves to the edge of the Great Door and they saw a great clear road leading to the horizon. Sam came galloping down the slope and swung the cart round so it skidded to a halt alongside the doorway in a cloud of rain-spray.

"Oh," cried Sydney, tears of relief standing in her eyes. She ran to the horse and kissed him. "Good old Sam, you've saved us, all of us. Oh, Sam."

As quickly as they could the Borribles clambered into the cart. Vulge was pushed from below and pulled from above because his wounds had stiffened so much that he could not climb the cartwheels unaided. Everyone was eager to get Sam on the move and escape to the streets; everyone that was except Knocker, who, with unbelievable single-mindedness, returned through the Great Door to retrieve the Rumble treasure box.

It was a foolhardy move. Smoke poured from the opening and the huge door-jambs were wilting and twisting under the effect of the immense heat. Once inside, Knocker found that the hallway was an inferno of flaming and falling timber; scorched bricks expanded and exploded from the walls like cannon shot. The Bunker ceiling dropped more every second as the whole Rumble edifice began to collapse, but Knocker heeded none of that and ran on, risking his life to get at the money.

Adolf and Orococco, against their better judgement, followed, not for the treasure, but to help Knocker if they could, for, in spite of his faults, they loved the chief lookout and were willing to risk their lives to save him.

Knocker came to the box all right, but he found it almost buried in fiery rafters and white-hot bricks. When he had kicked the box clear of debris, he discovered that it was incandescent, defiantly red and burning with a dangerous light. The handles were hot to the touch and the box itself would burn the skin of whoever tried to carry it, but Knocker grasped it and hauled the dreadful burden to his shoulders. The handle seared deep into the flesh of his palms and the brass-bound corners of the box smouldered through his clothing and down into his back. He staggered and slipped and Adolf caught him up and showed him on towards the doorway that Knocker could not see in his pain.

Orococco yelled, "Over here, Knocker, damn you!" Then, "Watch out, Adolf!"

The warning came too late. A dying Rumble had risen to his knees unnoticed, and with a sticker in his grasp he fell against Adolf and brought him down. The German scrambled to his feet immediately, though the spear had snapped off in his right thigh. *"Verdammt,"* he cried in agony and he pulled the broken shaft from his leg, kicked the Rumble in the head and killed him once and for all.

Orococco hurled Knocker from his path and ran towards the German who, blinded by the billowing smoke, was limping away into the heart of the fire.

"Adolf," he shouted, his heart breaking, "this way."

It was then that the ceiling of the hallway of the Great Door collapsed. With a roar like an avalanche the great red-hot timbers fell, bringing with them a lethal barrage of blazing stone. A molten, glowing wall reared up between Orococco and Adolf and the brave Totter was forced out of the smoking Rumble halls, his clothes aflame, his hair burning like a torch. Adolf was gone; lost in the heart of a volcano.

Once outside Orococco threw himself down and rolled over and over. Sydney jumped to the ground and beat him about the head to extinguish the flames that might have killed him. She helped him to his feet and he saw that Knocker, with the strength of a madman, was pushing the box up and into the cart. Chalotte leant over him, bashing as his smoking shoulders with the flat of her hand. An angry shout went up from the Rumbles. They had seen the box, and a shower of lances came over, some wounding the horse and making him lurch in the traces. Sydney and Orococco ran forward and, catching hold of the pain-crazed Knocker, they propelled him angrily aboard. Then Stonks stretched out a hand and helped them as they climbed up the spokes of the wheel.

"Where's Adolf?" screamed Chalotte. "Where's Adolf?"

"He's had it," said Orococco, his face tight with anguish. "The roof came down. I couldn't get to him. There's nothing we can do; we'll have to go. Nothing could live in there, nothing."

"You mean Adolf's been killed all because of a bloody box?" said Stonks. "What the hell's in it, anyway?"

Knocker jumped to his feet. "It's the Rumble treasure," he shouted, his eyes shining strangely with pain and something else. "It's money."

The others looked at him in horror and they knew then that Knocker had had a mission all along and hadn't told them; that Spiff had sent him to steal this treasure and take it home—and that for Knocker nothing else mattered.

"It is a bad thing, that box," cried Chalotte, "it has

killed Adolf and will kill more of us. It's bad luck; throw it overboard."

"Yes," said Orococco, "that is enough. The Rumbles might let us go easier if they see we leave the money. We've done what we came to do. Let's get off while we still have a chance."

"No," roared Knocker, his hand falling to the bloody knife at his belt. He looked wild, his hat was gone and his hair swung over his eyes. "You've all got your names, but I will get a second one if I can get the box back to Battersea. It's going with me, I tell you, and I'll kill anyone who tries to stop me." And to put an end to the argument he picked up a stone from the bottom of the cart and threw it hard at Sam's hind-quarters and, with no need for guidance, the brave horse bore the Adventurers away from the shattered remains of the Great Door.

The Rumbles had been terrified by the precipitate arrival of Sam and his cart and had retreated in panic, but when they saw the treasure carried from the Bunker they were roused to action and advanced en masse to prevent, even now, the escape of the Borribles.

They were wary of approaching the horse from the front but they did not scruple to run at the cart from the side and throw their lances with all the strength they could muster. The bravest of them ran alongside and tried desperately to climb on board, and some threw lances at Sam, hoping to wound him, to injure a leg or a hoof. But things had changed in favour of the Borribles. Inside the cart were the hundreds of stones they had loaded earlier, and this godsend was nearly as important as the arrival of Sam himself. Now the Borribles took out their catapults to fire broadsides of stones with telling effect and the Rumbles, though attacking constantly, were forced back to a respectful distance.

Sam pulled the cart along by the side of the hill that

covered the Bunker. The ground pitched and rolled beneath his hooves, as explosions and fires continued to devastate the Rumble stronghold. A hundred plumes of yellow smoke were hanging foul against the sky, mis-shapen and forlorn, like the clouds of burning dust above a hundred London crematoria. The heart of the Rumbledom empire had been consumed by a mysterious detonation and it would be many years before it could be repaired and rebuilt.

Sam headed into the dense mass of Warriors and they brandished their spears in fury. One slip from the horse under the onslaught of those flying lances and the escape would be over.

"Keep going, Sam," prayed Knocker, "as fast as you can."

But Sam veered suddenly, so violently as almost to tip the Borribles overboard.

"Hey, what's going on?" shouted Stonks.

"I don't know," cried Knocker, "it's Sam. . . ." He broke off and stood up in the driver's seat. "Look, look," he yelled, "over there."

Over there was back towards the hill they had just left with such difficulty and danger and Sam, for good reasons of his own, had decided to turn in that direction.

"Now, we're really in the cart," said Orococco.

There was a shout from the Rumbles and they too looked back towards the Bunker and then they ran to intercept the Borribles for they had seen a chance of victory. On the edge of the hillside, in the centre of an embattled gateway, at the very core of the explosions, three figures had appeared, silhouetted against high flames that leapt and danced behind them. Unless they were rescued within a minute or two, Torreycanyon, Bingo and Napoleon would be forced to retreat into the fire or die on the spears of the enraged Rumbles.

Knocker urged Sam to a gallop. "Oh, come on, Sam,"

he pleaded. "Oh, Sam, run, run, or we'll be too late. No more to die, not now, not now!"

The horse galloped on and the Borribles crowded to the front of the lurching cart, firing forwards and sideways to keep their enemies beyond lance range of the horse. Sam neighed as loudly as he could and the Rumbles fell back in dismay under his second onslaught, robbed yet again of the Borrible blood they had hoped to spill.

When Sam skidded and slid to a halt before the burning garage only Torreycanyon was able to get into the cart without help. Bingo and Napoleon, weakened by the wounds they had sustained in the Library, and their insides demolished by the near-suffocation of their trip along the ventilation shaft, had to be man-handled aboard. The fell into senseless heaps over the unconscious form of Vulge, and they knew nothing more until several hours later.

Knocker wheeled the fearless horse about once more to face the enemy troops, but courage was deserting the Rumbles. They knew now that their High Command had gone and there was no real cohesion in their ranks. Their principal Bunker had been completely ruined and was in flames about their ears. The workshops, the armoured car, the laboratories, the Library, the kitchens, the dormitories—the whole structure had been dismantled and their best warriors killed, slain in single combat or vanquished by stealth and cunning. They had tried everything and they had fought well but they had perished beneath wheels and hooves or they had been struck down by the unerring aim of the Borrible catapults. Demoralized, they fell back, and though they kept pace with the cart they kept well out of range and their numbers thinned as Sam cantered to the very confines of Rumbledom and to the main road that bounded it.

Sam halted. It was rush hour on a cold, wintry morning. The cars and buses zipped along the wet road, sending up a fine spray over the Borribles. Not one adult could be seen walking anywhere and no one seemed to have noticed the great battle. The Borribles gathered at the end of the cart and held on to the tailboard; even Knocker left his seat and came back to look. There in the falling mist and swirling rain stood several hundred Rumbles, leaning despondently on their spears. They could come no further; in the streets they would be recognised and caught. The Borribles had eluded them, sorely wounded it was true, but still they had escaped. Now the Rumbles would have to return to their shattered Bunker and salvage what they could.

The Borribles did not cheer, did not wave their catapults aloft, they simply watched as the Rumbles turned slowly and melted away between gorse bushes and trees, or went down into the hollows or up over the hillsides, until there was nothing to be seen but the blue-grey rain blurring the outlines of the black and green of Rumbledom. There might never have been a Rumble on the face of the earth and sadness filled the hearts of the victorious Borribles.

"Oh," sighed Chalotte, blinking, "I wish there'd been some other way."

"Maybe there was, maybe there wasn't," said Torreycanyon. "One thing is sure, once we got in there, we had to fight like the clappers to get out. They ain't so soft."

The moment of reflection was ended by Sam who saw a gap in the traffic and set off across Parkside and passed into Queensmere. The Borribles were heading into the broad calm of the residential area where Dewdrop had taken them stealing. They were safe from Rumbles now, but if the bodies of Dewdrop and his son had been found, the police would be looking hard for them, and of course, Sam.

Chapter 9

Knocker sat on the driving seat wrapped in Dewdrop's old mac. To the adult eye he looked a little short to be driving a horse but it was raining heavily and those few people who were moving in the streets ran by with their heads down. The other Adventurers had strung the canvas over the cart like a tent and in its shelter they were tending to each others' wounds and eating their provisions.

It was wonderful to lie down and ease the pain in the limbs and allow a colleague to cleanse one's wounds. They all took a turn and eventually Knocker left his seat and was replaced by Stonks, and Knocker had something to eat and lay back while Chalotte bound the gashes in his arms and legs and bandaged the burns on his shoulders and hands.

"These are bad wounds," she said. "You are a fool, you worried about the money when you could have escaped—and worse—Adolf is lost because of it."

Knocker did not answer. It was warm and dry under the canvas and the movement of the cart lulled the Borribles into a deep sleep. Napoleon and Bingo and Vulge had been cleaned up and fed but had hardly opened their eyes during the process and were now unconscious again. Sydney was keeping watch out of the back of the cart, but she too was so tired that Knocker could see her head dropping forward, as if it were going to fall off at any moment.

Torreycanyon was recounting his adventure to Orococco, who closed his eyes every five seconds, and Torreycanyon, who felt "fresh as a Rumbledom daisy", stopped talking and allowed the Totter to doze.

Sydney turned and said, "Torrey, if you're so fresh,

you come and keep watch and let me go to sleep, too."

Knocker waited. When it became silent inside the cart he turned his attention to the Rumble treasure box and touched it with an injured hand. It was sooty and still warm. Quietly, taking care not to awaken anyone, he shoved the box to the side of the cart behind him and disguised its appearance with a piece of old canvas and some discarded clothing. Then he leant his back against it so that no one could move it without his knowing.

He tried to keep awake, to guard the box and to relive the events of the past hours, but his head fell onto his chest and the horse plodded through the rain. Sam went calmly along the edge of the traffic, across by Augustus and over by the railway station of Southfields, down Replingham and past the opening to Engadine where they had been attacked and forced into the clutches of Dewdrop and Erbie. And all the Borribles slept, even Torreycanyon who should have been on watch, and even Stonks who should have been guiding Sam, but Sam paced on without need of command. He had heard talk of the Wandle and of King George's Park so that was where he went. He knew London as well as any horse, and he stepped out evenly for he realised the Borribles were exhausted. He halted gently by the traffic lights and paid particular attention when changing lanes and crossing roundabouts. He trudged on and on and Stonks snored in the driving seat and the others dreamed behind, at the mercy of chance. But luck stayed with them and the rain continued to fall in heavy drops and no adult had time to observe the horse and cart or think them out of place as they went slowly along the streets bearing the Borribles away from Rumbledom and towards the dubious safety of Wendle territory.

It was dusk when they awoke. Sam stood in a deserted side street by King George's, sleeping between the shafts, totally exhausted, all energy drained from him.

When the Borribles came to move their limbs they found that it was almost impossible. Stiffness and fatigue seemed to have fixed them in one position for ever. Stonks had fallen sideways onto the driver's seat and lay curled up in Dewdrop's raincoat. It was Torreycanyon who was the first to stick his head out into the moist evening air.

It had stopped raining and the street lamps shimmered gold in the wet roadway and made it dark, shiny and deep. Torreycanyon looked at his watch, five o'clock. He glanced at the name of the road and ducked under the canvas to check it on his street map in the light of his torch.

"Longstaff," he said. "Good old Sam, we're right near to King George's."

The others at up one by one, groaning as they realised how battered their bodies were. They huddled together for warmth and made a cold meal before continuing their journey. As they ate they argued amongst themselves about which route they should take for the return trip to Battersea. The easiest way of course was by boat through Wendle country to the Thames, the way they had come. But some of the Adventurers had their doubts.

"I think we should go back some other way," said Chalotte.

"What do you mean?" Napoleon looked up sharply.

"I didn't mean anything personal to you, Nap," she answered, a little embarrassed. "It's just that Flinthead gives me the creeps, a nasty feeling."

"Any other way must be safer," said Knocker, "must be."

Napoleon laughed a cool laugh. "It's too late, friends, you should have kept awake. Sam has brought us right up to King George's. We must have been sighted as soon as we crossed Merton Road. I should think there are Wendle lookouts all around us."

There was an uneasy silence under the canvas.

"Don't let's go bonkers," said Sydney at length. "The Wendles are Borribles, after all; they'll be pleased that our Expedition was a success."

"Anyway, we are in too bad a shape to go by any but the shortest and easiest way," said Napoleon. "Just think, you'll be home in two or three days."

"Remains to be seen," said Knocker.

Napolen laughed again. "You're being ridiculous," he said.

It was decided, after a little more discussion, that all they could do was to walk on as far as the banks of the Wandle and then camp there. Napoleon would make contact with a lookout and ask for the Adventurers to be taken back to *The Silver Belle Flower* and guided down to the Thames. After that everything would depend on the Wendles.

When they were ready, they clambered down the cart-wheels to the gleaming pavements and struggled into the straps of their haversacks. They were a sorry sight, limping and shuffling as they got into marching order. They looked grotesque, with improvised bandages round their heads and limbs. Vulge and Stonks had made themselves crutches from Rumble-sticks and could manage to get along only with help from the others. All of them moved badly and every step they took was a torture.

Knocker, in spite of his serious wounds and the feelings of his companions, went to the rear of the cart and threw aside the coverings that hid the treasure box from view. He dragged it towards him and hoisted it on to his injured back and, though he stumbled and nearly fell under the weight, nothing in the world would have induced him to leave it behind.

"You are very persistent, Knocker," said Chalotte. "How can you take that box after what has happened?"

"You'd be persistent if it was your name, wouldn't

you?" retorted Knocker, his temper short because of his feeling of guilt.

"Well, I don't like it much," said Torreycanyon, "but I'm sure Adolf would have understood about your second name." And he took one of the handles and helped Knocker lower the box from his shoulder so that they could carry it between them.

"So!" cried Napoleon Boot, shoving forward. "There it is, that's what you've been after all along, you scab. Selling us down the river, eh? You'd never have got it away without us. It's ours as well, you should share it out."

"Oh, let's throw it away before it stirs up more trouble," said Sydney.

"That's not very bright, now we've got it this far," butted in Torreycanyon. "I mean it's money, isn't it? A lot of it, too. Look at the way those Rumbles lived. They had everything up there, and a few things besides."

"We can't share it out between us yet," said Knocker, turning towards Napoleon and thrusting his face up against the Wendle's. "Spiff wanted to share it equally between all the tribes who had sent members on the Expedition. Each one of you will take a share back with him when he goes."

"Ha! Do you expect me to believe that load of old cobblers?" asked Napoleon, his face green in the light of the street-lamp. "You may trust Spiff, but I don't."

There was a dreadful silence under that lamp-post and some hearts sickened to think they had been so far and had done so much together and could now quarrel over a rotten box of money. Stonks said as much and he was backed up by Chalotte and Sydney, Bingo, Vulge and Orococco.

"Sod the money," shouted Stonks. "Here we are, dying on our feet, and you two argue. Let's get into the Park before the damn bread kills us all. We need a good night's kip. We can talk about the money tomorrow."

His voice woke Sam who nearly fell off his four feet. He neighed and turned his head. Sydney ran to him and the others followed, the money forgotten for the moment. They shone their torches over the horse and saw that his hide was caked with blood and covered with scratches and stab wounds.

"Here you are yammering on about money," cried Sydney angrily, pointing her finger at Napoleon and Knocker, "and the horse that saved us all is neglected by the lot of you."

They freed Sam from the traces, patted him down and expressed their sorrow at having ignored him for so long. Then they led him towards the Park and as Sam stepped out they noticed that he had a very bad limp, caused by a deep wound in one of his back legs.

"Look at that," shouted Sydney at them all, as if they'd each and severally been responsible. "Wounded like he is and brought us all the way down here. You ought to be ashamed of yourselves. Sam ought to be retired on that money."

The gates to the Park had been closed at dusk but Napoleon soon picked the lock and the Borrible team, Sam first, went into King George's. The Park was black and silent and the grass was wet but they had brought the canvas with them and when they reached the banks of the Wandle, flowing quiet and murky, they spread the tarpaulin on the ground and sat on it to keep dry. Soon the sky cleared of clouds, the stars appeared and the night turned cold, but the Adventurers wrapped themselves in their combat jackets and sleeping-bags and sat round in a circle, except for Sydney who tended and spoke to Sam for a long while before she regained her temper and rejoined the group.

Then began the story-telling, the moment that Borribles love above all others. They wanted to know who had done what and how, and in what order, and to whom. Bingo wanted to know what had happened to

Vulge, Vulge wanted to know what had happened to Torreycanyon, and Torreycanyon wanted to know how Chalotte and Sydney had fared. Napoleon told his story to Orococco, and Orococco told his story to Knocker, and Knocker's voice trembled as he recounted, almost as a penance, how Adolf had opened the safe. And there were tears in their eyes and lumps in their throats as they remembered the German and his mad, jolly voice and the way he had hooted at them. No one said anything to Knocker directly but there were looks and silences during the story of the safe and Knocker looked at the ground between this feet.

But the stories went on and past quarrels began to be forgotten because the Borribles looked at each other and realised how lucky they were to be alive. Never had Borribles had such an adventure and they even began to chuckle a little at their exaggerations, because exaggeration is an essential part of name-winning storytelling.

They were still talking when Napoleon suddenly stood up. "I can hear a Wendle scouting us from the other side of the river," he said.

Napoleon told them to switch off their torches and he went to the railings that bordered the river. He whistled softly, a slight variation on the normal Borrible whistle, and he was answered within two seconds. The others then heard him in conversation with a voice across the river.

"I'm going across," he announced when he returned. "Got to see Flinthead. You're to wait here; better get some sleep. You're quite safe, there's night patrols of Wendles all around. I'll be back before dawn. Be ready to leave. Don't try to go anywhere. You know they, we, don't like that." Then without a word of goodbye he turned his back and disappeared into the night.

"He's a funny bloke," said Bingo, "you never know where you are with him; nice and friendly one minute, saving your life and fighting with you, and then all of a sudden as cold and as straightlaced as the North Pole."

"I think," said Knocker with a worried expression, and looking at his box, "that he's just remembering he's a Wendle after all.'

Napoleon came back as promised just before dawn and the others rolled over in their sleeping-bags and, without getting up, looked at him. The tall shapes of the buildings on the far side of the Wandle were dark against the sky. Napoleon was just a darker shape. They couldn't see his eyes or his expression; only his voice told them that he was tense and tired.

"We're to stay here until it is nearly light," he began, "then I am to lead you across the Wandle, along the bank and then underground. We can rest, as we did before, for as long as we like, Flinthead said, and then they'll take us to where they've hidden the boat. Then we can go—you can go—as long as we tell our stories, all of them."

"What,' said Knocker, asking the question that was in everybody's mind, "about the money?"

Napoleon hesitated, then he said, "Flinthead didn't mention it, nor did I," and he went over to his sleeping-bag, unrolled it and slipped inside.

There was quiet for a long while. The sky lightened. Knocker got up stiffly and went and sat by Napoleon. After a while he touched the Wendle gently on the shoulder. He could see Napoleon's eyes now, they were open and staring at the sky.

"Flinthead said nothing about the money, eh?" he said.

Napoleon blinked and said, "That's right. I didn't tell him about it, did I?" and he tried to roll over on his shoulder but Knocker stopped him.

Bingo came over and joined them. Since the Battersea

Borrible had saved Napoleon's life and escaped with him from the Library he had got closer to the Wendle than any of the others, and he wanted to get between Knocker and Napoleon if trouble started. Knocker spoke again, low and even, and everyone listened. "I don't believe you. I think that we ought to go home some other way."

The silence deepened a notch or two. Napoleon sat up brusquely and grasped Knocker's arm.

"I've told you—you've got no bloody option," he said, between his teeth. "You're stuck all of you, there's Wendles all round. There's only one way out, and that's down the Wandle, the way we came."

Knocker was not put off. The others waited for the outcome, holding their breath.

"When you say you," he said to Napoleon, "does that include you in or out?"

Napoleon did not answer. A great struggle was going on in his mind and he could not speak while it continued. Lights came on in the building opposite and the sky was grey now. Soon they would have to make a move, one way or the other.

"Tell us what really happened," insisted Knocker. "Come on, straight up."

"You owe us the truth," said Bingo.

Napoleon got up and stepped over to the railings and looked at the surface of the Wandle as it floated by under its quilt of rubbish. Bingo thought for a second that the Wendle was going to run away.

At last Napoleon turned and spoke to them all, in a low voice so he wouldn't be overhead beyond the group. His words came all in a rush.

"I am telling the truth. I know you do not trust Flinthead, Halfabar or Tron, or even me," he began. "I know you do not like the Wendles, even though they are Borribles like yourselves, but remember the threat we have always lived under. I swear that Flinthead will ask only to hear your stories, will see that you get rest and food. He will take nothing from you, he is proud of us. After all, he's out of danger from the Rumbles for years to come. He told me how . . . how grateful he was . . . really."

There was silence and the others watched as Bingo walked over to the box and said, "Wish we'd never set eyes on the thing. Been a good Adventure apart from that."

Knocker spat. "My job is to take the box back and I'll do it even if I die."

"Even if we all die," said Chalotte.

"The trick," said Torreycanyon, "is to get it back without dying."

"They won't take it from us," insisted Napoleon. "They will wait to get their share. I'll be coming back to Battersea with you so that I can bring the Wendle share back to Wandsworth."

"It's only fair to share it out amongst everybody," said Chalotte. "I'm sure they'll see that."

"Yes," agreed Vulge. "They won't attack us, Napoleon is right. It would be Borrible against Borrible."

"It's happened before," said Orococco. "I'm for fair shares, let's hope we get them."

Napoleon raised his head. The blood had gone from his face and there were mauve patches under his eyes. He shook his head sadly at them. "If they wanted to take it, they would have taken it already--but you won't listen. They don't want it. Everything will be all right."

Napoleon's companions recognised the force of his argument, but they had been made uneasy by the discussion and looked about cautiously. There was not a Wendle to be seen.

"Come on," said Chalotte, forcing a laugh, "have we journeyed so far and survived so much that we are now going to jump at shadows?"

The others agreed with her but Knocker shook his

head and quoted a dark proverb. " 'The shadow cast by a Wendle is twice as long as his body,' " and he stared hard at Napoleon and tried to read the truth in the Wendle's eyes, but Napoleon's eyes wandered and looked elsewhere.

"We shall have to move soon," said the Wendle. "I can hear the early buses in the streets and it is nearly daylight."

Within a few minutes they were ready and they filed past Sam to give him a last pat and a stroke. They were subdued by the uncertainty that lay before them, by the sadness that lay behind them, and they hated themselves for deserting the horse who had helped them through so many dangers. Sydney was the last to squeeze through the gap in the railings. She had lingered to gather a handful of fresh grass for Sam, she wanted to wish him farewell alone.

"Goodbye, old Sam," she said, and she felt very mournful. "We can't take you any further because of the river, but I tell you, Sam, if I ever get out alive on the other side I'll find out where you are and I'll come back, however far it is, and I'll steal you away one night and you'll come back with me and you won't work again, Sam, ever."

When she had gone Sam ambled over to the railings and stuck his head over to watch the tiny figures marching along the towpath towards the dark and semi-circular hole where the Wandle disappeared under the streets of Wandsworth.

Napoleon led the way but his step was not springy or light. He looked unhappy, not at all like a Borrible returning home covered in glory.

Knocker and Torreycanyon followed along with the box and the others came behind them. They were still in a bad condition despite their night's rest and their appearance would no doubt give the Wendles more cause for derision than sympathy.

The silence along the towpath was uncanny and the saw not a soul, at least to begin with. It was only wh they glanced over their shoulders that they saw how the path had become crowded with heavily armed war riors who had materialized from the very bankside. Across the river they could see more Wendles rising mysteriously from the mud to stand watching as the Borribles marched by.

Bingo, who felt that his companions were allowing themselves to be over-awed by the Wendles, raised his voice in song and that London voice, bright and defiant, rang out over the river.

"Hurrah! Hurrah! The Battle's won!
The victors are marching from Rumbledom!
We smashed the evil furry crew,
We finished the job we went to do.
Let our great deeds and high renown
Spread to the ends of London Town.
Brave though bloody, here we come!
The victors returning from Rumbledom!

"Rejoice! The foe is overcome!
The victors are marching from Rumbledom!
We trounced the enemy through and through,
We finished the job we went to do.
Nothing can frighten us again,
We fear no monsters, fear no men.
Brave though bloody, here we come!
The victors returning from Rumbledom!"

With Bingo's example before them, the Adventurers determined to show the Wendles that they were not downcast and each of them sang loudly of his London Borough: songs that told of fine abandoned houses and good days of thieving and food.

Knocker laughed at the songs. He felt happier now they had committed themselves to a course of action.

There was no going back, so they might as well make the best of it.

All too soon they came up with Halfabar at the mouth of the sewer where the Wandle went underground. He was waiting for them and he smiled and inclined his head; the early morning sun of winter gleamed on his helmet.

"Welcome, brother Borribles," he said. "Napoleon has told us a little of your great Adventure. Your names were well won. Flinthead is impatient to hear your stories from your own lips. A great feast awaits you."

"There," said Napoleon to Knocker, "what did I tell you?" Knocker did not reply.

They followed Halfabar and his men underground and found their way by the light of the torches as they had done on their previous visit. Again the Adventurers smelt the smell of the River Wandle, penned and confined in its narrow tunnels, and the sweat of the Wendles, who guarded them on all sides, rose and stung their nostrils. Even Napoleon wrinkled his nose, so many months had he spent away that he was no longer used to the stench.

They left the river and the passage they took led them directly to the Great Hall, and there, as before, sat Flinthead, his eyes opaque. The Hall was not crowded this time, only the bodyguard stood by, heavily armed and numerous, their faces unsmiling beneath their war-helmets. In a line before Flinthead's stage were nine armchairs, and in front of them was a long table loaded with all kinds of food from the Wendles' store.

The Adventurers filed across the Hall, with members of the bodyguard at their side. They were directed to the armchairs and their knapsacks were taken and stacked behind them. Torreycanyon and Knocker dropped the burnt and valuable box in front of their seats, and when, on a gesture from Flinthead, they sat, they each put a foot on the Rumble treasure. Flinthead saw the movement and smiled indulgently. When all was still in the Hall he spoke and his voice was just the same as ever, kind, warm and solicitous.

"Welcome back," he said, and smiled again. "Your Adventure has been successful and we are proud, and not a little envious of it, though we grieve at your loss. If you are not too weary, I would like to hear of your exploits, in detail, for all we Borribles love a story of the winning of a name, and I think that there have never been names won like yours. Napoleon Boot has told me something, but I wish to hear it all from your own lips. There is food before you. Tell me your stories one by one, the rest may eat until it is their turn to tell." He pointed a finger at the end of the line away from Knocker. "You," he ordered, "begin."

So, Stonks it was, began. He told how he and Torreycanyon took the Great Door, how he defended it and how later he took the Rumble-skin, and what a fright it caused. The others ate, or aided the story with comments, correcting and enlarging the thread of the tale as it went along. Then it was the turn of Vulge, and Flinthead leant forward in his chair with great interest as he heard how the Chief Rumble had met his end. Sydney and Chalotte told of the assault on the kitchens and the subsequent retreat; then came Orococco, followed by Bingo, who told how he met with Napoleon in the great Library and how he had fought in single combat with the greatest Warrior in Rumbledom. Napoleon took up the story and told how he had shaken his namesake from the ladder and how Bingo had saved his life, and how, sorely wounded, they had squirmed and crawled their way to safety, to find Torreycanyon, who then must tell of his lonely fight in the garage and how he caused the Great Explosion which had put paid to the whole Bunker. After that, Flinthead asked of Adolf and what he had done, so Knocker related how the German and he had found Vulge, surrounded by the bodies of his enemies, and how the safe had been opened and the box discovered. And the Wendles heard the stories and leant on their spears and everyone relaxed, except Knocker, and Torreycanyon whispered that everyone seemed friendly and happy and that things would turn out fine in the end. But Knocker scowled and whispered back that things that happened could only be judged after they had happened, and then not always correctly.

But Flinthead turned his bland face to Knocker again and said, "And now you must speak further and tell us your own story, one full of colour, I am sure, and for one which I have been waiting with great interest, for were you not the writer, the Historian, and you will have seen and known things that the others did not know."

Knocker felt very uncomfortable and looked along the line of his companions. They sprawled weakly in the comfortable armchairs, their faces flushed with food and drink. They were too relaxed, too easeful, unable to defend themselves if the need arose. Knocker himself sat nervously on the edge of his seat, his feet tucked under him, ready to leap at the slightest hint of danger.

"My part was, in fact, small," he heard himself saying. "Adolf and I followed the others and discovered Vulge only after he had fought his great battle alone. Later it was a question of retreating slowly, grouping together and fighting our way along the tunnels to the Great Door where Adolf was killed, but if it hadn't been for Sam, the horse, none of us would be sitting here now." And Knocker went on to praise the horse and tell of the imprisonment under Dewdrop and his son, how they had escaped and taken Sam with them.

Flinthead cupped his chin in his right hand and rested the elbow on his knee. He swayed forward, listening with an attention that did not waver for a second. He was fixing every detail of the story in his own mind.

When the tale was finished he leant back in his chair, clasped his hands in his lap and beamed a cold smile at everybody, a brittle smile that was simply a movement of facial muscle with no breath of warmth in it.

"I hope, Knocker," he said, "that you will write down all these adventures as soon as you have time. There are so few good stories left. I look forward to it." He paused and looked round the Hall at the bodyguard, then he looked down at Knocker and smiled again and flicked his finger against his thumb, just once. There was a clash of armour and soldiers moved behind the Adventurers to hold them fast, deep in the soft armchairs, knives at their throats. Held all that is save Knocker; he had been ready, perched on the edge of his chair. He jumped forward, butted a warrior in the stomach and snatched his lance.

But there was another Adventurer who had not been made captive, Napoleon Boot. He too sprang from his armchair as if expecting trouble but his lance he did not seize; one was thrust into his hands and he was joined by a band of Wendles who rushed from the side of Flinthead's stage.

Knocker crouched, his spear held low. He was convulsed with a bitter rage. To come so far, to do so much, and then to lose everything through the treachery of a fellow Adventurer.

Napoleon stood opposite him, haughty, confident. "Drop that spear, Knocker, you have no chance. If you resist we will kill you."

"You thing of no name," screamed Knocker at the top of his voice, "you liar, deceiver, traitor. May you be un-named and cursed and your story told with a curse," and Knocker drew back his arm and cast the spear at the Wendle with every ounce of strength at his command, for he hated Napoleon with every fibre of his being. But Napoleon was ready. He knew that Knocker would throw the lance and he stooped under it and it struck a Wendle behind him and such was the force of the blow that the lance pierced the warrior and the blade stood out a handsbreadth behind his back.

The Wendle shrieked and fell lifeless to the floor, but his fellows leapt upon Knocker and bore him to the ground and he was cuffed and beaten and his hands were tied and at last he was hoisted to his feet. Blood trickled down his face and a bruise rose, brown and purple, on his forehead. He swayed weakly, but he swore at Napoleon Boot.

"You'd better kill me, you no-name-bastard-Wendle," he said, hissing the words, "for if I live, I'll kill you. I'll train a race of Borribles who will seek you out and put you through a mincer."

Napoleon ignored him and gave a sign and the other Adventurers were hauled to their feet and their hands bound fast. Flinthead rose from his chair and came to the edge of the stage.

"Well, there we are, nice and tidy." Again he clicked his fingers and the box was prised open to reveal the banknotes. "Hmm," said Flinthead, "very handy! Napoleon, you have done well, you shall be promoted to the bodyguard, co-captain with Tron and . . . er . . . choose yourself a second name while you are at it. I want you to see that your . . . friends are safely locked up. As for the box, that must be guarded day and night by members of the bodyguard, you will be responsible for it—with your life, of course. Take as many Wendles as you need." Flinthead looked down at the captives and smiled his smile of death once more but they did not watch his face. They stood looking at the ground, their shame too great to bear, tears of anger in their eyes. Only Knocker held his head up and shouted after the Wendle Chieftain as he left, "Guard yourself well, Flinthead. I'll ram that money down your throat before I'm finished. I'll skin you alive, you and your bodyguard of un-named, slow-witted, snot-gobblin' morons."

But Flinthead just waved a bored hand and without looking round he went from the Great Hall surrounded, as always, by the pick of his bodyguard.

When Flinthead had gone, Halfabar stepped up to Napoleon and gave him a warrior's helmet and a special jacket. Napoleon put them on and tugged the lance from the corpse on the floor and he rapped the bloody tip of it against Knocker's chest. "You shuddup, sonny," he said. "You're a nobody and nobody wants to hear you."

By way of reply Knocker spat directly into Napoleon's face and the saliva trickled down his nose. Angered, Napoleon twirled the lance expertly in one hand and caught Knocker a stinging blow across the head and Knocker fell to his knees.

Although bound and outnumbered by the bodyguard Knocker's companions stepped forward and stood fearlessly between Napoleon and his victim.

"Leave it alone," said Stonks, in an untroubled voice. "Leave it alone, you skinny fart, or I'll kill you."

"Yes," said Sydney, "aren't you satisfied with your day's work, yet, Wendle?"

Napoleon's face clouded over for an instant, then he shook himself and said to Halfabar, "Right, let's get them out of here."

The Adventurers were taken only a short way into one of the corridors before Napoleon halted them and opened a heavy iron door. With blows raining over their heads they were forced to enter a small and damp dungeon, where green slime dripped and oozed from the walls. It was lit by one weak electric bulb and there were no seats or beds, only some dirty and mildewed sacks piled in one corner.

Once they were in the cell Halfabar entered and, protected by others of the bodyguard, he cut the bonds from the Borribles' hands.

"Ain't that cosy," he said when he'd finished, and

leering into Orococco's face he added, "safe and sound the lot of you."

Orococco bared his teeth at the Wendle, making him jump backwards.

"I'm going to hold you under the water next time, friend, but I will not let you up until you have stopped breathing that stinking breath of yours. Couldn't you sprinkle a little deodorant on your cornflakes and make a few friends?"

Halfabar raised his hand to strike Orococco but he remembered in time that the Totter now had his hands free and so he contented himself with a sneer. He backed to the door and pulled it to; the noise of its closing and locking echoed up and down the tunnels and was still echoing long after the last Wendle footsteps had faded into the distance.

The Borribles stood disconsolate in their prison. They could not even look at one another and it was some time before they could talk. A mixture of shame, rage and hatred, despair and disbelief, held them tongue-tied. Speech was impossible. Quarter-of-an-hour went by, then half-an-hour, and the silence became hard and solid. At last Knocker broke into a stream of swearing that he kept rushing along for minutes on end. He thought of every Borrible curse he could remember and enlarged and embroidered on it. He went backwards and forwards through *The Borrible Book of Proverbs* and turned them into maledictions on the head of Napoleon Boot. He wove garlands of evil words around that Wendle's name and when he had finished and was breathless and his memory and mind were empty he felt better, and so did those who had listened to him and had joined in his song of hate with imprecations of their own.

"I still can't believe it," said Chalotte. "What made him do it?"

"Once a Wendle always a Wendle," said Knocker

bitterly and that was enough explanation for him and he said no more.

"I don't think we ought to be too downhearted," said Stonks in his flat, straightforward manner. "After all, we got there and back again and did what we said we'd do."

"I'm not blaming anyone," said Chalotte, looking at Knocker, "but if it hadn't been for that money, we'd have been on our way home by now."

There was silence but Knocker didn't look up, nor did he speak.

"Well, it's happened," said Vulge. "It's no one's fault; it's happened. After all, we're still alive."

Orococco laughed harshly. "Not for long, we ain't."

"It was such a dirty trick, coming from an Adventurer, after all he said, too," said Torreycanyon, and again they lapsed into a long and moody silence.

They were kept incommunicado for many days and nights. Food was brought to them but it was the meanest of cold scraps and it was flung at them through a barely opened door. They became weak through lack of food and more and more depressed as the days went by. Even if they managed to open the heavy iron door of their dungeon, they were certain to become lost in the tangle of culverts and corridors that was Wendle country, and on their heels would be warriors from the toughest of all the London tribes. Hard and dedicated they were, the Wendles, and they knew every inch of their own territory. They knew every tunnel, every fathom of the river and every yard of underground sewer within a radius of miles. The idea of escape receded further and further from the captives' minds, and their hatred of Napoleon Boot dulled to a slow burning ache.

One day, or night, some weeks later, the door to the cell opened quietly and, after a moment's pause, clicked shut. The Borribles did not look up, it would only be some inedible meal in a bucket.

When Vulge rolled over in his blanket, which was green with damp mould, like all the others, he saw, to his surprise, the slight figure of Napoleon Boot. Napoleon looked splendid. His helmet of tin was burnished and his orange jacket gleamed in the light of the electric bulb. His waders were new and shone blackly and they fitted tightly to his calves and thighs. He had two steel catapults in his belt and a double bandolier of the choicest stones. He looked proud and well-fed, though his face had once more taken on the green tinge that touched the complexion of all Wendles.

Napoleon raised a finger to his lips. The Stepney Borrible couldn't believe his eyes.

"What's going on?" he asked.

"We're getting out," said Napoleon, his voice quiet but tense with excitement.

Hearing this strange conversation, the others looked up and rolled out of their damp couches.

"Be dead quiet," said Napoleon whispering, "or you'll just be dead."

The captives rose to their feet, gazing at each other with puzzlement.

"Is this some new trick?" asked Sydney. She had liked Napoleon ever since the day he had stolen the boat in Battersea Park, and she had taken his deception very hard.

"I haven't got time to explain now," said Napoleon. "You'll have to trust me."

Knocker laughed quietly. "Trust the honest Wendle and end up in prison?"

"Kill him," said Torreycanyon, affecting to look at his finger nails.

Napoleon's face creased with anguish. "There isn't much time, don't be stupid."

"What are you going to do this time?" said Knocker.

"Let us loose in the tunnels so the bodyguard can practice on us? Hunt us down one by one and shove us under the Wandle mud when they catch us? I've heard that's one of your favourite sports."

"Oh, listen," said Napoleon quickly, "and listen well, because every minute we waste is precious. Flinthead knew all the time about the Rumble money, even before the expedition started. He sent me on the Adventure in the first place to keep an eye on you all, and find the money—and watch it."

"I could see that," said Knocker with a sneer, "that much was obvious."

"On the way back," continued Napoleon, "my job was to lead you into the Wandle and see that you suspected nothing, so that Flinthead could capture you and the money."

"You did it very well, didn't you?" said Bingo. "You fooled me completely—but then I only fought side by side with you in the Library. I thought we were mates. . . ."

"Shuddup," said Napoleon uncomfortably. "When we got back to King George's, I didn't know what to do. There was you lot on the one hand, my tribe on the other. I worried about it all the time. Anyway, we couldn't have got away at that stage, Flinthead had patrols everywhere. He doesn't mess about, you know. So there was only one thing I could do—go ahead with Flinthead's plan. It wasn't easy being hated by you all . . . and now, if I help you escape, I shall be hated by my own tribe. I'd like to see you in the same position. What would you make of it?"

"If all this is true," asked Torreycanyon, "why has it taken you so long to make up your mind?"

"I've been waiting for the right opportunity," said Napoleon. "It won't be easy getting out of here—and today's a good day."

"What's so special about today?" asked Chalotte.

"There was a big stealing expedition yesterday," said Napoleon, speaking more easily. "Most of us were out, hard at it. Now they're sleeping. There's to be a big celebration soon, and as Knocker said, it is likely that you will be released into the tunnels one by one for the bodyguard to hunt down. I . . . I . . . would be one of them; I couldn't stand that . . . so . . . well, there you are."

"Well," said Orococco, "I don't care whether he's telling the truth or a lie. I'm for getting out of here. Anything's better than staying in this hole, even a scrap with the bodyguard and a muddy grave in the Wandle."

"Would Flinthead really do that, just for the box of money?" asked Chalotte.

"Strange things have happened to these Borribles," said Stonks. "We don't know how far they'd go."

"You've got to believe me," pleaded Napoleon. "This is your only chance to get out. You know what they'll do with me if they catch me alive, don't you?"

They looked at him without speaking.

"They'll stake me out on the mud flats, at high water mark, and let me drown a little each day, until one day the water and muck will come a little higher, and then I will drown. You know, in the end I am being more loyal to the Adventure than anyone."

The eight captives looked at each other and pondered and at length Bingo sniffed, stepped forward and threw his arms round Napoleon and hugged him tight. One by one the others did the same, even Knocker, who came last, saying, "Well, whatever was in your mind when you betrayed us to Flinthead, let us hope that now you have come to a final decision. Tell us what to do, Napoleon. I for one am longing to see the sky again and walk through a market."

Napoleon relaxed when Knocker had finished speaking and he told them his plan. There were normally two sentries outside the door but he had sent them off to a guardroom, where they were resting. They would have to be dealt with first. In the guardroom would be found Wendle clothes and waders, arms and ammunition. They would steal what they needed and, as soon as they were disguised and armed, he would take them to *The Silver Belle Flower*. If they ran into Wendle warriors they would have to fight. Even if they got the boat under way, they still wouldn't be safe but they would have a good chance. Once they emerged onto the River Thames they would be out of danger, though still a long journey from Battersea Reach.

The Borribles agreed to the plan and gathered by the door, while Napoleon unlocked it and looked into the tunnel. He stepped out after a moment and motioned the others to follow him and they crept towards the guardroom, united again.

They overpowered the two off-duty guards and in a short time they were dressed as fierce Wendle bodyguards, wearing black rubber waders and orange jackets. They armed themselves with steel catapults and double bandoliers; there were Rumble-sticks in the room too and each Borrible took one.

"All we have to do now," said Napoleon, "is march along in an orderly fashion, and all being well we'll march straight onto the boat and no one will give us a second glance. It will just seem as if I am taking a fresh guard to one of the outlets."

Knocker jammed his tin-can helmet onto his head and said, "I want the money," just like that, calm, toneless

Napoleon looked at him in amazement. "Don't be mad," he protested. "It's kept right next to Flinthead's apartments. There's a squad of the bodyguard sitting on it all the time, day and night."

"That's right," said Knocker, "and you're Keeper of the Box, aren't you? I'm sure you can order them to stand up for five minutes."

"Straight up," said Stonks. "I never cared about the money from the word go, in fact I hate it, but I don't like being shoved into prison, half-starved, and then used like some stuffed hare at a greyhound track to be chased about in tunnels by a lot of tin-helmeted twits. It's the principle of the thing."

"I agree, man," said Orococco, "if we leave the money behind, old Flintbonce will be sitting pretty and laughing away all over his flat face. I'd like to put one over on him."

"Yes," said Sydney, "he ought to be shown that Borribles should treat Borribles fair and square, if nothing else."

"It's so dangerous," said Napoleon.

Knocker said, "Anyone against the idea?"

"Nobody takes my catapult away and tells me to piss off," said Bingo. "Nobody."

"Me neither," said Torreycanyon.

Vulge said, "Let's just say that this one's for Adolf."

It was this last remark that brooked no argument, only Chalotte had something to add. She shrugged her shoulders and smiled exhaustedly. "I think you're all mad," she said, "but how can I stay behind now?"

Napoleon sighed, looked at their faces, and gave in.

They formed up in pairs and, looking every inch as military and as ferocious as Wendle bodyguards, they tramped out of the guardroom and through the long sloping tunnels. They hummed the Wendle marching song as they went and any non-warriors they met hastily squeezed out of their way, or stepped into a side-tunnel to let them pass.

"This is the way to escape," said Bingo to Knocker, who marched beside him and behind Napoleon, "with verve and bravado. I shall compose a song about this when I get back to Battersea."

They marched for a long while but Napoleon led them with confidence this way and that in a maze of criss-crossing corridors. Not once were they questioned, not once were they given more than a brief disinterested glance. The power of the warrior class had been built up over a long period by Flinthead and now it was working against him. Warrior spoke only to warrior, ordinary Wendles kept their distance.

Soon the tunnels became more spacious and were gracefully arched and dry under foot. This was the old Victorian part of the sewers and no longer used except by Wendles. It was a warm and comfortable section and that was why Flinthead had established his quarters here, and the room where the treasure-box was held was getting nearer at every step. In a deserted part of the tunnel Napoleon halted his company and explained what he had in mind.

"It is nearly time for the guard to be changed," he said, looking at his watch. "You will pretend to be the new guard. You will march in, follow my orders exactly, and then I will march off with the old guard. I'll get back as soon as I can, on some pretext. We'll only have a few minutes before the real guard turns up, looking for me. They will discover the box gone and will raise the alarm. We'll have to run like a train to get to the boat. If anyone tries to interfere, hit him hard and run on. Remember these ain't Rumbles you'll be fighting, but Wendles, and the best of them."

They formed up again and marched another fifty yards, and then wheeled smartly into a wide guard-room, very comfortably furnished. At the far end of the room was an iron door, rather like the one that had held them in prison, but this door was larger and heavier and studded with huge rivets.

Napoleon yelled. "Guard, halt!" and the eight of them brought their rubber-heeled waders together as one man. "Oh, yes, very smart," said Napoleon, his face giving nothing away, and he went over to the door that led to the strongroom.

He rapped on the door with the butt of his lance—a special knock it was, too—and the Borribles stood stiff to attention. A flap in the iron door swung open immediately and a helmeted Wendle's face could be seen through the opening.

"I've brought the relief guard, sergeant," said Napoleon, and before the other could ask the question forming in his mind, Napoleon added, "I know I'm early but I'm on special business for Flinthead."

The Wendle guard nodded, closed the flap and the door swung open and he marched his men out and formed them up in a line opposite the new arrivals. He handed the keys to Napoleon and observed, "There's one man short."

"Yes," said Napoleon casually, "he'll be along in a minute. He wasn't ready in time. I couldn't wait."

The sergeant of the guard fell in at the head of his men and waited for Napoleon's orders.

Napoleon led his command into the strongroom and gave Knocker the keys. "Lock the door immediately, Wendle," he said in his sternest voice. "Let no one through but me," and without another look at the Adventurers he did an about turn and marched off with the sergeant and his eight men.

As soon as Napoleon had gone, Knocker closed and locked the door and leant against it, the sweat trickling down under his armpits.

The strongroom was small and the box stood on a table in the centre of it. Round the walls were comfortable armchairs for the guards and a couple of tables carrying food and drink. Wendle warriors wanted for nothing.

"Help yourselves to some grub," said Knocker. "It may be a long while before we eat again."

The Adventurers needed no second bidding but used the time to fill their stomachs, and their pockets, with food.

All too quickly came the special knock at the door and Knocker opened the flap. His heart missed a beat. It was not Napoleon but Halfabar standing there. Luckily he was alone and did not recognise Knocker under the Wendle helmet.

"Yes," said Knocker.

"You mean, 'yes, sir'," said Halfabar.

"Yes, sir," said Knocker.

"Open up," sneered Halfabar. "I saw you marching up here and I want to know why there's only eight of you instead of the normal nine. That cocky little Napoleon has slipped up on the job this time. Promoted over my head, he was. I'll screw him for that."

During this conversation Orococco had flattened himself against the wall and now he nodded to Knocker. Knocker unlocked the door, opened it and stepped back respectfully to allow the Wendle to enter. As Halfabar came across the threshold Orococco seized him by the throat and shoved him tight against the wall.

"My friend Adolf ain't here," he said between his teeth, "but I know he'd want me to look after you before we leave."

He shifted his grip and grabbed the Wendle by his scruff and seat, holding him up like a limp bolster. "Remember, Halfabar," hissed Orococco, "you can't live by bread alone," and he threw the Wendle into the room like a sack of spuds.

"Leave him to me," he cried, his black face intoxicated with pleasure and his eyes rolling as they hadn't done since the Battle of Rumbledom. But Halfabar did not rise. Orococco had thrown him into the room with such gusto that the Wendle had broken his head against the box of money. His tin helmet had split open like a rotten orange. It was wedged over his face and his ginger hair sprouted through the crest like rusty springs from a discarded mattress. Blood dripped from the box to the floor.

"There," said Orococco, breathing deeply, "did you hear his brains rattle like dried lentils when I shook him?"

It was Napoleon who knocked next and Knocker let him into the room. He started when he saw the body of Halfabar.

"It's all right," said Knocker, "he was alone and we made no noise. He did not have time to cry out, Orococco got him."

Napoleon nodded. "It's time to go," he said. "Most of the warriors are still sleeping. It's about one o'clock in the morning in the streets above, but they'll be waking soon for work. There are patrols coming and going too. It is all a question of luck now. As soon as they see that box they will know what we are up to."

The Adventurers left the strongroom at a trot, Stonks and Torreycanyon carrying the money. They followed Napoleon at a sustained and speedy run down the wide bricked tunnel that led to the River Wandle, the boat, and safety. They ran and they ran, making little noise on the rubber feet of their stolen waders. They brushed past one or two ordinary Wendles but they moved so quickly that the box was not seen and no alarm raised. They were halfway to the river before they ran into trouble. Rounding a bend at full tilt they came upon a small night patrol of warriors returning from the outside world.

"Stay where you are," shouted Napoleon. So used were the warriors to obeying, they stopped at once and for a minute did nothing. That minute was enough and the Adventurers sprang upon them and brought them down. But the noise of the scruffle attracted the attention of another patrol in one of the side tunnels and they saw in a flash what was happening, and worse, they saw the box.

They fired their catapults and hit Stonks in the kidneys and Orococco in the arm, paralysing both Borribles for a few moments. The Adventurers returned the fire and the Wendles ran off, but the clamour they raised made the very walls shake.

"That's it, now," shouted Napoleon, "they'll be on us in less time than it takes to steal a spud in Covent Garden. Run for your lives."

Knocker and Bingo took up the box and the convoy raced on. The smell of the Wandle got stronger and the floor of the tunnel sloped more and more steeply.

"We're getting there," panted Napoleon, "come on."

The clashing of weapons came from behind and all around them in the hundreds of side tunnels. Wendles slept all over the vast sewer complex and could be out of bed and dressed for an emergency faster than a crew of London firemen.

"If we don't get to the river first," said Napoleon, "we'll be up to our necks in mud before the night's out."

They redoubled their efforts and, though their lungs were bursting, they ran faster. Now Chalotte and Orococco took the box, not even breaking their stride as they snatched up the burden.

At last, with a cry of relief, they burst out onto the underground bank of the river, as dark green as ever, the tenacious mud bubbling just below the surface of the water. The tow-path was wide at this point and there rode their boat, *The Silver Belle Flower*, tied to the bank. Napoleon drew his knife and slashed the painter.

"In with the box. Stonks, round to the front, you've got to pull real fast till it's wide and deep enough to row; then we've got to go like Oxford and Cambridge gone bonkers."

He glanced up the tunnel. The noise of pursuit was getting nearer; any minute now they would be overtaken. Napoleon took Knocker by the arm.

"Knocker," he whispered urgently, not wasting a word, "see that tunnel just behind us? It goes straight

271

to the Thames; the river meanders. If we all get in the boat the Wendles will run straight down that tunnel and be at the outlet before us, cut us off and do for us. Two of us have got to stay here and stop them getting into that tunnel, give the others ten minutes', quarter-of-an-hour's grace, then they'll get away. Otherwise they won't. You and me?"

Knocker looked behind him and back up the tunnel from which the pursuers would issue. "Not you," he said. "You are the navigator, you know the Wandle and you know the Thames. I will stay."

"Not alone," Torreycanyon said, and pushed in between them. "Knocker is right; you must go. Two of us will be enough. Straight down that tunnel, you say? When we have dealt with the Wendles, we will catch you up."

"Wait a quarter-of-an-hour," said Napoleon, "but be careful when you go down the tunnel, there's a guard-room down there, too. I'd better stay, all the same, three is better than two."

"Then I will stay," said Orococco, who had leapt back out of the boat to see what they were doing. "Just make sure that Tooting's share of the money gets to Tooting."

Napoleon took off his bandoliers and gave them to Knocker, and the others in the boat, when they realised what was happening, each removed one of their bandoliers and threw it to the bank. Then they stood sadly, just looking at their three comrades.

"Oh, go on, Stonks, go on, run," shouted Knocker, and the boat jolted away and Napoleon leapt aboard as it left the shore. Knocker watched the boat spurt out of sight round the first bend, pulled steadily by the never-tiring Stonks. There had been no time for farewells and no time for pity.

"We'll never see them again," said Knocker.

"Well, we still got each other," said Orococco and he picked up the bandoliers.

"Let us go out with a fight," cried Torreycanyon excitedly.

"Yes," said Knocker, "whatever happens we've won and Flinthead and his pointed skull and his petrified grin will not laugh like we will laugh tonight."

"We'd better get into the mouth of the short-cut," said Orococco. "We can't possibly hold them here."

They crossed the Wandle, up to their waists in the foul slime of the river bed, and adopted defensive positions. As they took cover, an advance party of Wendles came careering out of the main corridor and a shower of well-directed high-velocity stones rattled around the Borribles' hiding-place.

"Man," said Orococco, "I'll go white with the shock."

"This is no time . . ." began Knocker, and then stopped and laughed instead, and they knelt in the gloom and laid their bandoliers and lances beside them.

Within a few seconds the open area by the landing stage had become crowded with Wendle warriors and Tron appeared in the midst of them, his face flushed with anger.

He instantly ordered a large detachment of his men to follow the course of the Wandle in pursuit of the boat. Into the branch tunnels he dispatched smaller patrols to make sure that the fugitives were not lurking there, but the main body of his troops he directed into the short-cut so that he could block the mouth of the Wandle with a considerable force before *The Silver Belle Flower* could ever get there.

"They can't get away," he shouted. "We'll have them yet, suffocating in Wandle mud."

"Let us hold our fire till they get halfway across," whispered Knocker, "and we'll soon see who is in the mud first."

Already the Wendles, ardent and fanatical, had plunged into the filthy water and were wading across.

Tron himself was carried shoulder high by two of his personal guard.

The three Adventurers loaded their catapults in the darkness and they waited until Knocker hissed, "All right, now!"

Three well-aimed stones each struck their targets and three Wendles disappeared under the mud. The Adventurers fired again and again and the rate of their fire was phenomenal, but the Wendles came on in spite of their losses, for they did not lack bravery.

"Aim for Tron," cried Orococco, "or his guards."

Knocker shifted his aim to one of Tron's porters, and his stone struck the bodyguard solidly on his helmet and he lost his footing on the river bottom and Tron was pitched face foremost into the Wandle.

"Swallow that!" said Knocker with relish.

Tron was pulled to the bank by his followers and the mud was wiped from him. This victory gave the three defenders a short breathing space but Tron was not a Wendle to allow his enemy to relax for long. Wave after wave of warriors he sent into the river, and although the Adventurers fired till their arms were aching, they could not stop the warriors crossing in force and spreading out to right and left of their tunnel.

When satisfied with his bridgehead Tron ordered his Wendles to attack. Fortunately only three warriors at a time could enter the short-cut and deadly work was done with knife and lance in the darkness, as Torreycanyon and Knocker and Orococco fought side by side for their lives and the lives of their companions.

Suddenly Tron's voice was heard calling on his soldiers to cease fighting for a moment and the attackers fell back. The three Borribles leant against the wall at the tunnel entrance, exhausted and nearly done for.

, "How long has it been now?" asked Knocker. "My watch is smashed."

"Quarter-of-an-hour," said Orococco triumphantly. "We've done it."

Tron called again. "You Borribles in there, you might as well come out, you're surrounded. The boat has been captured, we've got the box again. You are fighting for nothing, I tell you. Save your lives."

"Don't believe him," said Knocker. "It must be a trick, they've got clean away."

"Keep them talking, anyway," said Orococco, "it's not so dangerous as fighting."

"Show us the box," shouted Knocker hoarsely, "then we might believe you, Tron."

Tron laughed. "Your friends will be here soon, in chains, then you will see the box. Surrender, cause no more trouble and we might be lenient with you. You have fought well, that is enough."

"We would rather fight here than go back to your dungeons," shouted Knocker.

"There'll be no dungeons for you, friend," called Tron, his voice hardening.

"I can believe that all right," said Orococco quietly.

At that moment a runner bounded up and spoke to Tron. The crowd of warriors fell back and the onlookers saw Flinthead himself arrive, surrounded by his guard. His face was stern and cruel and he was dressed for war.

Flinthead took in the situation at a glance. He gave orders and his guards looked at the roof of the cavern where they stood, then they ran forward and climbed one upon the shoulders of another until the last man reached the ceiling and disappeared. A rope ladder was thrown down to the ground and half a hundred Warriors scrambled up it and went out of sight.

"What does that mean?" asked Knocker.

"It means trouble," said a voice behind him and the Adventurers spun round, weapons at the ready.

There stood Napoleon Boot, covered in mud and

gashed in the head, his helmet gone and his jacket torn.

"What's happened?" cried Knocker aghast.

"It's all right," said Napoleon breathing heavily. "They got away, I saw to it. They'll be out on the Thames by now, I shouldn't wonder."

He sank to the floor and leant his back against the wall.

"How did you get back here, man?" asked Orococco, kneeling beside the Wendle and inspecting his head wound. "My, that sure is a beauty!"

"When the boat was safely away," explained Napoleon, "I made for the short-cut. The guard had been alerted but they didn't know I was part of the getaway. As we were talking, some Warriors appeared along the Wandle and shouted to the guard to hold me. I had to fight my way out. They can't be far behind; not a lot of them, but enough."

"What's Flinthead playing at?" asked Knocker.

"He's sending Warriors up to the surface. They'll come down through a manhole behind us. When he's got us surrounded, he'll come and talk to us, or just starve us out. He can wait. He can't know yet that the boat is clean away."

"Well, it's nice to hear such things," said Orococco, "but why risk your life to come back to tell us?"

Napoleon hesitated and then went on. "I haven't told you all the story yet. There is bad news. Halfway down to the mouth of the Wandle we were jumped by a large night patrol coming back from outside. They saw the box, and guessed something was up and didn't wait to ask questions. Stonks went under the water with five of them on him, but he came back up again – alone. There was about twenty of them around the boat. They dragged the box out and we dragged it back in. We fought like double our number. Honest, Knocker, we fought like tigers."

"They got the box," said Knocker, in anguish.

"No, they didn't," said Napoleon, emphatically. "I'd have died, rather . . . after everything."

"Then you got it away?"

"Not that, either. We were fighting across the mud flats, they had it halfway to the shore, we came back at them, we did for every last one of them, and when we looked for the box, to get it back into the boat, there it was, sinking in the mud. We couldn't even get hold of a handle, it went down so quick. You know what that mud is like, like a live thing with the grip of a python. The mud is deep there, deeper than anywhere else along the Wandle. The old stories say it goes down to the centre of the earth."

There was a long silence. Then Napoleon spoke again. "I had to come back to tell you. I wanted you to know before anything happened that I'd done my best. The money's gone for ever, and even Flinthead can't get it where it's gone. But the others got away, Knocker, don't forget that. We done the Rumbles – and our Adventure was surely the best ever. That's what counts, isn't it?'

Knocker knelt by the wounded and mud-splattered Wendle and took his hand gently in his own. "You are right, sod the money! We have done great things and it has been a great Adventure. They will sing songs about all of us."

"Flinthead's going to sing one to us right now," said Orococco who had been watching the enemy. "Here he comes, to tell us no doubt what lovely treats he has in store."

"He'll go raving lunatic when he finds out about the money," said Napoleon, and the four of them inched over to the tunnel opening, knowing, but not saying, that they were doomed to an early and unpleasant death.

Chapter 10

"We'll have to go. We'll be picked up if we wait any longer." Bingo spoke reluctantly.

The others twisted in their seats and looked over the bows of *The Silver Belle Flower* to the distant bank. The far side of the River Thames was clearly visible and the silhouettes of the factories and gasometers stood sharp against the morning sky. From time to time the rowers clipped the water with the blades of their oars so as to stay on station opposite the Wandle. Boats and barges were passing by in increasing numbers and at any moment a police launch might appear, checking that all was well on Wandsworth Reach. The city was awake; from high above, on the Wandsworth Bridge roadway, came the unbroken hum of traffic on its way to work.

The survivors shifted their attention and gazed dejectedly at the wasteland that spread out on either side of the Wandle's mouth. Their eyes sought for some sign of their companions, but they saw no movement. Even the Wendle patrols had returned underground, shaking their fists at the five Borribles who sat off-shore waiting and hoping, their hearts heavy with a great sadness.

"They didn't stand a chance of getting away," sighed Vulge, "but I bet they gave a good scrap at the end."

"I hope Napoleon got back," said Bingo. "I hope they were all together when . . ." His voice trailed off and there were tears in his eyes. "Come on, we must go. There's no point in us getting caught as well."

Sydney, Chalotte, Stonks and Bingo leant forward to row. Vulge sat in the stern and navigated, searching for a group of two or three barges where they could hide through the daylight hours and clean themselves of the

Wandle mud that covered them still. The tide, strong as a waterfall, bore the boat through the cathedral arches of Wandsworth Bridge and Vulge saw what he was looking for almost immediately. He directed *The Silver Belle Flower* into a tiny haven of motionless water and hardly bothering to scrape the caked slime from their clothing the Borribles huddled together in the bottom of the boat in an attempt to keep a spark of warmth glowing amongst them.

It was deep winter; they had neither food nor blankets and the damp river wind gnawed at their shrinking bodies. All day they tried to sleep but the pangs of hunger and the hateful cold kept them restless and their wounds throbbed without respite.

Night rescued them. They watched the sun go down, blurred crimson into black smoke, and they took up their oars once more and warmed themselves by rowing. Though they were but four to power the strokes now the swift current of the Thames carried them homewards and though they were clumsy and stupid with fatigue and hunger they brought *The Silver Belle Flower* safely down the river. Just before dawn the next day the boat slid between the high-masted sailing barges and the embankment wall and ended its journey on the solid wedge of floating rubbish that had been marooned from the main stream for so long. They had returned to Battersea Churchyard. They fell forward on the oars, spent, bedraggled, filthy.

"Battersea," said Bingo, almost weeping with pleasure. "I can hardly believe it, lovely Battersea."

They helped each other over the high river wall and stood in the quiet churchyard and looked up at the green steeple. "It's a good feeling," said Vulge, "being back where you belong, with a good Adventure behind you, and friends to remember."

"It must be one of the best feelings there is," agreed Chalotte.

They went from the churchyard and out into Church Road. There was not much traffic about and not many people, which was just as the Borribles wanted, for they could not have passed as ordinary children. They had lost their helmets in their many fights and their pointed ears were plainly visible. They were covered in the dried mud from the Wandle swamps and most strange-looking of all were the Wendle waders they wore, and the orange road jackets.

"We'd better get off the streets," said Bingo, "before we're spotted."

Opposite to the Old Swan Pub, near the church, were a couple of Borrible houses, derelict and falling apart, their window spaces boarded up with rough planks and corrugated iron.

"They'll lend us some clothes and hats," said Bingo pointing over the road, "just to get as far as Spiff's."

Every London Borrible had heard of the Expedition against the Rumbles but every London Borrible had, long before this time, given the Adventurers up for dead. It took Bingo and the others half an hour to convince this Battersea household that they weren't attempting to perpetrate some Borrible subterfuge for stealing clothes. Once they had been convinced however they lent the clothes eagerly and were delighted to be the first to see the survivors of the Adventure to end all Adventures and proud to hear the first snippets of their stories.

The Adventurers waited until after eight o'clock before going back onto the streets. It was safer that way, for with the pavements crowded they could mingle with the kids on their way to school and remain inconspicuous. The traffic was building up, for many cars use Church Road as a short cut from York Road to Battersea Bridge, crossing the river to get to the centre of London. It was a very busy and dangerous road but to the Borribles it was friendly and welcoming. It was home.

They walked on until they came to the fork of Vicarage Crescent and Battersea High Street itself. They went past Sinjen's School, and they came up to Trott Street and the empty building where Spiff lived and where Knocker had lived as chief Battersea lookout all that time ago. But before they went in, with one accord they walked past the house and on to the market proper.

The stallholders were putting out their merchandise, the shops were open and there was a bustle and a friendliness that made each Adventurer feel glad to be alive. The pie-and-eel shop was preparing for its lunch-time trade and the smell of sauce and liquor was strong. The fish and chip shop was being swabbed out by an Indian who sang as he worked, a strange spicy song, and the surplus store looked reassuringly the same, a cross between a pawnshop and a junk-yard. The Battersea costers whistled and shouted at each other across the street and man-handled their barrows into position or stacked goods on them from the vans parked sideways and awkward across the road. Even when the stallholders shouted at the Borribles and told them to clear off to school, the Borribles only smiled at each other, selfconsciously indulging their nostalgia.

"Knocker loved it down here," said Chalotte, and they came away from the stalls, bringing with them a few things for their breakfast, for they were extraordinarily hungry. They took their provisions and went to report to Spiff.

He was waiting for them. Their arrival had been noted and reported and their story was eagerly awaited. Crowds of Borribles were in the house and more crowded in by the minute. The Adventurers had to push their way in to the basement and fight their way through an excited throng to Spiff's room. He was there, just the same in his orange dressing-gown, with a cup of tea held in front of his sharp face.

He bade the Adventurers sit down and eat the food

they had brought from the market. His eyes moved over them and he noted the absences, but his expression gave little away and he said nothing.

Other house-stewards arrived and sat on the floor or stood against the wall round the room. They all waited till Spiff gave the word for the story to be told. They would listen intently and, that very day, would each tell the stories to their households, and the stories would be told again and again from Borrible to Borrible, and so the stories of the Adventurers would become legend, one of the greatest legends ever. And new proverbs and sayings would be added to the Borrible Book and new ambitions would be born in the hearts of Borribles as yet un-named and some would yearn to have such an Adventure too. But many would find the Adventure unbelievable and say that no Borrible could have done such things and the whole expedition was a fiction and a fabrication, a good story, but not true. "Had anyone ever talked to those who had undertaken the trip?" the sceptics would ask. "Who's ever spoken to Knocker and Napoleon? Has anyone ever seen Orococco and Vulge? Oh, you heard of people who knew somebody who had met someone who had seen Chalotte or Sydney or Torreycanyon, but nobody had really met them."

But in Spiff's room that day were the listeners to and the tellers of a great Adventure, and the tellers still had the marks of their Adventure on them. Their scars were still soft and their muscles still ached and the listeners could see this and they knew the story was true and they would tell it as true and they would be believed. Only in the years to come would the story grow in the telling and lose its firm outline to become a great Borrible Legend.

The Adventurers finished their breakfast, and when Spiff's room was crammed with house-stewards and the doorway was crowded and the landing and all the other rooms too, he gave the sign and Bingo started the story at the beginning, from the moment they had rowed away from Battersea Churchyard. His companions listened, and added to his story if they thought he had forgotten anything, and sometimes they went on with it themselves and the story was thrown backwards and forwards amongst them and it grew and grew. And each one told of his own part in the destruction of the Bunker under Rumbledom, and the tale of the Great Explosion and Adolf's death brought forth deferential whistles from the house-stewards and they looked at the Adventurers with respect and nodded their heads.

Then, sombrely, the Adventurers told of their imprisonment by the Wendles and of the great dilemma of Napoleon Boot and how finally his cleverness had saved them. They told of the loss of the four friends who had stayed behind so that their companions might survive to thwart Flinthead's greed, to escape with the box of Rumble treasure, and how, after all, they had been lucky to escape with their lives alone.

When the great story was ended a heavy silence came over the room and the Adventurers looked at the floor, remembering the five who had not returned. The house-stewards were deeply impressed by the Adventure and indicated to Spiff, by signs and nods of the head, that they thought he ought to mark the occasion with a few well-chosen phrases.

Spiff, who could never resist the temptation of public-speaking, pondered. He took his teapot from the paraffin stove, poured himself a cup, put the sugar in and stirred well, before he deigned to pronounce a word. At last he stood up and cleared his throat.

"A great Adventure!" he began. "The threat of the Rumbles gone; their power destroyed. Their presumption and pride have taken a very serious knock; it will be many a year, if ever, before they come down here again. A day of great rejoicing it is, and one of sadness, also. Four of you did not return, and one German person, who joined in, only for the glory of the Adventure, has also perished. What can we do except try to remember them always, tell their stories and remember their names—good names; Torreycanyon, Napoleon Boot, Orococco, Adolf Wolfgang Amadeus Winston—and of course, our own chief lookout, Knocker. What second name is there worthy of his Adventure?"

Chalotte looked up and interrupted; there were tears in her eyes. "He went back into the hallway of the Great Door to get that box when he should have been escaping, and though it was blazing with flames and the rafters were falling in huge sparks, he picked up the box and carried it out and it was red-hot and the handle burnt into his hand—down to the bone—and he didn't care. His clothes were alight and I thought he was completely on fire. I think you could call him Knocker Burnthand. It is a good name."

There was a murmur of assent from everybody and many repeated the name to themselves to see how it sounded.

"Burnthand it shall be," said Spiff seriously, "and it shall be written in the book."

He looked at the five survivors in the chairs before him. "Your names, too, are confirmed. You have more than won them. You left here with empty words for your title but you return with names that are full of meaning, and every time they are heard now, great and generous deeds will be thought of. Great names they are, which will make every Borrible think of courage and cunning, loyalty and stealth, individualism and affection, every time they hear them." And Spiff, over-acting a little, recited the names like a litany, "Chalotte, Sydney, Vulge, Stonks and Bingo from Lavender Hill."

Spiff gave a sign and the stewards began to file past

the chairs and from the room. They left the house and ran through the busy High Street, back to their own dwellings so they could begin retelling the tale straight away. At their heels followed all the Borribles of Battersea, eager to hear the details of the Great Adventure, and soon Spiff's house was quiet.

He gulped his dark brown tea and looked at the Adventurers, still slumped in their seats.

"You must all be tired," he said. "Why don't you go to the rooms upstairs and rest? I'll see that there's some grub for you when you wake up. It would be a good idea for you to have a good long kip, you know." The five of them got up listlessly and left the room. The elation they had felt at arriving home and telling their story had gone and in its place was a rotten feeling of melancholia mixed with self-pity. They felt too a yearning love for the companions they had left to perish on the River Wandle and the immensity of the loss made an awesome gap in their minds.

They climbed the stairs like old cripples. On the second landing Chalotte, who was leading, turned and stopped the others; her eyes were wet.

"Oh," she said, only just holding back her sobs, "it all seems so useless now. We've won our names but lost our friends. Isn't it all so stupid?"

"Shuddup," said Bingo, "don't make things worse."

They went on upstairs without saying another word.

When he was alone, Spiff topped up his cup of tea and mused over what he had heard and he thought about the loss of Knocker and the others.

"I hate to think of what Flinthead did to 'em when he got his hands on 'em," he said to himself. "What a swine he is." He stirred in the sugar. "Shame about the money. I was never worried about the Rumbles at all, really. Couldn't have given a monkey's. It was the money; I could have done with that. Your average Bor-

285

rible don't know the value of the stuff, they don't know what it's about. I don't suppose we'll ever see any real money down here. Bloody nuisance! Ah well, there'll be another time, some time."

Douglas Hill
Galactic Warlord 80p

He stands alone . . . his planet, Moros, destroyed by unknown forces.
His one vow – to wreak terrible vengeance on the sinister enemy.
But Keill Randor, the Last Legionary, cannot conceive the evil force
he will unleash in his crusade against the Warlord and his murderous
army, the Deathwing.

Deathwing Over Veynaa 95p

The Robot's attack proved one thing – that the Deathwing was on
the Cluster with a weapon that could destroy a world.

Only a small rebellion in a minor solar system but it was part of the
evil master-plan of the mysterious Galactic Warlord. And it would
need all the special skills and courage of Keill Randor, the Last
Legionary, and his alien companion Glr, to defeat the Deathwing, and
save the planet Veynaa.

Day of the Starwind £1.10

The third action-packed adventure of Keill Randor, the Last Legionary
of Moros, and his alien companion, Glr. They set course for the
planet Rilyn in their search for the evil Warlord and his army the
Deathwing. Our hero must pit his wits against the savage fury of the
Deathwing army. Will Keill survive the struggle to avenge his
destroyed planet? The Deathwing *must* be eliminated!

Isaac Asimov
The Key Word and Other Mysteries 90p

It's hard work being a police detective – long, gruelling hours of investigation often lead to a dead end. Larry's fascination with his father's work involves him in a series of mysteries that have baffled the police. By using his wits and his interest in words, Larry solves the cases and helps in the fight against crime by sheer brain power!

Arthur C. Clarke
Dolphin Island £1.25

This exciting story is set in the 21st century. Johnny, who has run away from home, is shipwrecked in the middle of the South Pacific Ocean. Stranded on a raft, he is miraculously propelled by a pack of dolphins towards the famous centre for dolphin research. Johnny assists in training the dolphins, survives a fearful hurricane and unearths a horrifying underwater conspiracy.

You can buy these and other Piccolo books from booksellers and newsagents; or direct from the following address:
Pan Books, Sales Office, Cavaye Place, London SW10 9PG
Send purchase price plus 35p for the first book and 15p for each additional book, to allow for postage and packing
Prices quoted are applicable in the UK

While every effort is made to keep prices low, it is sometimes necessary to increase prices at short notice. Pan Books reserve the right to show on covers and charge new retail prices which may differ from those advertised in the text or elsewhere